Praise for
Last Chance for Justice

A delightful blend of healing, new beginnings, and the simplicity of the love that shines for a new season. *Last Chance for Justice* tugs sweetly at the heart with delicious hope for tomorrow.

—Janet Perez Eckles, author of best-selling *Simply Salsa: Dancing Without Fear at God's Fiesta*

Kathi Macias writes a hometown tale reminiscent of *Anne of Green Gables*, yet with a modern-day twist. She masterfully weaves a tale of mother-daughter love, complete with small-town gossips, a sweet romance, and a bit of mystery. I was enamored by the uplifting story, endearing characters, and the snuggle-down tale of loss, love, redemption, and discovery.

—Susan G. Mathis, author of *The ReMarriage Adventure* and *Countdown for Couples*

Kathi Macias's new book *Last Chance for Justice* is as inviting as Bloomfield, home to the annual Spring Fling Festival and lots of characters who will feel like old friends. You'll want to meander down Main Street and stop for lunch at Bert's Barbecue. And of course you'll cheer for Lynn Myers, the widow who returns to her old hometown and gets a fresh start in the old house next to the cemetery.

Last Chance for Justice is a delightful read you won't be able to put down. If you love stories that entertain and capture your heart, this one hits the spot! Can't wait for the next Bloomfield book!

—Kathy Howard, author of many books, including *Unshakeable Faith* and *Fed Up with Flat Faith*

Last Chance for Justice is a masterful story that blends the most important issues of life, love, and faith into one compelling contemporary novel. With realistic characters and a great plot set in a small town where life moves at a slower pace, the dialogue alone will keep a reader turning the page.

—Rita Gerlach, author

Once again, Kathi Macias hits her target square in the center! *Last Chance for Justice* strays a bit from her usual deeper, darker subject fare, but it surely doesn't lack in reader satisfaction. Rather, it has the perfect blend of mystery, sweet romance, and inspiration. As always, Macias delivers a fine, compelling story to capture a reader's heart and full attention. Couldn't put it down!

—Sharlene MacLaren, author and speaker

Last Chance for Justice is a lovely story about coming home and connecting to community. Mrs. Macias brought out some crucial and universal questions. How far do we go to honor the wishes of a departed loved one and how might that be part of God's plan? *Last Chance for Justice* explores honor and love in relationships from families to the delight of budding new love, a book you won't want to miss. (You won't want to miss any books by Kathi Macias!)

—Angela Breidenbach, speaker and author of
A Healing Heart

Love, mystery, and friendship are blooming in Bloomfield! In *Last Chance for Justice*, Kathi Macias weaves a refreshing and often humorous tale of a mother and daughter's journey home.

The deeply connected people and simpler pace of Bloomfield made me want to pack a bag and pay the small town a visit of my own.

—Julie Carobini, author, *The Otter Bay Novels*

Last Chance for Justice is a wonderful addition to the Bloomfield series of novels. It's homey and heart-warming with a touch of mystery. The cast of unique characters quickly made their way into my heart. And the setting of Bloomfield expanded to include even more of the town and countryside. A delightful and insightful read.

—Lena Nelson Dooley, multi-award-winning author of McKenna's Daughters, including the recently released *Catherine's Pursuit*

Pleasant characters, a cozy little mystery and a love story to boot. Kathi Macias's *Last Chance for Justice* lets us walk alongside Lynn as she wrestles with the death of her husband, her reluctance to embrace change and the hesitant but brave return to the hometown she left behind years before. As God unfolds His plans for her, for her daughter Rachel, and for some of the people of her quaint old hometown, it becomes wonderfully clear that His plan is bigger than her fear of change and her fear of what others might think put together. Deliciously heartwarming, *Last Chance for Justice* left me with a smile and a sigh—and a major craving for some sun tea.

—Rhonda Rhea, humor columnist, radio personality, and author of ten books, including *Espresso Your Faith* and *Get a Grip*

Last Chance for Justice

KATHI MACIAS

A *Bloomfield* Novel

Last Chance for Justice

PUBLISHING GROUP

Nashville, Tennessee

Published by B&H Publishing Group
Nashville, Tennessee

Dewey Decimal Classification: F
Subject Heading: MYSTERY FICTION \ LOVE STORIES \
INHERITANCE AND SUCCESSION—FICTION

Publishers Note: The characters and events
in this book are fictional, and any resemblance
to actual persons or events is coincidental.

1 2 3 4 5 6 7 8 • 17 16 15 14 13

To my Lord and Savior, the Author and Finisher of my
faith—and of my part in the Bloomfield project;
To my best friend and strongest supporter, my husband, Al;
And to my dear mother, whose flat apple pie is even
now calling me from heaven.

I can't wait to get old enough that I no longer
have to deal with peer pressure!

# Chapter 1

THOUGH IT WAS THE MIDDLE OF JUNE AND SUMMER WAS ALMOST officially upon them, the day itself seemed as drab and color-less as Lynn Myers's shoulder-length hair before her Clairol touch-up, and she had no reason to believe that tomorrow would be any different, which for the most part suited her just fine. Sameness represented security to Lynn, and she thrived on it—even pursued it with passion. But opposites attract, as they say, and life with Daniel had contained little, if any, sameness from day to day.

However, Daniel was gone now, and Lynn instinctively had resorted to routine to carry her through. So far, it appeared to anyone who didn't look too closely that her efforts had suc-ceeded—until the day she returned from grocery shopping and spotted the official-looking letter protruding from the white metal mailbox on the outside wall next to her front door.

She snagged the envelope, along with three nondescript occupant offerings, on the way inside. Smiling, she offered a brief hello to her ten-year-old cocker spaniel, Beasley, who lay in his customary spot on the braided rug next to Lynn's favorite chair. Beasley opened one eye and wagged his stub of a tail in greeting, and Lynn proceeded to the kitchen and set her groceries on the table. Still holding the envelope, she flipped it from front to back twice and even held it up to the light, as if she could determine its contents in the process. Why didn't she just open it? She started to, several times, but instead decided to put her groceries away first. No sense deviating from her usual method of doing everything "decently and in order," as the Bible dictated. But what was it about that envelope that jacked up her heart rate and dampened the palms of her hands?

Lynn's aversion to change was nothing new. Born and raised in a small town where the annual Spring Fling Festival was the biggest event on the calendar, Lynn grew up believing she would always live in Bloomfield, surrounded by the same familiar friends and walking the same familiar streets. Then she met Daniel, a man too handsome for his own good—and hers, too, she'd been warned—but her heart hadn't listened. And because Daniel was only in Bloomfield to visit relatives for the summer before returning to his home a few hundred miles away, eighteen-year-old Lynn had a decision to make.

Admittedly, she'd been torn. Her avoidance of change, combined with her loyalty to family and friends in Bloomfield, beckoned her to do the sensible thing and say good-bye to the good-looking young man who had blown in and out of town, capturing her heart in the process. But the letters and phone calls he sent her way once he returned home drew her in a way she'd been helpless to resist. She'd prayed, she'd worried, she'd even argued with herself. Why leave a perfectly good little town with nice people and comfortable surroundings to live in a sprawling metropolis of nearly 100,000 residents, none of whom she'd ever met? She wouldn't even know which grocery store had the best bargains or the freshest meat, or which stoplights were preprogrammed and which could be tripped by the weight of a car idling in just the right spot. Why not continue to live at home and attend the nearby junior college, as she'd originally planned, and hope that one of the few sensible and eligible bachelors in town would one day notice her and pop the question so she wouldn't have to make so many adjustments?

But ultimately she acted in a way many in Bloomfield had described as "completely out of character," and she accepted Daniel's romantic and urgent proposal of marriage, following him "to the ends of the earth." When people asked her why—and many did—she simply told them she was in love. She'd known the moment her best friend introduced her to Daniel Myers on that bright June day less than a week after her high school graduation that her heart would never again be her own. And for some unimaginable reason, he felt the same about her. They met in the gentle heat of early summer and were married less than six months later, while the cold, harsh wind of winter blew outside the little church where their friends and family had gathered to wish them well and to place silent wagers on how long they would last.

Thirty-five years, Lynn thought as she reached to slide the new box of baking soda onto its proper place on the spice shelf. *We lasted thirty-five years—and then You took him home, Lord.* She sighed. *I know You have a right, and I know You never make mistakes, and I'm grateful for the time we had together; truly I am. But, oh, Father, You know my heart. You know how much I miss him and wish we'd had just a few more years together.*

Blinking away tears, she turned back to let her eyes settle on the old butcher block table in the middle of the room. That table had hosted so many family meals and discussions over the years, but it now appeared as lonely as Lynn felt. The envelope lay where she'd left it, right next to the final bag of groceries. Should she give in and open it? No, she'd finish her task and put away the last of her small purchases first.

She ignored the temptation to sit down and rest, something she never grappled with before Daniel died. Was this nagging sense of exhaustion part of her grief process? She'd heard somewhere that it could be, and since she was only in her midfifties and relatively healthy, why else would she feel this ongoing need to crawl into bed, pull the covers over her head, and just sleep?

She reached inside the bag, emptying the items one by one and placing them in a neat row before transporting them to a more permanent, predetermined spot where they would wait, neatly and quietly, until she needed them.

One loaf of whole wheat bread, which will last for a month if I keep it in the refrigerator. It wouldn't have lasted a week if Daniel were still around and Rachel lived at home. She shook her head. *They're gone now,* she reminded herself. *Both of them. So finish what you're doing and stop daydreaming. You'll just end up crying again.*

With everything put away at last, she had no more excuses. She sat down and picked up the envelope, shaking it one more time before tearing an opening at the end and slipping out the neatly folded letter. She was surprised when a small key slid out of the envelope and rattled onto the table. Puzzled, she swallowed and spread the letter out in front of her.

"Dear Ms. Myers."

Lynn hated that form of address.

Ms. indeed! Why do I have to be a "Ms." just because my "Mr." died? I was a "Mrs." then, and I'm a "Mrs." now. Must I suddenly change my entire identity just because Daniel moved on ahead of me?

She knew she was overreacting, but she didn't care. The fact that the letter opened with what she considered an offensive salutation did not bode well for the remainder of its contents. She could smell the word "surprise" lurking in every line.

She read on, her grip tightening on the paper in an unconscious effort to keep her hands from shaking. Her heart raced as a lump formed in her throat.

Myron? Dead? If she hadn't already been sitting, she would have fallen smack-dab into her chair—or possibly even onto the floor. She would never have imagined this in a million years.

Well, all right. Maybe by then. After all, no one lived that long. But now? Already? This soon, when her only brother wasn't even seventy yet? Wasn't it enough that she'd lost her beloved Daniel in what she considered the prime of his life, even though AARP had been sending him membership invitations for several years? Did she have to lose her only sibling as well? And why hadn't she been told sooner? Why now, several weeks after the fact? As the next of kin, shouldn't she have been notified immediately so she could plan the funeral?

As she read on, she got her answer. Though Myron had not felt well in awhile, he had kept that fact to himself. Even his doctor, lawyer, and pastor didn't realize the gravity of his situation until the last few days. In addition, the terms of Myron's will included the stipulation that Lynn not be told until at least a couple of weeks after his death, as he didn't want a "big to-do," just a quiet burial in the cemetery next to his home. Apparently, the town of Bloomfield had honored the request, but the time had come for Lynn to claim her inheritance.

Inheritance?

How could she even think of such a thing while still reeling at the news of Myron's death? So far as she knew, Myron had always been healthy. But then, so had Daniel, and he was gone, wasn't he? Besides, who knew Myron well enough to make a call on his health? He'd been quiet and relatively noncommunicative, even as a child, and a virtual recluse since his one true love left him at the altar decades earlier. Even their parents, who had lived less than three miles away from their only son, had seldom seen him during his adult years.

Moving into that big old house next to the cemetery certainly didn't help any. Myron, what were you thinking? But then, that was the problem, wasn't it? You never let anyone know what you were thinking.

Grabbing a tissue from her pocket, she dabbed at the tears that threatened to run down her cheeks and forced herself to read on.

"*. . . has left his entire estate, including his house, to you . . .*"

Lynn reread the statement several times. So that was her inheritance, that monstrosity that looked like something from a horror film. Myron had left it to her? And what was she supposed to do with it? Certainly not live there! Why, she hadn't even been back to Bloomfield since . . . since . . .

Her mother's funeral. Had it really been nearly ten years, not only since her mother died but also since she'd set foot in the town where she'd been born and raised and thought surely she would die and be buried as well? The realization that once both her parents were gone she had ceased to visit Bloomfield—including her only sibling, now deceased—made her cheeks grow hot with shame.

"Forgive me, Lord," she whispered. "How could I have neglected Myron like that? For all I know, he was sick and needed me. But here I was, miles and miles away, busy with my own life and then feeling sorry for myself when my husband died, wondering what I was going to do with the rest of my days. Oh, poor Myron! Why didn't I at least try harder to reach out to him after Daniel died? It's not like I didn't have the time, or . . ."

The words stuck in her throat as tears spilled over her cheeks, and she didn't even bother trying to stop them. As she wept softly—for the unexpected loss of her estranged (and yes, somewhat strange) brother and the still-fresh grief over the death of her husband, as well as the memories and confusion that swirled in her mind—she found herself wondering if God was trying to tell her something.

"I know," she sniffled. "I've been on a long and disgusting pity party since Daniel died. But Lord, he was my life! You knew that, but You took him anyway. Now I have nothing—no direction, no purpose. I don't even have my daughter anymore. Rachel's a grown woman with a fresh degree from Bible college and a whole lifetime of choices and opportunities ahead of her. What have I got? This old house that's in need of more repairs than I can ever afford and reeking of memories that rip my heart out fresh every morning, not to mention Rachel's education bills looming over my head. Now I've got another house to worry about—and an ugly one at that! What in the world am I supposed to do with it?"

Lynn realized she was once again whining at God, but her prayer life had been reduced to little else these past months. It was a wonder He still loved and listened to her, but she knew He did. At the moment, it was all she had to cling to.

Just some direction, Lord, she prayed silently, mopping away her tears and calming her sobs. *That's all I'm asking for—really. Am I supposed to sell Myron's house and use the money to pay*

*my bills? That would be the logical thing, wouldn't it? And You
know I've always been one to appreciate logic—despite the fact
that I married a man who didn't know the meaning of the word.
I know what he'd do if this happened while he was alive. He'd
say it was our big chance for an unexpected adventure. Instead of
selling that house, he'd sell this one, take an early retirement, and
off we'd go to live in my brother's mausoleum in Bloomfield—
right next to the town's only cemetery. That sure would have
rekindled the gossip fires about Daniel and me, wouldn't it? The
very thought sounds terrifying, but Daniel's green eyes would
have lit up at the prospect. Why can't I be just a little bit like him,
Father? Just a little—*

"Mom?"

The sound, as much as the name, nearly jolted Lynn from
her chair. Jerking her head upward, she had to remind her heart
to stop tap-dancing so close to her ribs. It hurt—and besides, it
was dangerous. It was just too much for one day—first the letter about Myron, and now this. How many surprises could one
woman endure?

"Rachel?"

Why did her daughter look so much taller than normal? Was
it because she'd piled her long black hair on top of her head?
Because she was dressed in a T-shirt and shorts that revealed her
suntanned legs that seemed to stretch to forever? Or just because
she was standing in the kitchen, directly in front of her mother
and miles from where she was supposed to be?

Lynn frowned. "What are you doing here?"

Rachel's expectant smile faded only slightly. "Gee, Mom,
not a very warm welcome. I thought you'd be happy to see me."
Then it was Rachel's turn to frown. "Are you crying? You are.
Oh, Mom, you're missing Dad again, aren't you?"

Lynn waved away her daughter's concern and ignored her question, instead lifting herself from her seat and crossing the small space that separated them. Wrapping her arms around her daughter, she let the flood of emotions that had assailed her since opening the letter melt away into the joy of realizing her daughter was home.

"I didn't expect you for another few weeks," Lynn said, pulling back and tilting her head slightly to gaze up into her only child's face. "What happened?"

Rachel's frown deepened. "Never mind why I'm home early. I'm just glad I am. It looks like you need some cheering up." Her frown disappeared as a grin spread across her face. "And that's one of the reasons I'm here. I know I told you I was going to stay at the college for most of the summer before moving on to something more permanent, but the temp job I was supposed to get fell through, so I decided, what's the point? Why not come home and hang out with Mom?"

Rachel's green eyes sparkled, tearing at Lynn's heart with the memory of Daniel and what she'd always called his "dancing eyes." She blinked to rid herself of the painful reminder and tried to refocus.

"So here I am," Rachel announced. She shook her head. "And not a minute too soon from the look of things. Come on, let's sit down and talk. I have an idea I'd like to run past you."

Her curiosity piqued, Lynn sat back down with Rachel across from her and waited. Why did people—particularly those closest to her—continue to insist on springing surprises on her, thinking she'd be pleased? Sometimes she wondered if they knew her at all.

"Here's the deal," Rachel said, a conspiratorial tone teasing her delivery. "I know we both miss Dad, and I know if we stay here in this house and do nothing but think about him every day, we'll end up sitting here at the table crying. So I was thinking . . ."

She paused—for effect, Lynn knew, though she continued to wait silently for her daughter to finish.

"Why not go on an adventure together?" Rachel asked. "A vacation or short trip or . . . something. Anything away from this house and everything familiar that breaks our hearts every time we look at it. What do you think, Mom? I know it's not your style to do something so spontaneous, but . . . would you at least consider it? Please? For me?"

Lynn's mouth nearly dropped open. Why did she feel as if she were caught up in the midst of a conspiracy? *What are You up to, God? This is just too much to be a coincidence. If Daniel were still alive, I'd think he put Rachel up to this. But You? Was this Your idea? Did You send her here? Judging by Your track record, I'd say that's a definite possibility.*

"Mom?" Rachel leaned forward and reached across the table, taking one of Lynn's hands in her own. "Did you hear me? What do you think? Are you up for an adventure? Something new and different? You can even pick the place—anywhere you want to go. You name it; I'll pack and have the car loaded before you know what hit you."

I think I know what hit me, Lynn mused. *It was a Mack truck with my name on it.* Out loud she shocked herself by saying, "Actually, I think it's a good idea, though I must admit it's not one I'm completely comfortable with. But though I can't explain it, I think God is behind the whole thing."

Rachel's grin nearly split her face. "Mom, that's fantastic. Awesome! So where do you want to go? Do you have any ideas, any place special in mind?"

Lynn pressed her lips together in one last feeble attempt to regain her sanity and nix what could very well be a fiasco at best. For someone who hated surprises or change, her life seemed to be careening out of control—not to mention the fact that they didn't exactly have a lot of extra money lying around to blow on frivolous, spur-of-the-moment activities. Thanks to wise planning on Daniel's part, Lynn had enough to get by if she used her resources wisely. But vacations? Trips? Adventures? Not in the budget.

Still, they did have two old houses now, didn't they? One right here where they sat, and another much larger and even older, propped up right next to a cemetery in Bloomfield. Didn't she owe it to her late brother, her only sibling and the last remaining member of her family of origin, to at least check out the possibilities before making a decision?

She sighed. "Actually, yes, I do," she said, watching her daughter's face for a reaction. "I'd like to go back to Bloomfield. I know you didn't know your Uncle Myron well and we haven't even seen him since your grandmother died, but he passed away, and he left us his house. I think we should go and check it out."

Rachel's eyes widened until Lynn thought they'd pop right out of her face. At last she said, "That scary old house by the cemetery? That one? He left it to us?"

Lynn nodded.

Rachel appeared to gather herself as she swallowed and took a deep breath. "I'm sorry about Uncle Myron, Mom. I know he was your only brother."

Lynn nodded again. "Thank you, sweetheart."

In the questioning way she'd had since she was a little girl, Rachel raised one eyebrow and offered a crooked grin. "It would definitely be an adventure, wouldn't it?" Before Lynn could nod yet again, Rachel laughed. "Then I say, let's go, Mom—you, me, and Beasley. What are we waiting for? Bloomfield, here we come!"

Chapter 2

LYNN'S THREE-YEAR-OLD CREAM-COLORED TOYOTA COROLLA had scarcely 15,000 miles on it—most of those logged before Daniel died. The 400-mile trip to Bloomfield was the longest drive Lynn had ever made in the sensible, economical car, and she imagined the trip back home when they'd finished up their business in her old hometown would be her last such lengthy journey. After all, she lived within five miles of her favorite grocery and drug store, shopping mall, and beauty shop, so where else did she need to go? Even her doctor's office and the hospital were less than ten minutes away, so she imagined herself driving her current car right up until she passed on to glory and no longer needed it.

I could probably even leave it to Rachel after that, she mused, peering at her daughter who had insisted on driving most of the way on their trip to Bloomfield. Her black hair once again piled on top of her head, the twenty-two-year-old beauty hummed along with the song blaring forth from the golden-oldies station. She tapped her fingers on the steering wheel in time to the music, keeping her eyes straight ahead as she focused on the road.

Lynn smiled. *No doubt the old Toyota will still be running even then,* she told herself, *but I can't imagine anyone wanting it at that point, especially Rachel.*

They'd parked Rachel's old beater, a multicolored twenty-year-old Honda Civic that had logged more miles than any ten normal cars, in the garage before leaving, loaded a couple of suitcases in the Toyota's trunk and Beasley in the backseat, and headed out first thing the previous morning. With one stop at a decent but inexpensive motel overnight, they now neared their destination and planned to be there in time for lunch. Rachel had already expressed her desire to stop at the one barbecue place in town, and Lynn had agreed, but as the car purred down the winding, two-lane road, through the green hills that so far hid their destination from sight, her stomach clenched and the desire for food eluded her.

Why did coming back to Bloomfield make her tense up? She'd loved growing up there and had such fond memories of the little town and its friendly residents—until right before she'd married Daniel, of course. At the age of eighteen, she'd left with what she imagined to be speculative gossip ringing in her ears, tainting her otherwise pleasant memories of her hometown.

Maybe that's the problem, she thought. *It's all about memories—good, bad, or otherwise. The past. Everyone in my family is gone now. There's no one here to welcome us home, no one I'm really close to anymore. Have I made a terrible mistake by coming here?*

Lynn shook her head and turned to look out the passenger side window. Colorful splashes of wildflowers brought the verdant hillsides to life, and she couldn't help but think of the many summers she'd spent as a child in this idyllic setting. For the first time since her mother died, she wondered if she should have made more of an effort to stay in touch with some of the Bloomfield residents she'd grown up with, people who had known and loved her family, despite what they might have thought of Lynn's impulsive decision.

It wasn't because they didn't approve of my decision, she told herself. *I didn't bother to stay in touch because I was so happy with Daniel. We had our own life, our own family, and somehow I thought it would always be that way. Even with Rachel off at college, I had my husband, our church, our friends.* She sighed. *Everything's different now. Our home is so empty without Daniel there, but would it be any better in Bloomfield?*

"You okay, Mom?"

Lynn blinked and turned her head toward her daughter. "Did you say something, honey?"

Rachel's brow creased before she looked back at the road. "I asked if you're okay. I heard you sigh."

Lynn smiled. Nothing much got past Rachel. She might have her father's looks and zest for adventure, but the two Myers women were close. Lynn would have to be careful not to let her apprehension and insecurities put a damper on Rachel's enthusiasm over their adventure.

"I'm fine," she said, using her most reassuring tone. "Really. It's just . . . well, I haven't been home in awhile. Not since your grandma died."

Rachel nodded. "So . . . you still think of Bloomfield as home?"

Lynn raised her eyebrows. *Bloomfield? Home?* No, not really, but hadn't she just said that? Home was where she'd lived with Daniel. Bloomfield was simply the town where she'd grown up. Why would she call it home?

"I . . . I'm not sure. I don't think so, but . . ."

Rachel flashed a quick smile and turned down the volume on the radio. "It's okay, Mom. I imagine we always think of the place we grew up as home, even when our family's not there anymore. It doesn't take away from what you had with Dad. Where the three of us lived together while I was growing up will always be my home, even when I move on and have my own family and life somewhere else." She shrugged. "That's just the way it is, don't you think?"

"I suppose."

Lynn turned back to gaze out the window, only to spot the bright green WELCOME TO BLOOMFIELD sign up ahead. "Stop," she said, wondering why she made such a request. "I want to see the sign."

Without question, Rachel slowed and pulled to the side of the road. Wordlessly, Lynn opened the door and stepped out into the noonday sunshine. One lone pickup truck rattled past as she walked forward and stood in front of the sign, admiring the multicolored flowers that topped the large, rectangular welcome that proclaimed Bloomfield as HOME OF THE ANNUAL SPRING FLING FESTIVAL and populated by 9,978 people.

Lynn squinted through her sunglasses, smiling in spite of herself at the memory of the Spring Fling and how much the annual event had meant to her mother. *She was so active in the garden club,* Lynn thought. *And why not? Mom could grow anything, anywhere. Not like me.* Her eyes moved then to the population figure, and she couldn't help but wonder if her brother's death had lowered it by one. *Surely someone's had a baby to offset it by now*, she thought, wondering who kept track of such things and how often they updated the sign.

She sensed her daughter's presence before she felt her hand around her waist. "We're here," Rachel said.

Lynn nodded. Yes, they were. They were here, back in Bloomfield. Such a quaint, quiet little town. And they would be here only for a short time. So why did she feel as if everything familiar was about to be turned upside down?

She swallowed and looked up at her daughter, who also seemed to study the Bloomfield sign. "I'm ready if you are," Lynn said.

Rachel smiled down at her. "Maybe we should let poor Beasley out to run a few minutes before we head into town for lunch."

Lynn nodded. The faithful spaniel had endured a lot more hours in the car than he was used to and would no doubt appreciate a quick romp. She watched Rachel return to the vehicle, open the back door, and let the grateful dog out. As he hurried into the grass beside the road, with Rachel at his heels, Lynn shot up a prayer for whatever adventures lay ahead. Though she had no idea what those adventures might be, she could relax in the care of the One who did.

Rachel made sure Beasley had been fed and watered and relieved himself before loading him back inside the car. Then Rachel and Lynn climbed into the front seat and off they went, slowing down to observe the 25 miles-per-hour speed limit as they cruised Main Street and headed for the barbecue place at the far end of town.

Bert's Barbecue was one of Rachel's favorite memories of her few visits to Bloomfield. According to her mother, the eatery had been around forever, though no one seemed to know where the restaurant had gotten its name. Lynn said she'd asked her dad more than once, since there was nowhere he liked to eat more than Bert's, but even he hadn't known.

"That was before my time," he'd explained, though Lynn's childlike mind had grappled with the concept of time before her parents. Rachel smiled; she could certainly relate to that. She also remembered her mother explaining that Myron had been her parents' only child for fifteen years until Lynn came along—"the best surprise ever," her father often proclaimed—but it meant Lynn's parents were older than most of her friends' mothers and fathers. In grammar school, Lynn said it had been difficult even to conceive of a Bloomfield before her parents' time. And if Bert's Barbecue had been there, serving up their delicious pulled pork sandwiches and baby back ribs from the little hole-in-the-wall establishment at the end of Main Street, then Bert must have been so ancient that it was no wonder no one remembered him.

Rachel nearly chuckled at the memory of her mother relating that story. "I no longer use the word 'ancient' to describe people in their fifties or sixties, or even seventies, the way I used to," she'd announced. "But I suppose it's all relative and just becomes more so as the years roll by."

As far as Rachel was concerned, her mother was still young and vibrant, though her recent weariness concerned her. Rachel hoped their visit to Bloomfield would perk her mom up a bit and help her start resolving her grief issues.

As they continued down Main Street, Rachel couldn't help but wonder if the sights were evoking a bit of nostalgia for her mother.

"So, Mom," she ventured, "what do you think? Has Bloomfield changed at all?"

Lynn turned toward her daughter, and Rachel thought she detected a hint of tears in her eyes, though she couldn't be sure.

"Change?" Lynn said, a thin smile teasing her lips. "Somehow the word just doesn't work in tandem with Bloomfield, does it? I mean, look over there." She pointed, and Rachel snuck a peek before looking back at the road. "The bank where my parents did business is still in the same spot, with the same sign out front and the same guard sitting on a bench in the shade." Lynn paused. "No, wait. It's definitely the same guard—Clyde Something-or-Other—but he has changed. He's still dozing on the job like he always did, but he has a paunch now. See? The buttons on his uniform are stretched to the max." She chuckled. "I remember him as being tall and rather well-built, even somewhat imposing. Of course, I was a child then. Now I wonder if he'd even notice someone walking right past him wearing a ski mask and carrying a sawed-off shotgun, looking to rob the place."

Rachel laughed out loud. "Really, Mom, when has anything like that ever happened in Bloomfield? Then again, maybe that's the heart of Bloomfield's unchanging charm, right?"

"Unchanging." Lynn repeated the word as if it evoked memories of the past and ponderings for the future. Rachel imagined it did, at least for her mother. After all, the town and its charm might not change, but people did. The bank guard had grown older and heavier during her mother's absence—as had Lynn and everyone Lynn knew from her childhood and even her last visits before her mother died. Time marched on . . . even in Bloomfield. Perhaps those were the very thoughts parading through her mother's mind right now.

At last, Rachel spotted the barbecue joint where her mother had introduced her to some of the best food she'd ever tasted. From the first time her parents had brought her to Bloomfield to visit her grandparents, Rachel had fallen in love with Bert's and insisted on eating there at least once on each of their rare return visits. Today would be no different.

Pulling into the dirt-and-gravel parking lot, Rachel maneuvered the Corolla into a cool, shady spot and cracked the windows for the now-snoozing Beasley. Both women knew he'd be fine while they went inside to eat.

The welcome bell tinkled as Rachel pulled open the door and held it for her mother. She noticed her mom take a deep breath and hesitate before she stepped inside, and Rachel shot up a silent prayer that their meal would be a pleasant one for both of them.

The smoky, sweet aromas assailed her nostrils and revved up her appetite meter, causing her mouth to water. The buzz of conversation didn't stop completely upon their entry, but Rachel was certain it dropped a few decibels as she and her mother removed their sunglasses and allowed their eyes to adjust. Rachel spotted a couple of empty stools at the counter, but instead aimed for the one vacant booth toward the back of the tiny room, knowing that's what her mom would prefer. She imagined it was unusual to find any available seats at Bert's at all, particularly during lunchtime, so she didn't want to hesitate and risk losing the one table that looked inviting.

"Seat yourself," a voice called from behind the counter. "I'll be with you in a minute."

Rachel saw her mother nod, though she didn't glance toward the owner of the voice as they made their way to the back booth.

No doubt Lynn knew exactly who had called out to them and had chosen not to respond.

"That's Jolene Trump," Lynn whispered as they settled across from one another in the booth. Rachel couldn't help but notice that her mother had chosen the side that would allow her to keep her back turned toward the rest of the room. "That woman must be a hundred if she's a day," Lynn continued in her hushed tone, leaning across the table so Rachel could hear. "She was working here when I was a kid, and she was no spring chicken then."

In moments the woman zeroed in on their table, bearing two glasses of water and two menus. Rachel smiled in welcome, noticing the white waitress uniform, covered by a frilly yellow apron that looked like it had been around nearly as long as Jolene. Hands covered with age spots and blue veins, yet surprisingly steady, placed the water and menus on the table. Lynn's head was bent, as if fascinated with the menu in front of her.

"I'd tell you our specials if we had any," said the woman, chuckling as she spoke, "but we don't. We just fix the same thing every day, take it or leave it. Most people take it. And they like it too. Been here before? You don't look familiar."

Rachel glanced at her mother once again, waiting for a response. At last Lynn raised her head and looked into the wrinkled face of the woman who Rachel had heard was famous for declaring that she couldn't quit working at Bert's or both she and the eatery would die. A lot of people in Bloomfield, including Rachel's grandfather, had speculated over the years that she might be right.

Lynn's smile appeared forced. "Jolene, it's good to see you again. It's been a long time."

The old woman's faded blue eyes widened, and her forehead wrinkled a bit more. Rachel realized their waitress was probably trying to raise her eyebrows, but she didn't have any—didn't even make an effort to draw them on as so many older women seemed to do. The thought brought a curious question to Rachel's mind as she noticed that her mother's eyebrows had grown thinner and lighter recently. Would she soon have to resort to those awful penciled-on brows that left women looking as if they were perpetually surprised? Rachel certainly hoped not.

"Lynn Cofield? Is that you? Why, I haven't seen you since . . ." Jolene paused, frowning as if trying to focus on a long-ago time. Her face softened as the memory obviously returned. "It was when your mama died, wasn't it? Oh my, that's been awhile now. What—five, ten years? Maybe more."

Lynn blinked, and Rachel wondered if she was fighting tears.

"Nearly ten years," Lynn answered, her voice surprisingly calm. "Yes. And it's Lynn Myers now." She smiled, no doubt in an effort to temper the correction, Rachel mused. "I haven't been a Cofield since I got married more than thirty-five years ago."

Jolene lifted her head and nodded slowly, her short, blue-gray perm bobbing with her. "Ah yes, I remember now. You up and married that stranger that came into town, didn't you? Nearly broke your poor mama's heart, moving out of Bloomfield the way you did. And so far! Why would you want to move so far away? Always seemed to me you two could have settled down here. Nothing wrong with living in Bloomfield, you know. I've been here all my life, and I can tell you, it's a fine place to live."

Lynn bit her lip, and Rachel could only imagine the effort it took to restrain her words. After all, her mother hadn't exactly moved to the ends of the earth; four hundred miles wasn't far at all. Besides, she had to go where her husband worked, didn't she? Rachel was proud of the way her mother held her smile as she spoke.

"Yes, Bloomfield is a fine place to live. And now my daughter, Rachel, and I are here for a few days—maybe longer—to get things settled with my brother's estate."

The woman's eyes widened even farther. "Your brother's estate? Of course! Myron Cofield. He did pass away recently, didn't he?" She leaned down slightly and lowered her voice to a near whisper. "I even heard some scuttlebutt that you might be coming back for that reason, but then I forgot all about it, especially since I didn't hear anything about a funeral. Strange, don't you think? But then, Myron was a strange one—no offense intended." She grinned and raised herself upright again. "Well, so here you are, you and your daughter. You gonna stay up at Myron's old place?"

Lynn hesitated. "I'm . . . not sure yet. As soon as we eat, we thought we'd head over there and see if it's livable. If not, we'll get a room at the bed and breakfast here in town."

Jolene nodded. "That's what I'd do, for sure. The bed and breakfast is a fine establishment—good food and nice, clean rooms. But Myron's place?" She shivered. "You couldn't pay me to stay there, not even for one night. The house is bad enough, but that groundskeeper, old Jason? A lot of people say he's harmless, and I'm sure that's true. But he loves hanging out at that old cemetery just way too much, and that's not normal if you ask me."

Rachel wanted to say that indeed no one had asked her, but she figured if her mother could restrain her words, so could she.

"So," Jolene said, pulling her pencil and order pad from the yellow apron's front pocket, "you two ready to order or do you want to study the menu for a while?"

Rachel breathed a sigh of relief, sensing her mother was glad for the change in subject. "I'll have a pulled pork sandwich," she said, buying her mother a little time, "with cole slaw and fries and a root beer. I'm starved."

Jolene scribbled the order and then looked at Lynn.

"I'll have the same," she said, smiling in what Rachel imagined was an attempt at levity, "but hold the fries and make it a diet soda. I'm trying to get rid of these extra fifteen pounds I've been carrying around for a while now."

Jolene smirked as she wrote down the order. "Just like nearly everybody else around here, trying to lose weight. Doesn't do much good though, does it? Everybody I see keeps carrying around those extra fifteen or twenty pounds, no matter how many diet sodas they drink." She shrugged. "Me? I don't worry about it. At my age, who cares?"

She cackled as she walked away, and Lynn leaned forward, whispering once again. "How fair is it that she can say something like that? Jolene's never worried about her weight a day in her life; she's always been as skinny as a rail. She doesn't understand that some of us are calorically challenged."

Rachel smiled, knowing her mom wasn't being mean or catty, though "calorically challenged" had become her way of referring to herself lately. Reaching across the table to pat her mom's hand, Rachel changed the subject. "The news of our arrival should be all over town by the end of the day, don't you think?"

Lynn appeared surprised for a moment. Then she nodded. "I'm sure you're right. Now that Jolene knows we're here, everyone from one end of Main Street to the other should know by sunset."

By the time Lynn and Rachel returned to the car, complaining all the way that they were so full they never wanted to eat again, Beasley greeted them with enthusiasm. His ears were on high alert when they opened the doors, and he looked at them anxiously, as if waiting for the all-clear to jump out of the car.

"Just a few more minutes, Beasley," Lynn said, reaching back to ruffle the soft golden fur on top of the dog's head. "As soon as we get to Myron's place, I'll let you out to run, I promise."

The dog seemed to accept her at her word and lay back down on the seat as Rachel pulled out of the parking lot and headed in the direction of Cemetery Drive, which would take them to their destination.

Couldn't they have named the street something else? Lynn wondered. *Who on earth names a road Cemetery Drive?* She sighed. *People in Bloomfield, of course. There's a cemetery at the end of the drive, so . . .*

She shook her head. Only her brother would have wanted to live in that ugly mausoleum next to a cemetery. And now the place belonged to her. She still hadn't decided if that would turn out to be a blessing or a curse.

It took less than five minutes to reach their destination. Rachel pulled the Corolla into the long, weed-infested gravel driveway and parked while Lynn found herself wondering just what this so-called caretaker named Jason actually did around there. Apparently, his caretaking didn't extend to Myron's place—correction, her place—as the driveway showed signs of neglect; although the adjoining cemetery looked fairly decent by comparison. And surprisingly, though the house could use a coat or two of paint, she had to admit that it didn't look as bad as she'd expected.

She climbed out of the car and opened the back door to let Beasley out. She stood next to the Toyota and looked up at the somewhat eerie two-story home, once again wondering what had possessed her brother to want to live here alone for those many years. Had his heart really been so broken by his fiancée's rejection that this had become his hideaway from the world, or had his mind been broken too?

She shuddered as she once again forced her eyes to the right, toward the sprawling cemetery that seemed to spew forth from the side of the big old house and spread out in waves across the adjoining countryside. At the far corner, just beyond the oldest headstones, sat a small building—more of a shack than anything else—and Lynn recognized it as the place where Jason lived. Myron always assured her that the strange man was harmless and that the two otherwise male recluses enjoyed one another's limited company. When Lynn saw the tattered curtain on the building's one window move, she realized they were being watched.

"Let's go inside," she said, reaching for Rachel's hand. "We may as well see what we're up against here. If it's as bad as I think it is, we'll climb right back into the car and get that room at the bed and breakfast, I promise."

Rachel laughed as they approached the expansive porch graced by three old rockers that appeared to wait for them. "Don't worry about it on my account, Mom. You know I love a good adventure. Staying in this old place tonight would be fun."

Fun? Lynn raised her eyebrows and glanced at her only child. *Most definitely Daniel's daughter. I love her dearly, but I sometimes wonder if she didn't just skip my genes entirely.*

Opening her purse, she fished around for the key that had been mailed to them with the letter informing her of Myron's death and her inheritance. After she'd assessed the inside, she and Rachel would go out to locate Myron's grave and pay their final respects. But for now, she had to face the inside of a house that had given her chills even when Myron still lived in it. However would she deal with it now that he was gone and the house belonged to her?

Taking a deep breath, she placed the key in the lock, fought to turn it, and finally succeeded, pushing the door open with a creak that would have wakened the dead . . . who were unnervingly close by, she reminded herself.

She tightened her grip on Rachel's hand, and the two of them stepped inside.

 Chapter 3

"EEEEW," RACHEL COMPLAINED AS THE CLOSED-UP BUILDING unleashed its musty odors on the intruders. "This place stinks! It smells like somebody died in here."

"Somebody did," Lynn reminded her, "though I don't think that's what you smell. I understand the groundskeeper found Myron nearly right away after he died, so it's not like he was lying here dead for long."

"You're right. Sorry, Mom." Rachel squeezed Lynn's hand before letting it go. "I guess it's just the smell of an old house that hasn't had any windows open since before Uncle Myron died."

"And probably not many before. I can remember this place being closed up and stuffy no matter what time of day or season we came to visit. It was part of Myron's eccentric recluse persona, I suppose."

"Ya think?" Rachel's laugh had a nervous edge to it as the two took a couple of tentative steps farther into the entryway. "Eccentric is putting it mildly."

Lynn smiled. Her confident, daring daughter seldom showed any misgivings, but Lynn sensed them now. Not that she could blame her. Lynn was having her own confidence crisis at the moment.

"Where are the lights around here?" Rachel asked, running her hands along the walls. "You don't think the power's been turned off, do you?"

Before Lynn could answer, an overhead light flipped on, and the two women jumped as they turned back toward the door. Framed by the outside sunlight, a man who appeared to be in his mid- to late sixties stood in the open doorway, staring at them, a gleam in his dark eyes that did nothing to calm Lynn's already fragile nerves. She'd met Jason before, so it wasn't as if she didn't recognize him, but knowing his identity did not attest to his character. The man was so genuinely strange that he made her late brother look normal by comparison.

Lynn swallowed. "Jason," she said, trying to steady her voice, "it's nice to see you again. I'm Lynn Myers, Myron's sister, and this is my daughter, Rachel. We've met before. Do you remember?"

The old man squinted his eyes as if studying them while searching his memory banks. "Sure," he said at last. "I remember. I don't forget nothin'. Got a memory like a steel trap, I do."

Rachel offered her hand, though Lynn sensed her daughter's hesitancy. "Hello, Mr. . . . ?"

"Just Jason," he said, scarcely touching her hand in response. "Don't like bein' called Mister."

Rachel nodded and withdrew her hand.

"I knew you was comin'," Jason said. "Myron told me if anything ever happened to him to watch out for you 'cause you'd be swoopin' in to claim your inheritance." He shrugged.

"Don't matter to me. Myron promised I could live in my little house out back as long as I wanted, whether he was here or not. Said he put it in his will."

His lined face grew hard then, as if daring the women to challenge him. Since Lynn hadn't yet seen the will, she declined to do so. That would have to wait until she'd met with the estate lawyer and found out the details of the inheritance. Meanwhile, she'd have to put up with the odd caretaker and his cantankerous ways.

Before she could answer, Beasley bounded in the door, nearly knocking Jason down in his enthusiasm. Waiting for a negative reaction from the groundskeeper, Lynn blinked in surprise when he instead leaned down and patted the dog on his head.

"Hey there," he said. "You must be Beasley. Myron told me about you. Said his sister mentioned you in a letter but he never did get to meet you. Don't know why no one brought you here to visit us before." He raised his head and shot an accusatory glance in Lynn's direction before returning his attentions to the receptive animal. Beasley's short tail wagged along with his entire rear end, and it was obvious the two had made an immediate connection.

Great, Lynn thought, sending a silent scolding toward Beasley. *A fine watchdog you are!*

Pushing away the temporary interruption caused by Beasley's entrance, she forced a smile as she tried to pick up the conversation where they'd left off. "Yes, well, thank you for that information about Myron's will, Jason. I . . . I'll be meeting with Myron's lawyer tomorrow. For now, we just wanted to check out the house and see if it will work for us to stay here for the few days we'll be in town. If not, we'll just go to the bed and breakfast and get a room there."

"Nope," Jason said, shaking his head. "No need for you to do that. I cleaned up the kitchen and a bedroom and bathroom too, just 'cause I knew you'd be comin'. Course, I didn't know there'd be two of you, so I didn't clean but one room. I can clean another one if you'd like. There's plenty of 'em."

"Oh, no, that won't be necessary," Lynn said, holding up her hand. "Rachel and I can share a room. That's no problem at all. We appreciate all you've done already."

Jason paused before nodding. "Good. Follow me and I'll show you which room you can use."

As the man stepped past them, headed for the stairway, Lynn caught a whiff of body odor that nearly knocked her over. She glanced at Rachel, whose eyes watered as she wrinkled her nose. Quite obviously, their host wasn't big on baths or showers—or clean clothes either, for that matter. Of course, that didn't matter a whit to Beasley, who scrambled up the stairs behind him.

Keeping a safe distance, the two women followed. Lynn marveled at the solid condition of the handrail and the steps beneath her feet. Even the dark mahogany paneling that dominated the house seemed in mint condition, though it could no doubt benefit from a good scrubbing. The building was certainly old and musty, but at least it seemed to be in decent condition. Still, she couldn't help but wonder at the cleanliness of the room that awaited them, considering who had done the so-called cleaning.

Jason reached the top of the stairs and turned immediately to his left, stopping at the first room and pushing open the thick wooden door. The smell of lemon oil was a pleasant surprise, almost offsetting Jason's presence as the two women stepped past him into a bright, spacious room. Two sets of heavy damask curtains were drawn back to reveal sparkling clean windows, and even the sunrays that shone through them seemed nearly devoid of dust particles.

Lynn felt her eyes widen as she took in the king-sized four-poster bed in the middle of the room. The quilted comforter that covered it looked fresh-from-the-cleaners ready, giving her hope that the sheets and blankets were equally pristine. Spotting the door that opened into an adjoining bathroom, Lynn sidestepped toward it to peek inside. The porcelain, claw-footed tub sparkled as brightly as the toilet, sink, and small shower. Stunned . . . and grateful . . . Lynn smiled to herself.

Still, should they stay or head back into town? Rachel had indicated she liked the idea of staying here, that she would consider it an adventure. But it was an awfully big house for the two of them to rattle around in for the next few days—especially with Jason hovering close by.

She turned back to see if she could catch her daughter's eye and get a feel for what Rachel wanted to do, but the first thing she noticed was that Beasley had already hopped onto the padded bench at the foot of the bed, making himself right at home as he curled up and prepared for a nap.

"Looks like we're staying here tonight, Mom," Rachel said, grinning as she looked from Beasley to Lynn and back again.

Lynn nodded. "It certainly appears that way, doesn't it?" She turned her attention toward Jason, who waited in the doorway. "This is lovely. Thank you, Jason."

He nodded, and Lynn thought she spotted a slight twitch on the right side of his mouth. Was that his version of a smile? If so, it was the only one she'd ever seen from the man.

"There's clean towels in the bathroom closet," he said, "and I stocked the refrigerator and kitchen cupboards with a few things. If I forgot something, just let me know and I'll go to

town and pick it up. I promised Myron I'd take care of you."
He squinted his eyes once again before adding, "And I always
keep my promises."

Lynn wondered why the man's words seemed to steal what
little sense of assurance she'd managed to gather upon seeing the
cleanliness of the room. If Beasley wasn't already snoozing and
Rachel so obviously determined to stay here, she'd still insist on
going into town to rent a room.

*Oh well, what harm can one night do? We'll see how it goes
between now and morning and decide then about tomorrow.
One day at a time.*

"Thank you, Jason," she said. "I'm sure we have everything
we need. We'll be just fine. We won't be bothering you for anything else."

Their eyes locked for a moment as Lynn wondered how the
man would respond to her obvious dismissal. Would he honor
her wishes and go quietly—and leave them alone after that? She
certainly hoped so.

At last, he nodded and broke eye contact. "Well then, I'll
be going. I have things to do in the garden, after all. You know
where to find me if you need me."

The two women waited until they were certain Jason had
reached the bottom of the stairs and then gone outside and
closed the door behind him. "The garden?" Rachel said, raising
a quizzical eyebrow in her mother's direction. "I didn't notice a
garden outside."

Lynn nodded. "I'd forgotten, but Myron told me once that
Jason referred to the cemetery as his garden and the various
deceased who are buried there as his plants. A little macabre,
don't you think?"

"More than a little. But hey, it goes with the setting." She smiled then and slid her arm through her mother's. "Okay, enough about creepy old Jason and his garden. Let's go check out the kitchen—and the rest of the house too. Maybe if we open the place up, it'll smell better. I mean, it is summertime, right? Let's get some fresh air in here and see what happens." She laughed. "Too bad we can't air Jason out too. He sure could use it."

Lynn joined in her daughter's laughter, as the two of them headed downstairs, leaving Beasley to nap in peace.

"Hey, at least there's coffee," Rachel called over her shoulder as she opened and closed cupboards and rummaged around. "And several cans of soup and tuna. Looks promising so far."

She turned and watched her mother pull open the door of what had to be a thirty-year-old refrigerator. "Does that thing even work?" Rachel asked.

"Surprisingly so," Lynn answered. "Everything in here is good and cold. Let's see, there's a quart of milk and some eggs and bread. The basic condiments too—mayo, ketchup, mustard. And even some cheddar cheese. I'd say we can get by for a day or two, don't you think?"

"Definitely," Rachel agreed. "Even the dishes and silverware seem relatively clean, and there's a coffee pot and a few pans besides. It may not be the best stocked kitchen in the world, but it's functional."

Lynn closed the refrigerator and turned toward her daughter. "Well then, are you still okay with us staying here? I mean, it's not too late to change your mind. I have no problem with packing Beasley back into the car and heading for the bed and breakfast."

Rachel stood in front of the countertop, leaning back against it as she stretched out her long, blue-jeaned legs in front of her. "I know this is going to sound weird, Mom, but I like it here—smell and all. Well, not Jason's smell, but the house. We've got most of the windows open now, and it's already fresher, don't you think? I vote for staying—not just for a day or two, but for as long as we have to be here to settle things for Uncle Myron." She frowned, remembering something Jason had said. "Do you think your brother really did make a provision in his will for Jason to stay here for the rest of his life? It would make sense, wouldn't it? After all, where else would he go? He's been here like forever, right?"

Lynn smiled. "That's just like you to be concerned with Jason's future. Compassion is another trait you inherited from your father. He never could stand to see someone suffer, and you're exactly the same way." She shook her head. "How many times did you bring home a wounded kitten or befriend the new kid at school? Remember that time you actually ended up in a fistfight trying to defend a smaller child from a bully?"

Rachel felt a blush creep up her cheeks. "All right, Mom, enough about me. What about Jason? Do you think Uncle Myron provided for his future by writing him into the will?"

"I wouldn't be surprised. Myron cared about Jason. He was one of the few people he allowed into his life, and it's only natural that he'd want to provide for him after his death. But I suppose I'll find all that out tomorrow when I see the lawyer."

Rachel smiled. "You're right. We'll worry about that later. Meanwhile, I'm hungry again. I know, I know. We just had lunch an hour ago. But I need dessert, and I just spotted a bag of chocolate chip cookies in the cupboard. How about if I make some coffee and we sit outside on the porch and have a snack?"

"Now that's a great idea," Lynn said, a smile teasing her lips. "And like Jolene pointed out, those extra pounds just keep following us around no matter how many diet sodas we drink anyway, so let's just go for it."

Rachel grinned. It was good to see her mom smiling and enjoying herself again.

The afternoon sun warmed Lynn, making her drowsy, but she used it as an excuse to snag a second cookie. The sugar, combined with the caffeine from the coffee, would help her stay awake. Strange. Before Daniel died, she scarcely ever considered taking a nap; now she found herself longing for one at least once a day. She knew from recent experience, however, that when she allowed herself the luxury of a daytime nap, it meant she wouldn't sleep well that night. It would be hard enough sleeping in a strange place, sharing a bed with her daughter, and knowing that a "garden" full of corpses was planted just yards from their room. But at least she knew the corpses were harmless; she still wasn't so sure about Jason.

"Want some more coffee, Mom?"

Lynn turned toward her daughter, who sat in the rocker next to her. They'd done their best to clean the seats before settling into them, and now Lynn had to admit they were surprisingly comfortable.

"Sure, you might as well top it off," she said.

Rachel stood to her feet and took the nearly-empty mugs into the house, returning a moment later with them full to the

Chapter 4

"MRS. MYERS? LYNN MYERS?"

The attractive young woman—probably in her mid-thirties, Lynn decided, qualifying her as young so far as Lynn was concerned—stepped up to the porch but stopped at the bottom of the steps, lifting her head to lock hazel eyes on Lynn as she waited.

She looks familiar, Lynn mused but dismissed the thought and regrouped. "Yes, I'm Lynn Myers. And you are . . . ?"

The woman's face broke into a grin, considerably softening her demeanor. For the first time Lynn noticed their visitor's brown ponytail, and it struck her as incongruous with her otherwise professional appearance. "I didn't think you'd remember me," she said, climbing the three wide steps to the porch, where she once again stopped, this time immediately in front of Lynn. "I'm Bailey McCullough. You might remember my parents, Jim and Leila. We lived over on Fourth Street—still do, actually."

Lynn raised her eyebrows. Lively, energetic Bailey McCullough, that cute little girl with the pigtails, always racing up and down the sidewalk in front of their house on her bright brim and steaming. She'd barely sat back down when the dog raised his head and looked down the long driveway toward the street.

"Who's that?" Rachel asked. "Looks like we have company."

Lynn followed her daughter's gaze and zeroed in on the dark SUV now crunching its way down the dirt-and-gravel driveway. It pulled up directly behind Lynn's Corolla and stopped. Mother and daughter waited, coffee cups in hand, until the driver's door opened and a woman stepped out.

"Do you think she's here to see us?" Rachel asked.

Lynn didn't take her eyes off their visitor as she answered. "I sincerely doubt she's here to see Jason, and no one comes out here without a specific purpose—unless, of course, it's to visit someone in Jason's 'garden'—and then they usually take the other driveway that bypasses the house and leads straight to the cemetery. So yes, I'd say she's most definitely here to see us, but I can't imagine why."

"Looks like we'll find out soon enough," Rachel said, setting her coffee down on the small wrought iron table between the rockers and rising from her chair.

Lynn followed suit, her imagination threatening to shoot off in all directions, while her inner surprise meter registered a violent protest as it hit "tilt." Whoever this woman was and whatever she was doing here, Lynn was not pleased at all. Civilized people should have the courtesy to call ahead and make an appointment rather than showing up unannounced on someone's doorstep—even in Bloomfield. Small town or not, there was no excuse for being rude.

Lynn took a step forward, her daughter at her side, ready to confront whatever unexpected issues were about to be unleashed on them. She hoped her expression appeared as confident as she

meant it to be, but underneath all she wanted was for Daniel be standing next to her, ready to battle unseen foes and cha pion their family's causes.

You're being silly, Lynn Myers, she scolded herself. *The la is probably just dropping by to say hello or something.* But confident stride of their approaching visitor, briefcase in ha told her otherwise.

red two-wheeler? Well, hadn't she turned into a lovely young woman! But that still didn't explain her visit.

"I do remember," Lynn said, offering a smile. "And of course I remember your parents. Are they doing well?"

A flicker of pain skipped across Bailey's face before she answered. "My dad died a couple of years ago. It's just Mom and me now. I moved back in with her not long after Dad died and I came back to Bloomfield."

An unreasonable pang of guilt pierced Lynn's heart as she considered how much her own parents would have loved having her close enough to visit daily, but she shook it off.

"That's nice," Lynn said, her guard up as she spoke. "I'm sure your mom appreciates having you there."

Rachel cleared her throat then, and Lynn turned toward her. "I'm sorry. Bailey, this is my daughter, Rachel. She's come here to help me sort through my late brother's affairs." She moved her gaze back to their guest. "I'm sure you're aware of that situation."

Bailey nodded. "I am, and I'm very sorry to hear about your loss. In fact, that's why I'm here."

Aha. At last. The reason for her visit. Lynn smiled and indicated the three rocking chairs behind them. "Why don't you sit down and tell us about it? We just cleaned these chairs a short while ago, so I promise they're safe." Turning back to Rachel she said, "Honey, why don't you get Bailey a cup of coffee? There's still plenty left, isn't there?"

Rachel beamed as she headed for the front door. "There sure is. And cookies too."

"Oh, I don't want to be any trouble," Bailey objected as she settled herself into the middle rocker where Rachel had been sitting earlier.

Lynn ignored her impulse to ask Bailey to move down one chair. What did it matter? Besides, it would probably be easier to visit this way. "It's no trouble at all," she assured her. "Rachel enjoys waiting on people. She's always trying to do something for me." She chuckled. "But what can I say? It's one of the few traits she inherited from both my late husband *and* me. He loved helping people, and I'm afraid I'm a classic helicopter mom, always hovering."

Bailey smiled and nodded. "You sound like you're related to my mom. Then again, maybe it's just a mom thing in general. I remember my grandma being that way."

Rachel reappeared on the porch, carrying an extra mug of steaming coffee, and set it down on the table between Bailey's chair and Lynn's. As Rachel retrieved her own cup, she asked, "Would you like anything in that? There's some milk in the fridge and sugar in the cupboard. Mom and I drink it black, so I hadn't bothered to get it out. It's no problem to get it, though. I should have asked before I went inside."

Bailey waved her off. "This is fine just as it is." When Rachel held out the small plate of cookies, Bailey nodded and took one. "Thank you. I hadn't expected such a warm welcome when I headed over here."

Rachel sat down in the far chair and tilted her head. "Why is that?"

Bailey's gaze skidded from Rachel to Lynn and back again before she answered. "Well, it's just that . . . even when your uncle was alive, it was well known that he didn't particularly like visitors. And now that he's gone and the only one around is old Jason . . ." Her voice drifted off and she offered a weak smile. "But I'm the only society columnist in Bloomfield. Seriously, could the town sustain two? Anyway, when the news hit yesterday that you were on your way, I got the assignment to come out here and interview you."

Interview? News? Society columnist? Lynn was stunned. Had she really been gone so long that she'd forgotten how a simple visit from a former resident could stir up the town's tongues until absolutely everyone knew about the event? No. That part she hadn't forgotten. But newsworthy? That was a little hard to buy.

"You want an interview?" she asked, retrieving her own mug full of barely warm coffee and clutching it between her hands. "Why in the world would you want to interview me?"

Bailey smiled and sipped her java. "Mmm, delicious," she murmured before setting it down on the table and picking up her briefcase. "As I said, I'm the society columnist for the *Gazette*." She glanced from the notebook computer she pulled out of her briefcase to Lynn and said, "You're familiar with it, I'm sure."

Lynn nodded. As far back as she could remember, there had been exactly one newspaper in town, and nearly everyone read it. She wondered if that still held true in this new Internet age. She'd heard most people got their news online these days, but then again, she wasn't most people. Lynn liked the feel of real newspapers and magazines and books in her hands, and she couldn't imagine that changing anytime soon.

"When I graduated from high school and went off to college," Bailey explained as she fired up her computer and settled it onto her lap, "I studied journalism and ended up landing a reporter's job at a decent-sized daily in the next state. But I missed Bloomfield, and when Dad died and I found out the *Gazette* had this opening, it just made sense to come back home." Her smile seemed apologetic as she shrugged. "That's how I ended up working part-time at the *Gazette*, reporting on the Spring Fling, weddings, church bazaars, fund-raisers . . . and, of course, visitors in town." She dug into her briefcase and pulled out a digital camera. "I double as photographer too. Hope you don't mind, but I'll need a photo or two to go with the article."

Lynn watched Bailey as she spoke, and she had to admit she liked the young woman's sincerity. Despite that, she wasn't so sure she appreciated being singled out for a newspaper interview, not to mention photos. True, she had grown up in Bloomfield, where everyone knew everyone else's business or at least did their best to find out, but Lynn liked to think of herself as a private person. Daniel, on the other hand, had never met a stranger and was so completely trusting of others that she doubted he ever had a secret in his life.

"So," Bailey said, apparently satisfied that her notebook was primed and ready to go, "where should we start? I know you're here to settle your uncle's affairs, since the news of your planned arrival came to me via your lawyer." She turned and flashed a smile at Rachel before returning her attention to Lynn. "But we didn't know about your daughter coming too. That'll add an interesting aspect to the story."

Lynn wanted to ask just how dull Bloomfield had become that a visit from a former resident and her college-aged daughter qualified as interesting, but why bother? Bailey was just doing her job, and it didn't appear the pleasant but determined young woman would give up and leave without a story, so Lynn might as well give her what little information she could. How that could add up to an actual piece for the *Gazette* she couldn't imagine, but she'd do her best and "let the chips fall where they may," as her father used to say.

Before they could start, an anxious bark interrupted them from behind the closed front door.

"Beasley," Rachel said, hurrying from her seat to let him out. "He knows we have company."

"I hope you don't mind dogs," Lynn said. "He's friendly, I assure you."

Bailey's face lit up as Beasley circled and sniffed. She held her hand out, and the excited animal immediately placed his head beneath her touch. "I love dogs," Bailey said. "And Beasley looks like quite a gentleman."

"He is," Lynn said, her sense that she could trust Bailey now affirmed. Then again, Beasley had taken to old Jason, hadn't he? Maybe the dog's instincts weren't what they used to be.

Either way, they had an interview to do, so they might as well get to it.

●

"I like Bailey, don't you, Mom?"

Lynn watched her daughter clear away the cups and now-empty cookie plate and carry them inside. Lynn and Beasley followed close behind.

"Yes, I do," she admitted. "She seems like a very nice person—professional too, but without being stuffy, if you know what I mean."

Rachel chuckled as she set the plate in the sink. The old kitchen had no dishwasher, but the huge porcelain sink would hold a lot of dishes, and Lynn had always enjoyed washing them by hand. She and her mother had often done the task together when she was little, and the memory tugged at her heart as she positioned herself at the old round table in the corner of the room. The heavy, dark wood resembled most of the paneling in the house, though it bore a few scratches and nicks that had no doubt accumulated over the years. Lynn imagined her brother had eaten nearly all his meals right where she sat; she certainly couldn't picture him using the long, rectangular table in the dining area. If she were going to stay here in this house, she knew she'd get that dining table polished and ready for regular use . . . but since she had no plans to stay it really didn't matter.

"I thought the same thing," Rachel said, turning from the sink and crossing the linoleum floor to take a seat opposite her mother. "She did a great job with the interview, and I can't help but think she'll do just as good a job writing it up. But she's so natural and . . . I don't know, down-to-earth, I suppose. Must be that Bloomfield upbringing."

Lynn smiled. "Oh, I don't know. You didn't grow up in Bloomfield, but you're pretty natural and down-to-earth yourself. You don't have a pretentious bone in your body."

Rachel beamed. "Thanks, Mom. That's one of the nicest compliments you've ever given me."

"Really?" Lynn chuckled. "I guess I must not have given you enough compliments over the years if that's one of the best."

"So . . . what do you want to do the rest of the day?" Rachel asked. "I know we didn't bring much with us, but we probably should unpack what we have, don't you think? Then maybe we can drive into town for supper or something."

"Supper? Are you thinking of eating again?" She smiled and shook her head. "I don't know where you put it. And you never gain an ounce. Just wait until you get to be my age. All I have to do is think about food and I gain weight."

"Are you kidding, Mom? You look great for your age."

"For my age. Ah, those are the key words, aren't they? I'm

in my midfifties, so I guess I should be happy that I can still fit through the doorway and get around without the help of a walker, is that it?"

Rachel's laugh burst up from deep within her and seemed to echo off the high ceilings of the huge old house. "Oh, Mom, you are *too* funny! Seriously."

"If you say so," Lynn answered, swallowing her own laugh in the process. "All right, let's get unpacked and then head back into town. I'm not up for the Fancy Schmantzy tonight, but no more barbecue. Let's go for something a bit lighter, shall we?"

Rachel frowned. "The Fancy Schmantzy. I remember eating there once with you and Grandma, but that was a long time ago. It's the only really nice place around here, isn't it?"

Lynn nodded. "You're absolutely right. And it really is nice—for Bloomfield anyway. Maybe we'll dress up and go there right before we leave to head back home."

"Dress up? I don't know if I brought anything formal."

Lynn laughed. "Don't worry, honey. It doesn't have to be formal. Just not holey Levi's or overalls. There are plenty of other places in town where we can go dressed like that."

Rachel looked down at her T-shirt and jeans and smiled. "Then I guess I don't even need to change after I unpack."

"Not unless you want to," Lynn said. "Now, let's get those suitcases upstairs and get to work. The sooner we get done, the sooner we can go eat . . . again."

All the way into town, Rachel had lobbied for the steakhouse on Wren and Sidewinder, while Lynn had countered with "anything light." They'd finally compromised on one of the two Chinese restaurants in town and now sat across from one another in a booth at the Eastern Dragon Inn.

"The name of this place always makes me wonder if there's a western dragon somewhere," Rachel commented as she perused the menu. "When you and Grandma first brought me here, I was actually scared of all those fire-breathing creatures decorating this place. I thought the food was going to burn my tongue."

Lynn smiled. Rachel had never told her that before. Strange, the things children imagine and yet keep to themselves. But then, she'd done similar things when she was young.

"So what looks good?" she asked, hoping they might share an order of rice and chop suey, or something equally simple.

"Egg rolls," Rachel said. "We have to start with egg rolls. And soup. Other than that . . ." She paused, a slight frown creasing her brow as she continued to study the seemingly endless list of possibilities. After a moment, her eyes focused on a particular item and her face lit up. "Number eighteen, stir-fry shrimp and veggies," she announced, looking over the top of the menu. "Doesn't that sound delicious?"

Lynn shrugged. It not only sounded just fine to her, but it also sounded like she was getting off easier than she'd expected. "Sure, why not? Number eighteen it is."

After the waiter took their order and left them with a steaming pot of tea, Rachel quickly filled their two small cups and poured sugar into hers. Lynn resisted the temptation and forced herself to drink it straight, though she much preferred it sweet.

"So," Rachel said as she sipped her tea, "tomorrow's the big day when we meet with the lawyer. What do you think will happen?"

Lynn was pleased to hear Rachel say "we" rather than "you" in reference to the next day's meeting. She had so hoped her daughter would accompany her, though she knew Rachel didn't like getting up early unless absolutely necessary. Their appointment was at nine, so as far as Lynn's daughter was concerned, that was early.

"I have no idea what to expect," Lynn admitted, "though I can't imagine it will be too complicated. After all, the letter said Myron left everything to me. Of course, if Jason's right about being able to stay in that old shack for the rest of his life, that will throw a real fly in the ointment when it comes to trying to sell the place."

Rachel frowned and set the cup down. "You think you'll do that? Sell it, I mean?"

"It's the only thing that makes sense. We certainly can't afford two houses. I can just barely keep my head above water with one. In fact, selling Uncle Myron's place will really help a lot with upkeep on the other one, not to mention the rest of my bills and expenses."

A light blush tinged Rachel's cheeks as she dropped her gaze. When she looked back up, Lynn saw a hint of tears in her green eyes. "You mean, like my college tuition, don't you? I know that's been so hard on you, Mom. Really, I do. And I'm going to start paying you back and covering my current expenses as soon as I can, honest."

Lynn's heart constricted as she realized the guilt trip she'd put on her daughter. "Oh, honey, I didn't mean it that way," she said quickly, setting her cup down and reaching across the table to cover Rachel's hand with her own. "I'm just so glad you were able to go to college and get your education, and I don't mind paying for that one bit. You have your whole life ahead of you now, sweetheart, and I'm glad you're facing it with your college diploma in hand."

Rachel's smile appeared tentative. "Mom, I know you don't mind paying my college expenses, and I know you're glad I went to college and graduated. But that doesn't mean it hasn't been hard on you—or that I don't appreciate it. Because I do, more than you can imagine. And just as soon as we get things settled and know where we're going to live, I'll start working on lining up a job so I can start paying you back."

It was Lynn's turn to frown. "What do you mean, where we're going to live? We're going to live in the house we've always lived in. Where else would we live?"

Rachel's cheeks flushed again, and she shrugged. "I don't know. Here, maybe? In Uncle Myron's house?"

Lynn thought her jaw would drop to the table. "Live in Uncle Myron's house? Why on earth would we want to do something like that?"

Rachel shrugged again. "Seriously, I don't know why. I guess because . . . because I like it there. And I think I like the idea of living in Bloomfield too."

Lynn felt her eyes grow wide. This was a turn of events she certainly hadn't anticipated. Then again, she'd had more surprises lately than anyone should have to contend with—even people who liked surprises. And the good Lord knew, she wasn't one of them.

"I really don't think that's an option," Lynn said. "At least, not a viable one. The only thing that makes sense is to sell it. You can see that, can't you?"

Rachel paused. "Mom, you always tell me that I should pray before I make decisions . . . and you're right. But don't you think you should do the same?"

Lynn nearly gasped at her daughter's words. Pray about living in Myron's ugly old house? Why should she think God would even want her to consider such a thing? Still, Rachel had a point. Lynn truly had drilled it into her daughter's head that she needed to ask God for guidance before making major decisions. The question in front of her now was, would she practice what she preached . . . or at least ask God's opinion on the matter?

The answer unnerved her. She did not even want to consider the possibility that God's plans wouldn't line up with her own.

# Chapter 5

"HARRISON AND HARRISON," RACHEL READ AS THEY MADE THEIR way down the hall toward the wooden door with the lettering on the smoked-glass window. "I didn't know there were two of them."

"Well, there are . . . sort of," Lynn answered, shifting her shoulder to straighten her purse's leather strap. "Chuck's son joined him in the practice some years ago and now pretty much runs it himself. Chuck is actually semiretired and just handles a few cases for friends now and then. He and Myron knew each other for years, so that's how he ended up dealing with his estate. I understand the son is out of town, but Chuck said he'd come in just to meet with us."

"Interesting," Rachel commented, reaching for the door handle. "I'm looking forward to meeting him."

They stepped into the reception area, which wasn't much more than an old desk piled high with papers and files, a chair on rollers behind the desk, and three plastic chairs sitting against the wall where an obviously artificial hanging plant occupied the corner and was sprinkled with dust. The reception area was basic at best, with no actual receptionist in sight.

The women looked at one another, raised their eyebrows in unison, and shrugged. Rachel cleared her throat. "Hello?"

No answer.

Lynn spotted a small, domed silver bell on the desk and stepped over to ring it. The tinkle made her jump, but she stood her ground with Rachel at her side, waiting. They were rewarded seconds later when one of the two doors at the back of the room opened and a tall, hefty man with thick gray hair stepped out.

He smiled when he spotted them. "Can I help you?"

Lynn wondered why the man appeared surprised to see them. It wasn't unusual that he wouldn't recognize her on sight, since they hadn't seen one another in years, but shouldn't he at least have expected her arrival?

"I'm . . . Lynn Myers," she said, taking a step in his direction and wondering if she should offer her hand in greeting. "Myron Cofield's sister." She glanced back briefly before returning her gaze to the man in the rumpled suit jacket and crooked red tie. "And this is my daughter, Rachel. We . . . have an appointment." She glanced at her watch to confirm she had the time right. "At nine o'clock."

A warm smile spread across his face, and Lynn thought he suddenly looked ten years younger. "Of course," he said, stepping toward her and holding out his hand. Lynn took it and appreciated his firm grasp as he continued to speak. "Yes, Mrs. Myers . . . Lynn. Of course, I remember now. You do have an appointment, and I'm sorry my receptionist wasn't here to greet you when you came in. My son is out of town for a few days, so he gave her some time off too. Since I only work part-time and maintain a reduced caseload these days, I really didn't need her here. I hope you don't mind."

Lynn nodded. "I understand. Not a problem, Mr. Harrison."

"Please, call me Chuck. Everyone else does. Besides, it's not like it's the first time we've met, right?" He pushed the door open to his office and nodded them inside. "Come on in. Make yourself comfortable. Can I get you some coffee or water?"

"No thanks, nothing for me," Lynn said, stepping through the door.

"Me neither," said Rachel. "I'm fine, thanks."

Chuck closed the door behind them and indicated the two cushioned chairs in front of his desk, which was nearly as cluttered as the one in the reception area. The room itself was slightly less basic than the outside one, but a far cry from luxurious.

The women settled in across from Chuck, and though his smile was warm and his manner comfortable, Lynn felt her stomach clenching up once again. What if there were unexpected provisions in the will, snags and loopholes, or . . . ?

Stop it, she told herself. *You were managing just fine before you knew about any of this. What's the worst that can happen? You don't get the house. Do you really care? Do you really want it? Calm down and listen to what the man has to say.*

As the chitchat subsided and Chuck opened the will and began to read, pausing occasionally to explain a few minor points and asking if they had any questions, which they didn't, Lynn felt herself relax. So far, so good. Nothing unusual or difficult or unexpected. She began to breathe normally again.

"So as you can see," Chuck said at last, laying the document down in front of him, "it's all pretty cut and dried. Myron wanted to keep it simple, pretty much the way he lived his entire life, and he wanted you to have everything to do with as you please. Of course, he did specify that he wanted Jason to be able to stay on as long as he wishes, caring for the cemetery and helping out as much as he can, though that's a bit limited these days." He directed his smile at Lynn. "You know how it is when we get older—just can't do as much as we used to."

Lynn nodded. He was right, but she was still a bit concerned about how Jason would affect the eventual sale of the property— which, of course, was the only sensible thing to do with it.

"I . . . assume the provision for Jason holds even if the property is sold," she ventured.

Chuck raised his eyebrows. "Are you planning to sell? Myron said you probably would, but he hoped you wouldn't. He said he sure would like to see the old place stay in the family." He glanced at Rachel and flashed her a smile, and Lynn wondered if he envisioned the old manse being passed from generation to generation. She nearly shuddered at the possibility of her future grandchildren growing up next door to a cemetery.

"I am considering it," she said. "After all, I already have a home, and I certainly don't need two. Just the upkeep alone, not to mention taxes and insurance . . ." Her voice trailed off as she felt Rachel's hand on her arm. She turned to look at her daughter, whose green eyes flashed a silent plea. Lynn frowned. What was her daughter trying to say? Was Rachel really that enamored by the place already? Did she truly want to stay there—live there instead of the home where she grew up?

Lynn's heart raced at the thought, and she knew she had to say something to end the meeting and escape the office, which suddenly seemed much smaller than it had moments earlier.

"I . . . I need to think and . . . and pray about it," she stammered. "I really haven't made any firm decisions yet."

Lynn caught Rachel's relieved smile first, then turned and saw a similar expression on Chuck's face. What was this, some sort of expanding conspiracy? Why in the world would anyone want her to live in that awful house, back in this cloistered little town of Bloomfield, where most of the residents remembered her as the flighty girl who'd cut and run when Prince Charming arrived on the scene?

Worst of all, if she ever did do something as crazy as moving back to Bloomfield, she'd have hundreds of headstones and a very strange and odoriferous groundskeeper for neighbors. What had she gotten herself into?

"I think Bailey did an amazing job on our interview, don't you?" Rachel commented as she finished reading the piece aloud to her mother. "And the two pictures she included are super."

"I suppose," Lynn conceded, resisting the urge to sneak a peak at the photos as she steered the Corolla down Cemetery Drive. Rachel had insisted on picking up a copy of the paper as soon as they'd left the lawyer's office and then reading the article out loud while Lynn drove. "I must admit, she stuck to the facts and didn't try to sensationalize the story—such as it is. I mean, really, a former Bloomfield resident and her daughter are in town to settle an estate. How is that a story? It's not like we're moving back here or anything. And from the sound of things, nearly everyone in town knew we were coming almost before we knew it ourselves."

She risked a glance at Rachel, just in time to see her shrug.

"It's a small town, Mom," she pointed out, still focused on the paper. "The rest of your observations are redundant. We're news because there isn't much else going on. We missed the Spring Fling by a few months, so everyone's looking for news, and it seems like we're it."

Lynn knew her daughter was right. Still, she wished the town folks weren't making such a big deal about their being there. In a matter of days, a week or so at most, they'd be gone again.

Wouldn't they?

Of course we will, she reassured herself. *Just because Rachel has taken some quaint, romanticized interest in this version of small-town America doesn't mean we're moving back here.* She nearly shuddered at the thought. *Leave our perfectly good home to live in Myron's monstrosity? Ridiculous.*

She pulled into said monstrosity's driveway just in time to see Jason skulking around the corner toward the cemetery entrance. One of the chairs on the porch rocked slightly. Had a breeze come up and stirred it, or had the groundskeeper been sitting there, watching and waiting for them? Since the other two chairs sat perfectly still, she imagined it was the latter.

She also imagined Myron had encouraged or at least accepted Jason's familiarity with the property, even though technically he was a caretaker for the cemetery only. She knew now that whoever ended up living in the house would have to put up with Jason's hanging around, and that would cause a problem when she went to sell it . . . which she assured herself she would do at the first possible chance. Rachel would simply have to accept it. Besides, what sort of future opportunities could her college-grad daughter expect to find in a place like Bloomfield? Lynn and Daniel hadn't sacrificed to send their only child to Bible college just so she could get a job at a local diner or drugstore. No, indeed they had not. Surely God had grander plans for Rachel than that, and Lynn would do whatever she could to see that her beloved daughter fulfilled them.

"How about if I make some tuna sandwiches?" Rachel offered as she climbed out of the car. "We can sit outside and eat them on the porch."

Lynn had to admit that sounded like an excellent idea. The day couldn't be lovelier, with a clear blue sky overhead and the temperature hovering in the upper seventies. Though Bloomfield occasionally had an extremely hot day or two in the summer and a brief cold snap in the winter, for the most part the weather was ideal. And today was certainly no exception.

"That sounds wonderful," Lynn said. "I set a big jar of sun tea outside before we left this morning. It's no doubt ready by now. I'll get that while you make the sandwiches."

In less than fifteen minutes they were settled into their rockers, their tea in frosty glasses on the small wrought iron table between them, and their sandwiches on paper plates in their laps. After greeting them excitedly upon their return, Beasley now snoozed contentedly in the noonday sun, just a few feet away. Lynn had to admit to feeling the first nostalgic tugs at her heart as memories of growing up in this cozy little town danced through her mind.

It's not the same, though, she reminded herself. *Mom and Dad are gone, and so is Myron. I hardly know anyone anymore. I haven't been in touch with my childhood friends in years, other than an occasional wave as I passed them on one of my infrequent visits—and that's been years ago now. I always meant to stay connected with them, but life just got in the way somehow.*

She imagined it was the same for her Bloomfield friends. Did they even remember her after all these years, or care what went on in her life? And if they did, were their memories positive—or did they still think she had made a terrible mistake by leaving Bloomfield behind thirty-five years earlier? She shook her head. Even if she did decide to sell the other house and stay here—which she wasn't about to do—how would she ever go about reconnecting with the town's residents and changing their opinion of her? At best, she'd be as much an outsider as someone who showed up here for the first time. No, moving back to Bloomfield simply wasn't an option.

"Mom?"

Her daughter's voice snagged Lynn's attention and pulled her back to her late brother's front porch. She turned to Rachel and smiled. "Yes, dear? I'm sorry. I was daydreaming a bit."

Rachel nodded. "It's a perfect day for it." She paused then and set the last few bites of her sandwich on her plate before looking back at Lynn, her green eyes serious. "We haven't gone out to the cemetery to pay our respects at Uncle Myron's grave yet. Do you think we should?"

Lynn raised her eyebrows. She had said she would, and she knew it was the right thing to do, though everything in her resisted the thought. She still felt a bit hurt that no one had contacted her immediately when Myron died so she could arrange for the services. Then again, at his request there had been none, and Chuck Harrison had pointed out in Myron's will that he specifically requested Lynn not be notified for at least two or three weeks simply so she could not push for a service he didn't want. It was the way he had requested it, and his lawyer had honored his wishes. On the other hand, if she'd been more attentive to her brother over the years, perhaps things would have been handled differently. And, of course, if she'd stayed in touch with some of her former Bloomfield friends, one of them might have alerted her to Myron's passing.

But several weeks had passed now since Myron's death, and the lawyer had assured her that the headstone had been put in place just before she arrived. She could think of no reason to put off saying their final good-byes any longer.

She nodded. "You're right. As soon as we finish lunch, let's head out there and find Myron's plot. Chuck said it would be fairly near the back side of the house, rather than in the newer section with the other freshly dug graves or even near Dad and Mom's plots. Apparently Myron wanted to be buried as close to his home as possible."

"Should we take some flowers?"

Lynn frowned. She wished they'd thought of it while they were in town. She knew there were at least two florist shops in Bloomfield. But they were back home now, and she didn't feel like driving into town again to buy a bouquet or plant. She glanced around the property and considered another option. "Maybe we could put together a decent arrangement of wild flowers. There are plenty of them scattered around the place, and it's what Myron would have preferred anyway."

Rachel readily agreed. They finished the last of their lunch and carried their paper plates and glasses into the kitchen. With Beasley pacing between them and sniffing at every leaf or blade of grass along the way, they set about picking flowers for their bouquet. Lynn still wasn't sure why she experienced such apprehension about their outing; after all, it wasn't as if she hadn't been to this cemetery before. Her parents were buried there, as well as her grandparents on both her maternal and paternal side. She should no doubt stop at their graves as well. But Myron . . .

Was it because he was the last member of her family? Or did it have something to do with the fact that she felt guilty over not having paid more attention to him, made more of an effort to cultivate a closer relationship? Whatever the reason, she felt as if she'd opened a Pandora's Box—and everyone knew such a thing could only produce all sorts of unwelcome surprises.

It didn't take long to locate Myron's grave. It was the only one that still had that freshly-dug appearance amidst the immediately surrounding ones that had obviously been there for years. Lynn and Rachel had left Beasley snoozing in the house, deciding it would be easier than trying to watch him and make sure he didn't attempt to start digging. Still, they'd have to keep a close eye on him while they were here. Beasley had never spent any time at a cemetery and was completely unaware of accepted protocol.

She pushed thoughts of Beasley from her mind as she stood over her brother's grave. "Myron Nelson Cofield," Lynn read aloud, her head bowed as she stared down at the simple headstone. "Beloved son, brother, and uncle." Lynn raised her head to peer at her daughter. "I'm glad it says that. It's important for people to know that, despite the fact that he was a recluse, he was loved by his family."

Rachel nodded. "I wish I'd known him better," she said without looking up.

A pang of guilt stabbed Lynn's heart. It had been her responsibility to ensure that her only child and only sibling get to know one another and have a good relationship. But she'd allowed herself to become too busy to pay attention to the things that really mattered, and right now she didn't feel too proud of herself. "I wish you had too. But that's my fault, not yours."

Rachel, cradling the bouquet in one hand, reached out with the other and laid it on Lynn's arm. "It's no one's fault. It just happened, that's all."

Lynn nodded, wishing she could believe her, but she knew better.

"Tell me about him," Rachel said.

Lynn looked at her again, but her daughter's head was bowed as she contemplated her uncle's headstone. "He was a wonderful big brother," Lynn said at last. "Quiet, reserved, but generous. Always looking out for me. And he lived at home until he was in his late thirties. I left home ahead of him, for that matter, even though he was fifteen years older than me. But then he met Roxanne, a real beauty who moved into town and knocked him right off his feet. When she agreed to marry him, everyone said he was like a new man. His feelings ran deep—always did. When Roxanne changed her mind and moved back to where she came from, Myron was devastated. I don't think he ever got over it." She glanced around the cemetery and toward the house before returning her attention to Rachel. Tears stung her eyes, but she blinked them away. "Apparently, he just didn't feel like he wanted to stay at home with Mom and Dad after that, and so he ended up here."

Rachel remained silent for a moment, and then she knelt down and laid the flowers on the grave, just below Myron's headstone. "Goodbye, Uncle Myron. I look forward to getting to know you better in heaven one day."

The tears pushed out from Lynn's eyes onto her cheeks then, but before she could speak, she sensed they were no longer alone. Lifting her head, she spotted Jason standing just a few yards from them. The look on his face told her he'd overheard their last exchange.

"A good man," he said, nodding as he squinted at them.

Rachel's head tilted upward as she too became aware of the man's presence.

"A good man and a good friend," Jason said. He took a step toward them. "Just ask Last Chance. Myron was the best friend Last Chance ever had—even though they hardly knew each other—only met a few times when Myron was just a kid, not long before Last Chance died. Myron always wanted to help him, but then he died too. And now . . ." Jason shook his head. "That's why you have to stay, you know. To finish the job. All I could do was bury 'em side by side, like Myron asked. Can't do nothin' to finish what your brother started. It's not my job."

He took another step in their direction, and Lynn felt herself draw back, even as Rachel rose from her knees to slip an arm around her mother's waist.

"It's up to you now," Jason said. "'If somethin' happens to me before I solve the mystery about Last Chance, tell my sister to help him.' That's what Myron told me before he passed on. So I'm tellin' you, just like he asked me to." He pointed toward an old grave directly to the right of Myron's. "There he lays, right next to your brother. Last Chance and Myron, just waitin' to see if you'll do the right thing."

The lazy caw of a circling crow split the silence as the three of them stared at each other. At last, Lynn found her voice. "And just what is the right thing?" Lynn asked, annoyed with the slight tremble that crept into her words. "What sort of unfinished business did my brother leave behind?"

Jason's smile resembled a slow sneer as he cackled. "That's for me to know and you to find out, ain't it?" With that, he turned and began to move away in the direction of the old shed where he lived. "I'd advise you to start with Myron's journals.

I never seen 'em up close, but I know he kept everythin' there. I don't read much, so there was no point in me lookin' at 'em. If this business with Last Chance was important to Myron— and it surely was—then you just might find somethin' about it recorded there."

As he disappeared inside the hovel he called a home, Lynn and Rachel turned to one another and raised quizzical eyebrows. What in the world was that all about? Lynn had no idea and was relatively certain she didn't want to know. But before they turned to walk away from Myron's grave, she couldn't help but peek at the plot on the right. She read the epitaph out loud. "Here lies Last Chance Justice. Beloved son and brother . . . and a man of mystery and sorrows. May he one day rest in peace."

A chill passed over Lynn as she forced her eyes away from the weathered headstone. She had no idea what any of it meant, and she had even less desire to find out.

All the more reason to tie up the loose ends of Myron's estate and get out of town, she told herself. *Whatever business my brother was working on regarding this Last Chance guy is dead and buried with him. And that's exactly where I intend to leave it.*

Chapter 6

AFTER A BRIEF STOP AT LYNN'S PARENTS' AND GRANDPARENTS' graves, mother and daughter returned to the house, neither speaking of Jason's visit until Rachel finally broke the silence.

"You know we're going to have to go in there. Into Uncle Myron's library, I mean. I peeked in there last night and saw a big desk sitting there, in front of rows and rows of cobweb-covered books. The room needs some serious cleaning, but I'm willing to do it if we can start going through his things and maybe find out what all this Last Chance business is about."

Lynn stood in the middle of the kitchen, studying her daughter, who once again leaned up against the counter, her long legs stretched out in front of her. Instead of jeans, she wore cream-colored slacks and a short-sleeved peach blouse. With her dark hair hanging loose around her shoulders, she looked even lovelier than usual. But Lynn knew that behind that sweet, attractive exterior lay a determined, adventurous young woman who wouldn't be easily dissuaded from digging into what she no doubt saw as a fascinating mystery. To Lynn, it seemed more of an annoyance or distraction, something she couldn't possibly foresee as bringing them good results. Besides, she'd grown up in this town. If this Last Chance thing was that big a deal, why didn't she remember hearing about it? And why in the world pursue it now?

The gleam in Rachel's eyes gave her the answer. Not only did her daughter love a good mystery or adventure, but she was also the ultimate champion of underdogs. Whoever this Last Chance was, Rachel seemingly saw his cause as one that fit his last name—Justice.

Lynn sighed. "I suppose it can't hurt. From what Chuck told us this morning, it will take a few days to get everything finalized with your uncle's estate, so we're going to be hanging around here until then anyway. Maybe this will give us something to do besides sit out on the porch and eat."

Rachel laughed. "That's for sure. We've only been here a little over twenty-four hours, and already my pants are getting tight."

Lynn rolled her eyes. Her daughter's metabolism operated at double-time. She seemed able to eat most anything without gaining an ounce—and how Lynn envied her that! Of course, she had to admit that she'd also been like that once, though it seemed eons ago.

"All right," she agreed, "though I don't believe you for a minute about your pants. But I did see some basic cleaning supplies in the cupboard on the back porch, over that ancient washer and dryer—which, by the way, we should try out just to see if they even work. You go grab some scrubber and disinfectant, and let's see what we can do with that library."

Before long, a fresh lemony scent began to wend its way into the air, rising up to the high-beamed ceilings, and even enhancing the fragrance of the old leather-bound books as the odors of must and dust dissipated. Lynn reveled in how good it felt to establish cleanliness and order in a room, and the sensation invigorated her.

"What next?" Rachel asked, her cheeks flushed and her hair now pulled back in a ponytail. Some sort of dark smudge marred her once-clean peach blouse, and Lynn groaned.

"Oh, Rachel, I should have insisted you change into your old clothes before we tackled this. Look, you've ruined your blouse."

Rachel glanced down, then she looked up and shrugged. "Haven't you ever heard of a dry cleaner, Mom? I'm sure even Bloomfield has one or two."

Lynn opened her mouth to answer, but the ancient sound of chimes interrupted her. She'd forgotten about Myron's melodic, if somewhat eerie, doorbell, and now it seemed they had company. Had Bailey come back to see how they liked the article? She certainly couldn't imagine who else would be at the front door.

Tucking her hair behind her ears and hoping she didn't look quite as disheveled as she felt, she led the way to the front of the house, with Rachel following close behind. Beasley reached the door first, barking and growling a warning. It seemed it hadn't taken long for him to feel territorial about this place, and in some ways Lynn was glad. No harm letting people know that a watchdog prowled the premises.

Gingerly, she opened the door, reminding herself that she needed to find some oil to stop the creaking. "Yes? May I help you?"

"Lynn Cofield?"

Two men stood on the porch, one with a salt-and-pepper military-style crew-cut who appeared to be just a few years older than Lynn, and the other a tall, handsome younger man in his mid- to late twenties. The older man offered an apologetic smile.

"Forgive me. Lynn Myers, of course. I always relate you to your parents, I'm afraid."

The light came on in Lynn's memory as she recognized Pastor Brunswick, the senior pastor of Bloomfield Community Fellowship Church, where her family had attended for as far back as anyone could remember. Pastor Brunswick had come to Bloomfield Community after Lynn moved away, and they'd met several times over the years, but not since his hair had begun to gray.

"Pastor Brunswick," she said, smiling as she motioned them inside. "Please, come in. Rachel and I were just doing some cleaning. Can we offer you something? Some sun tea perhaps? We just made it this morning."

"That sounds wonderful. Thank you so much." His smile broadened. "I was so pleased when I heard you were in town and so looked forward to seeing you again. I'm sorry we didn't call ahead, but . . . well, I don't know your cell phone number and wasn't sure if Myron's landline was still functional, so we decided to take a chance and drop by. Besides, we saw your car in the driveway, so we figured you were here."

"I'm glad," Lynn answered. "And don't worry about not calling ahead. Myron's phone is still working at the moment, but probably not for much longer. There isn't much sense in keeping it connected if no one's going to be here."

The pastor raised an eyebrow. "You're not planning to stay, then?"

Lynn stifled a frown. What was it with these people? Why in the world would they all think that, just because Myron died and left her this huge, dusty old place, she would suddenly decide to move in? Honestly.

"Let's go into the kitchen, shall we?" she said. "Rachel and I haven't had much chance to straighten up the rest of the house yet, but Jason did a fairly decent job on that room."

She realized then that she hadn't introduced Rachel, and she quickly amended her oversight. "You've met my daughter, Rachel, haven't you, Pastor?"

He smiled and offered his hand, speaking directly to her. "A couple of times, yes, but not since you turned into a charming young lady. I think the last time we met, you still had braids or a ponytail."

Lynn saw Rachel's cheeks flame as she took the pastor's hand, and she couldn't help but think it had something to do with the good-looking young man who couldn't seem to take his eyes off her.

"And this is John Currey, our new youth pastor. John just moved to Bloomfield and joined our staff about a year ago. I like to take him with me on visitations to help him get to know people a bit better."

This time it was John's turn to blush as he shook Lynn's hand and then Rachel's, his eyes lingering on the younger woman even after they released their grasp. The two mumbled some basic greetings, and Lynn was certain she felt an electrical current arcing through the air.

Ignoring the sensation and its fascinating implications, she led the way to the kitchen. Even Beasley had welcomed the visitors by then, having received pats and "atta boys" all the way around. Lynn and Rachel filled four glasses with ice cubes and tea and set them on the table as they all settled in.

"And how is your wife?" Lynn asked after she'd sipped her tea. "I'm afraid I don't remember her name."

A light in the pastor's eyes seemed to dim as he answered. "Georgia. Her name was . . . Georgia." He cleared his throat. "She . . . passed away a couple of years ago. Cancer."

Lynn's heart caught as she recognized the signs of loss in the man's voice and expression. She knew them only too well. "I'm so sorry to hear that," she said. "I . . . had no idea."

He nodded. "And I'm sorry about your brother," he said, obviously glad to change the subject. "He kept to himself quite a bit, but he never missed Sunday services or failed to give generously to any need we had." He dropped his eyes briefly before looking back up, and Lynn couldn't help but notice what a kind face he had. His brown eyes telegraphed sincerity. "He didn't let on to anyone how poorly he was feeling until the very end. I felt bad about not at least having a memorial service for him at the church, but his will specified no services, so we had to honor his wishes."

Lynn nodded. She felt bad about it too, and more than slightly guilty at her obvious neglect, but it seemed there was nothing to be done about it now.

"On a lighter note," Pastor said, his face brightening as he spoke, "I wanted to be sure to invite you and Rachel to church on Sunday. Surely you'll be here at least that long, won't you?"

"Oh, yes," Lynn said. "At least. Possibly longer. I don't want to leave until I know we've tied together all the loose ends."

Lynn noticed a smile tug at the corners of John's mouth, and she knew she'd given the answer he hoped to hear. She cut her eyes toward her daughter, who seemed to be working awfully hard at appearing disinterested, but Lynn knew Rachel far too well to buy it.

So, it was settled. They would all see each other again on Sunday, two days from now. In the meantime, Lynn sensed a tug to return to the library and finish up the cleaning so she could begin searching for . . .

For what? She had no idea. And why did she care? She had no answer for that question either. Still, she had some time on her hands with nothing specific to do. Maybe she could learn a bit more about her reclusive brother if she rummaged through his things. After all, he was gone now and had left everything to her, so it wasn't like she was snooping or intruding on his private life. Myron was in a much better place, and he no doubt didn't care a whit what happened to the material possessions he'd left behind. She might as well sort through them and see what she could find.

She tried to pull her mind away from Myron and the strange comments Jason had made about a man called Last Chance and some unfinished business between him and Lynn's brother. Would she discover what that business might be? And if she did, would she wish she hadn't?

On second thought, maybe it was best left alone. Lynn knew she could probably walk away from all of this—Myron's house and his unfinished business as well—but she sensed it wouldn't be easy convincing Rachel to do likewise. Especially now that she'd met the handsome youth pastor named John Currey.

She smiled and focused in on Pastor Brunswick's words about the church picnic on Sunday, immediately following the morning service. Something told her she and Rachel would be attending. And why not? She'd always enjoyed church outings, and it might be fun to see a few of her friends from decades ago, though she couldn't help but wonder what they'd think of her after all these years. Still, she hadn't been to the town's main park, with its charming gazebo and walking paths, in years. Might as well see it one time before she and Rachel packed up and left Bloomfield to head back home once and for all.

The library was now spick-and-span, and Rachel and Lynn had even broken away for a quick fast-food meal in town before kicking off their shoes and unwinding a bit over a pre-bedtime cup of herbal tea. But now Rachel and Beasley were sound asleep, and Lynn found herself staring into the darkness at an unseen ceiling. She'd thought sure she'd drop right off after such a busy day, but her mind ran at double-time. If she stayed there much longer, she'd no doubt fall into the abyss of missing Daniel and end up crying, which she wasn't about to do with Rachel sleeping next to her.

Moving slowly, she slipped out of bed, careful not to awaken her daughter. Beasley raised his head as she donned her robe and slippers, but she patted his soft fur and whispered to him to go back to sleep. Then she padded softly to the door and let herself out into the hallway where a couple of soft lights she and Rachel had left on earlier now lit her way down the stairs.

Would another cup of tea help her sleep? She doubted it. But she'd spotted some instant hot chocolate in the cupboard and figured she'd give that a try.

By the time the steaming cocoa filled her cup, she knew she wanted to start going through her brother's things—not that she really expected to find much, but maybe it would make her drowsy enough that she could head back upstairs soon and catch some shut-eye.

Pleased at the clean, lemony fragrance that greeted her as

she opened the library door, she set her steaming mug down on top of some papers on Myron's desk and settled into his over-sized leather chair. If she were going to stay here—which she wasn't, she reminded herself—she'd have to replace the chair with something that fit her. Myron had been quite a bit taller and heavier than she, so she could easily picture him sitting in this massive seat.

She pulled open the top right-hand drawer, which turned out to be stuffed with old receipts, some dating back several years. Apparently, her brother had been faithful in retaining his paperwork but not very diligent in using it for income tax preparation.

Lynn smiled at the thought. Myron had always been some-what of a packrat, so even if she didn't come across anything important in his desk drawers, she could easily dispense with most of it.

She pulled a trash can from underneath the desk and began dumping everything dated beyond the past seven years. It didn't take long before the container was almost full, and she hadn't even started on the left-hand drawers yet. She had nearly finished her hot chocolate, so she picked up the cup and the trash can and carried them to the kitchen, placing the cup in the sink and emptying the can into the larger trash receptacle in the corner. As she thought of the size of Myron's house and all the nooks and crannies where he may have stuffed things, she realized she could have a full-time job on her hands just going through all he had left behind.

But did she really need to do that? She sighed. Yes, probably so—especially since she was going to sell the place. She certainly didn't want strangers coming in and going through her brother's personal things—better to do that herself. She'd enlist Rachel's help again in the morning, and they'd plow through it a lot faster together.

She returned to the library and plunked back down in the chair. Time to start on the drawers on the other side of the desk.

She pulled open the top one and nearly laughed aloud. Paper clips—hundreds, thousands of them, of all colors and shapes and sizes—seemed to stare back at her. What in the world had her brother been thinking? An army couldn't use all these paper clips, not in a million years!

Determined, she scooped them from the drawer into the trash can, and then opened the next drawer. There, on the very top, sat a dark brown, leather-bound book. Beneath it were several others just like it. Her eyes widened. What were they? Ledgers? Records? Or was it possible they were personal journals, entries that might give her more insight into her beloved but reclusive brother?

Last Chance. The name spoken by Jason rang in her ears. Might she learn something about him as well? And why did it matter? If she hadn't seen his headstone in the cemetery next to Myron's, she would have dismissed Jason's words as the ramblings of a less-than-stable old man. But she had seen it, and as strange as the name was, it seemed obvious the man had, at one time, existed, living right here in Bloomfield. But so what? A lot of people lived—and died—in Bloomfield. Well, maybe not a lot compared to most places, but enough that Last Chance Justice couldn't have been all that unique. Could he? Why had Myron been so concerned with this particular man?

She pulled the top book from the drawer and opened the front cover. Sure enough, Myron's handwriting recorded his daily events in dated order. She'd never realized her brother kept a diary of sorts, but obviously that's what she had discovered. Would she invade his privacy if she read them?

He's dead, she reminded herself. *He no longer cares whether or not you read what he wrote. In fact, since he left everything to you, he probably knew you would find them one day, and therefore intended for you to read them. And have you really got anything else that pressing to do with your time right now?*

She sighed. The decision was already made. She would read Myron's journals and see what secrets, if any, her brother might have left for her to discover. She only hoped she wouldn't be unduly surprised or upset by what she found there. It seemed she'd had enough surprises in the last few days to last her several lifetimes.

By the time Lynn finally stumbled up the stairs to bed, her eyes were bleary and felt as if she'd rubbed them with salt. She hadn't intended to read for so long, but a particular entry at the very end of the first journal—which apparently was Myron's last— had hooked her.

"I've got to find out what happened to the money," he wrote. "It might only be seven dollars and fourteen cents, but it was enough to besmirch a good man's reputation. If it's the last thing I do in this life, I must clear his name. I've got a couple of ideas that just might help."

The entry was dated two days before Myron died. Had he been able to accomplish his goal? Had he found the missing seven dollars and fourteen cents? Somehow she doubted it. But why was it so important to him? And who was this "good man" he had mentioned? Could it be Last Chance Justice, the man buried next to Myron in the cemetery?

Though Lynn had gone back to the beginning of the journal and continued to read through to the final entry at the end, hoping to find more clues along the way, she had simply grown too sleepy to press on. At last she had closed up the top journal, nearly overwhelmed to think there were five more in the drawer, and who knew how many others somewhere else, that might or might not contain the answers to this small-budget but apparently big-stakes mystery. She would have to get some sleep and tackle it again tomorrow, this time with Rachel's help. The two of them could get a lot more reading done together than Lynn could on her own.

She cracked the bedroom door and peered inside. Beasley raised his head but lowered it again when Lynn shushed him. She tiptoed across the floor, pulled back her side of the covers, and slipped beneath them, drifting off nearly as fast as her head hit the pillow.

Chapter 7

"MORNING, MOM," RACHEL MUMBLED AS SHE ENTERED THE kitchen and headed straight for the counter. She had clipped up her long dark hair on top of her head, with several strands spilling downward. She still wore her pajamas.

"I smelled the coffee from upstairs," Rachel said as she snagged a mug and filled it. "It was a nice way to wake up, but I have to admit, I'm a bit surprised that you're up already. I woke up last night around midnight and you weren't in bed."

Rachel turned toward the table and noticed her mother's smile. "What?" Rachel asked, sitting down across from her. "Did I say something funny?"

Lynn shook her head. "It's just . . . the way you look this morning. It took me back to so many mornings when you were little, coming to breakfast in your pajamas."

Rachel returned her mother's smile. "Those are great memories for me too, Mom. But you haven't answered my question. Why weren't you in bed last night?"

Lynn sipped her coffee before answering. "I had trouble falling asleep, so I thought I'd go down and start going through your uncle's things, now that we've got the room cleaned up."

Rachel hugged her cup with both hands, enjoying the warmth. "Did you find anything?"

"I did. Want to hear about it?"

Rachel laughed. "What do you think? You know it doesn't take much to get my curiosity stirred up."

After only a brief pause, during which Rachel was sure she saw a glimmer of light dancing in her mother's eyes, Lynn said, "I found his journals. Six of them. For all I know there may be more somewhere, but I just started on the most recent one last night." She took another swallow of coffee. "One of the last entries, written not long before he died, intrigued me."

Rachel leaned forward. "Really? What did it say?"

"It alluded to the loss of seven dollars and fourteen cents, and someone whose reputation was apparently damaged by the incident. Myron wrote that he wanted to find it so he could clear the man's name . . . if it was the last thing he did on this earth."

Rachel felt her eyes widen. "Apparently he wasn't able to," she said, leaning back in her seat. "But really, seven dollars and fourteen cents? How important could it be?"

"Important enough to cause Myron to enter it in his journal and to express his desire to resolve the issue." She paused before adding, "And I imagine it was important to the other man too, if it somehow damaged his reputation."

Rachel frowned. "Seriously, Mom, can someone's reputation really be damaged over such a small amount of money? And who do you suppose the man was?"

Lynn shrugged. "I don't know on either count, although I suspect he may have been referring to Last Chance Justice.

Though it doesn't appear they knew each other well, Jason said Myron was the best friend Last Chance ever had because he was so determined to clear his name. It just makes sense that he's the man Myron meant, don't you think? I hope to find some clues as we read through the rest of the journals."

"We? Sounds like I've been drafted."

"You have," Lynn admitted. "There are six journals full of entries. I figure we can get through a lot more of them in a whole lot less time if we work together."

"But what are we looking for? What if we read them all and don't find anything? And how will we even know if we do find something?"

"Three more I-don't-know questions. But we can try, right? I can't explain why this has suddenly become so important to me, Rachel, but it has. Maybe it's because I feel so bad about not spending more time with Myron before he died, and it helps to think I might be able to finish something that he started. And yes, I'm nearly positive that it all has something to do with the man named Last Chance Justice who's buried next to your uncle."

"The one Jason mentioned."

Lynn nodded. "Exactly."

"It could just be a wild goose chase."

"It could. But what if it isn't? Whatever it is, it was important to my brother—so important that he wanted to take care of it before he died. But it doesn't appear that he did. And now that I've inherited his entire estate, I somehow feel like this mystery came with it." She frowned. "Does that make any sense?"

Rachel smiled. "Not really. And to be honest, a missing seven dollars and fourteen cents hardly constitutes a full-blown mystery. But hey, if you feel obligated to give it a shot, then count me in." She set her cup down and stood to her feet. "But I'm not turning sleuth on an empty stomach. How about some scrambled eggs? Then I'll jump into the shower and we can get started. Sound like a plan?"

"Sounds like a great plan to me. Scrambled eggs it is, and then we'll get moving."

As it turned out, it took a bit longer than expected to get to the journals. By the time they finished breakfast and cleaned up the dishes, then showered and dressed, Beasley sat by the front door, fussing to go outside for a walk. Lynn didn't feel comfortable yet with letting him run far on his own—not only because she feared he might get lost but also because she didn't trust him not to start digging in the cemetery. The thought made her shudder, so when Rachel suggested they all take a long stroll, she readily agreed.

"It's really beautiful here, isn't it?" Rachel said as they made their way down Cemetery Drive to the main road. "The weather is nearly perfect."

Lynn laughed. "Today, yes. And for the most part, you're right. The weather in Bloomfield really is decent nearly all year long—not that much different from where we live, actually."

Rachel shrugged. "It's more than that, though. I love the small-town atmosphere, the way everyone knows everyone else. There's a real sense of . . . oh, I don't know, community, I guess. Like you belong to some big, extended family or something."

"I sure can't deny that," Lynn conceded. "Although sometimes there's a bit more interaction than I care for. I often wonder if that isn't why your uncle moved here next to the cemetery.

Maybe it was the only place he felt he could get any privacy. He always was a rather private person anyway, and when his fiancée left him, he just wanted to escape from everyone's knowing glances and prying eyes. Not an easy thing to do in Bloomfield."

"So Uncle Myron never dated anyone after Roxanne dumped him?"

Lynn flashed her daughter a disapproving glance. Maybe Roxanne had dumped Myron, but the word seemed a bit harsh and demeaning.

"Sorry," Rachel said. "After she left him."

"No, he never did. In fact, he scarcely dated anyone before he met her. Roxanne was his one and only love, period. When she broke his heart, that was it for him. Mom said he just drew more inside himself and almost never went out at all. And with his job as a freelance architect, he was able to do most of his work from home, away from other people. When the place by the cemetery went up for sale, he surprised everyone and bought it. Got it for a song, from what I understand. After all, who else would want the place? I suppose, for his purposes, it was perfect for him."

"Sad, though," Rachel said. "His whole life, I mean. To think that one woman's rejection could affect him so deeply that he decided to spend the rest of his life alone."

"True. But that's exactly what happened. Other than going to church on Sunday, he almost never left home."

She paused to watch Beasley chase a squirrel up a tree, then called him back before they went on. "I suppose that's why he and Jason became friends. From what I understand, Jason already lived on the property when Myron bought it. He sort of came with the place, so I guess it's not unusual that your uncle would put a stipulation in his will that would allow Jason to stay on." She sighed. "It's going to make it tougher to sell, though."

Rachel stopped and tilted her head toward her mother. "So you're still planning to do that? Sell Uncle Myron's house?"

Lynn frowned. "Why would you think I'd do anything else? Seriously, Rachel, whatever would we do with such a huge house? It's not like we need all that room. And next to a cemetery? Do you think we could really get used to living somewhere like that? Besides, we have a perfectly good home already. I thought you were always happy there. Why would you want to move?"

Rachel looked puzzled. "I . . . I don't know. I've been asking myself the same question, and I really don't have an answer. But I really am hoping you'll at least pray about it before making your decision."

There it was again. Another admonition to pray, along with an unreasonable nudge toward staying on at her brother's house in Bloomfield rather than doing the sensible thing and returning home. The strangest part of the entire situation was that she would actually consider it—though she wasn't ready to admit that to anyone, including Rachel.

"Let's head back," she said. "I think Beasley's had enough exercise for now. We can take him out again this evening. I'd really like to get going on those journals."

Rachel's eyes lit up. "Me too. And you know what? I've been thinking about it, and I hope we find a pile more of them. Then at least I know we'll be staying in Bloomfield until we finish reading. And who knows how long that could take . . . or where it might lead us?"

Lynn rolled her eyes and shook her head, but she knew she hadn't fooled her daughter. Rachel was right. There was no way they were leaving town until they had done everything possible to honor Myron's dying wish and to solve the mystery of the missing money—even if it was only seven dollars and fourteen cents.

With only a brief stop to fix a couple mugs of soup, the women worked straight through the day. By evening they'd managed to put together a few obscure pieces to the puzzle but certainly not enough to explain it, let alone solve it.

"So it is about Last Chance," Rachel said, closing up journal number five. "At least we know that much now. Apparently, Uncle Myron had always been fascinated with the story of Last Chance and considered him a friend, even though they only met a few times."

Lynn nodded. "And even though Myron was just a child then, he mentions Last Chance's kindness and his gentle demeanor. The young man made quite an impression on my brother. And that's really saying something, since he didn't spend much time around people." She sighed and shook her head. "In my case, I was so much younger than Myron that I really don't remember any of it. But you'd think I would have heard of Last Chance somewhere along the way, wouldn't you? In a town this size, how could I have missed knowing about someone with such an unusual name?"

"Not to mention such a damaged reputation," Rachel added with a chuckle. "Let's face it, the crime rate in Bloomfield is nearly nil—a jaywalker once in awhile, or maybe a parking ticket or two—so even something as small as seven dollars and fourteen cents going missing could stir up a lot of wagging tongues, I suppose."

Lynn frowned. "Maybe. But it all would have had to happen under some really strange or unusual circumstances, don't you think? And if it was a big enough deal for Myron's concern after all these years, then surely someone around here knows more about it."

"We could always ask Jason."

The thought had occurred to Lynn more than once that day, but she wasn't ready to go there . . . yet. Maybe she could get Pastor Brunswick aside at the church picnic the next day and see if he could shed some light on it. And there were bound to be others at the outing that she knew from her past. Perhaps it was time to reignite some old friendships and see what she could find out that way, though the thought made her uneasy at best.

"What's going on in your mind?" Rachel asked, squinting at her mom. "You look like something's brewing in there."

Lynn smiled, feeling her cheeks heat up a bit in the process. "You caught me," she admitted. "I was just thinking that we might be able to find out something from Pastor Brunswick or someone else at the church picnic tomorrow." She shrugged. "It's possible, isn't it? Surely in this close-knit community, where families have lived for generations, somebody knows the details of the missing money, even though it happened decades ago."

"You'd think so," Rachel commented, a slight change of expression passing over her face. "So . . . do you think that youth pastor will be at the picnic? What was his name again? John, I think."

Lynn didn't even try to hide her smile. "I think you know exactly what that youth pastor's name is—John Currey. And a very handsome youth pastor he is, at that. I'm sure he'll be there, along with a good portion of the citizens of Bloomfield." She nodded, her grin widening. "It seems tomorrow could prove to be quite an interesting day—in more ways than one."

Rachel scraped her chair back and stood up, startling a snoozing Beasley in the process. His surprised yip gave Rachel what Lynn imagined was a welcome diversion. "I'm going to take Beasley out for another walk," she announced. "Do you want to come along?"

Lynn rose up, a bit slower than her daughter, stretching her tired muscles in the process. "I think that sounds like a good idea for all of us. And when we get back, I'll be ready to eat. We really haven't had much since those eggs this morning."

"I saw a can of stew in the cupboard," Rachel said. "I'll heat that up and butter some of that wheat bread in the fridge. But you know, Mom, we really should go shopping on Monday and stock up on a few more groceries."

Lynn opened her mouth to argue that they wouldn't be around long enough to make a shopping trip worthwhile, but she thought better of it and bit back her words. Rachel was right. It's not as if they were moving in or anything, but there was no reason not to have enough food on hand for several days. It would take at least that long to wade through this mystery of the man called Last Chance Justice—a strange name, if ever she'd heard one.

Chapter 8

THOUGH A FEW FACES HAD COME AND GONE OVER THE YEARS, while others just grew older, Lynn felt as if she had stepped back into her childhood. Bloomfield Community Fellowship Church hadn't done much to upgrade its sanctuary in the thirty-five years since she moved away. The polished wooden pews gleamed as hard and shiny as they always had, with the front ones on both sides having special brass plaques attached to the ends to honor former congregants considered pillars of the nearly one-hundred-year-old building. Lynn remembered visiting a friend's church in another town when she was about eight and being impressed with the soft cushions that covered their seats. She'd wondered why Bloomfield Community couldn't do the same but had never had the nerve to ask.

Even the muted burgundy carpet, though spotless, appeared identical to the one she'd walked over every Sunday as a child. Surely it had been replaced since then, though not surprisingly with one exactly like the last.

Lynn smiled as she and Rachel slid into a pew on the right,

five rows back from the front. She couldn't help but wonder if some of her aversion to change and surprises hadn't come about as a direct result of growing up in Bloomfield. Had she been born and raised in New York, for instance, would she have been more adventurous and daring? Possibly. Then again, she wouldn't have been in the right place at the right time when Daniel showed up on the scene, and she didn't even want to contemplate what her life might have been without her beloved husband.

Wordlessly, she squeezed Rachel's hand, pushing aside the many memories of sitting beside her husband in church. Her daughter flashed a smile and then turned back to study her bulletin. Lynn opted to do the same.

She'd recognized many members of the congregation as she and her daughter made their way inside, but there hadn't been time to stop and chat since the service was nearly ready to begin. If there was one thing her parents had drilled into her over the years, it was never to arrive late for church—or anywhere else, for that matter. Lynn had learned the lesson well. If she was going to reconnect with anyone, it would be after the service at the picnic. She made a mental note to remind Rachel that they needed to swing by the only deli in town open on Sunday and pick up some sandwiches on the way to the park since there hadn't been enough food left at the house to pack a picnic lunch that morning. She only hoped Beasley would continue to sleep peacefully in the car, not waking up and yipping to be let out.

The organ began to play, and the slight rustling and whispering that was part of the pre-service routine settled down as everyone stood to their feet. Lynn shifted her attention from the bulletin to the choir that had entered and taken its place in the rows behind the pulpit. Was that Jolene Trump in the back corner? My goodness, it was! Not only did she still wait tables at Bert's Barbecue, but she still sang in the choir. Lynn couldn't help but smile and shake her head. More power to her. Jolene was as much a firecracker as ever.

The choir director was new, though—at least, to Lynn. She watched the short, heavyset woman raise her hand as the choir members eyed her closely. On cue, the singing began, and a wave of homesickness swept over Lynn, nearly knocking her back onto the pew. What in the world was wrong with her? She'd had moments of nostalgia before, but nothing like this. She shook her head, determined to ignore the feeling and participate in the service. After all, she was here to worship God, not to peruse the congregation or analyze her emotions.

Enough of that, Lynn Myers. You're letting your accumulated feelings get the best of you. You've lost both parents and your husband, and now your brother too. You're bound to feel more emotional than usual. All the more reason to keep your focus where it belongs.

Pulling a hymnal from the pew in front of her, she opened to the words she knew by heart and began to sing. She didn't need the printed lyrics, and even if she did, she could read them from the projected image on the wall. But right now, she wanted to keep her head down and her eyes off everyone else.

The chicken salad sandwiches were tightly wrapped and waiting in the cooler, along with cold drinks and fruit, while Beasley lay quietly beside the trunk of the massive shade tree where Lynn had secured him on a tether for the duration of the picnic. She was relieved that he had slept peacefully in the backseat of the car throughout the service, though he'd been more than slightly excited when she and Rachel came out of church and rejoined him. She was also glad he was old enough now to accept his stationary position during the event—unlike when he was a puppy and would no doubt have wrapped himself around the tree numerous times by now—but he was still adventurous enough that he would have run off to join the kids on the playground or the young adults batting a volleyball back and forth. She smiled at the thought, knowing the greatest danger would have been Beasley's nose for food. No one's lunch would be safe with her always-hungry cocker spaniel on the loose.

Even with their stop at the deli, she and Rachel had arrived at the park in time to snag a prime location in the shade. Though the temperature hovered in the low eighties and there was a slight breeze, it was still much more comfortable sitting under the tree.

Lynn glanced at Rachel, who leaned back on her elbows on their large plaid blanket, munching an apple and watching the surrounding action through her sunglasses. Her dark ponytail hung down behind her, and she'd made a pit stop in the church bathroom to change into some modest calf-length pants and a sleeveless blouse. Even in such casual attire, the girl was gorgeous. Lynn couldn't help but wonder how all those young men at Bible college had let her escape . . . but she was glad they did. Unlike Lynn, who opted for marriage instead of college, Rachel had graduated and received her degree. Though Lynn didn't regret marrying Daniel one bit, she occasionally wished she'd waited and finished school first.

"Excuse me. Lynn Myers?"

The male voice cut into her thoughts, and both Lynn and Rachel raised their heads to discover its source. Even Beasley looked up and issued a yip of greeting.

Lynn raised her eyebrows. The tall, good-looking young man with the wavy dark hair standing above them looked vaguely familiar, but . . .

"Yes, I'm Lynn Myers," she answered. "And you are . . . ?"

His smile included his warm, dark eyes, and Lynn couldn't help but wonder if Rachel noticed.

"I'm Hayden Blackstone, Norm and Ida's son. You remember me, don't you? You knew my mom. She was a couple years ahead of you in school."

Lynn pushed to her feet and stood facing the young man, although she had to look up to do so. "Well, Hayden, of course I remember you. I just don't remember you being so tall and handsome and . . . and grown up. My goodness, where have the years gone?"

Hayden chuckled. "You sound like Mom. She's always saying things like that."

"Is she here?" Lynn asked. "I'd love to see her again."

"Not yet, but she and Dad should be coming over soon. They had a couple things to do first."

A slight brush against her arm alerted Lynn to the fact that Rachel had also stood up and waited for an introduction. She smiled. "Hayden, this is my daughter, Rachel. If you two ever met, it's been so long ago that I'm sure you don't remember."

"I doubt it," Hayden said, stretching out his hand to shake Rachel's, his eyes glued to her face. "I can't imagine that we'd have met and I could have forgotten, no matter how long ago it might be."

Lynn glanced at Rachel in time to catch the color rise to her cheeks. Apparently, her daughter hadn't missed the inferred compliment in Hayden's words. The memory that she'd heard Hayden had been married briefly and then divorced flitted through her mind, but she brushed it away. As far as she knew, he'd always been a good boy and came from a decent and respectable family. Besides, a handshake at a church picnic didn't constitute a relationship.

When Rachel and Hayden had finished exchanging pleasantries, Lynn heard her daughter say, "Why don't you sit down and join us for a cold drink?" Before she could sit back down herself, the two young people had plopped down on the blanket and unscrewed the lids from iced apple juice bottles.

Well then, she told herself, *you may as well settle down too and keep an eye on things.* Situating herself next to Beasley, she smiled and quickly joined the conversation. As the three of them discussed Hayden's family, his accounting job, and various other aspects of Bloomfield life—carefully avoiding his marriage-and-divorce history—Lynn relaxed, reminding herself that Rachel was an adult now. And besides, they were only in town for a few more days.

Another male voice interrupted them. This time four heads—three human and one canine—looked up to find John Currey standing above them, his smile a bit stiffer than Lynn remembered from the previous day.

"Mrs. Myers," he said, nodding in her direction, "and Rachel. So glad you decided to accept our invitation and come to the picnic." He cast a quick glance at Hayden and nodded a greeting before returning his attention to Rachel. "I thought I'd make a point to personally invite you to join us for a couple of games. They're about to start, and they're really a lot of fun. What do you say? Interested?"

Rachel's dark eyebrows rose, and Lynn recognized her momentary discomfort. Was she obligated to accept John's invitation, since he and Pastor Brunswick were the ones who originally told them about the picnic and encouraged them to come? From the looks that had passed between John and Rachel the previous day, Lynn imagined her daughter wanted to say yes anyway. But now she was caught up in a conversation with another handsome young man, and Lynn had no idea whether or not Rachel was ready to end it quite yet.

Lynn smiled. This was a situation her daughter was going to have to resolve for herself.

Within seconds it appeared she had made her decision. Graciously, Rachel stood up and said, "I'd love to join you, John." She looked down at Hayden. "How about you? Why don't we all go? It sounds like fun."

Hayden didn't hesitate. He jumped up, ready to accompany them both, but quickly turned back to Lynn. "You're coming too, aren't you, Mrs. Myers?"

Lynn smiled up at the threesome and shook her head. "Not just now. I think I'll stay here and keep Beasley company. But you all go on and have a good time."

She watched them walk away, Hayden on one side of Rachel and John on the other—one tall, broad-shouldered young man with sandy blond hair, the other equally well-built gentleman with dark hair. It seemed this visit to Bloomfield had just become a bit more interesting . . . not to mention, complicated.

Lynn's stomach growled, and she wondered how much longer she should wait for Rachel and her escorts to return before giving up and digging into the sandwiches on her own. She had just about opted to do so when a middle-aged couple sauntered her way.

"Lynn, is that you?" the woman called as she neared, picking up her pace. "Hayden said you were here."

Lynn smiled and stood up to greet the Blackstones. Both had put on a few extra pounds over the last decade or so, but then, who hadn't? Well, Jolene Trump, of course, but otherwise . . .

"It is so good to see you again," Ida said, reaching out to encircle Lynn in a welcoming hug. She pulled back so they could see one another. "How long has it been? Nine, ten years? More?" Her smiled faded slightly. "I think it was at your mom's funeral, wasn't it?"

Lynn nodded, surprised at the ease with which the old lump in her throat reappeared. She thought she'd replaced the one from her mother's death with the one from Daniel's and now Myron's, but perhaps they were one and the same after all.

"Yes, it was," she said, refusing to allow the hint of tears that burned at the corners of her eyes to succeed in undoing her. "And yes, that was just about ten years ago now." She shook her head. "It doesn't seem possible, does it?"

"It surely doesn't," Ida agreed. "But you look wonderful, Lynn." She turned back to her husband. "Doesn't she look wonderful, Norm?"

The balding, pleasant-faced man, who stood only inches taller than his wife, nodded. "Wonderful," he agreed, still nodding.

Beasley was on his feet by then, sniffing around the two newest interlopers and glancing up anxiously at Lynn. When she patted the top of his head and assured him that all was well, he settled back down.

"Well, you two look pretty good yourself," she said. "And Hayden? What a handsome young man he's become. It was so good to see him again, though I scarcely recognized him."

Ida beamed. "He is handsome, isn't he? Tall, too. Norm and

I can't imagine where he got his height or his good looks, but we're certainly proud of him."

Lynn caught the look of embarrassment on Norm's face, and she wondered if Ida had any idea how her words might have impacted him. Apparently not, as she continued right on.

"He's an accountant now, you know," she said. "Has his very own office right downtown on Main Street." She leaned in as if she were confiding a nugget of great importance. "And quite successful, I might add. There's only one other accountant in all of Bloomfield, and she's just part-time." Her smile spread farther as she leaned back again. "Hayden is full time and has nearly all the important clients in town."

Lynn wasn't exactly sure how to respond, but she knew she had to say something. After all, it was obvious Ida was proud of her son. And why shouldn't she be? He had obviously done well for himself so far.

"That's wonderful," she said, wishing she'd come up with a slightly more original adjective. "No wonder you're proud."

Ida nodded, but her smile faded as she lowered her voice. "And now that he finally has that terrible Marissa fiasco behind him, he can get on with his life."

This conversation became more awkward by the moment. Lynn glanced over the Blackstones' shoulders, hoping to see Rachel and her bodyguards coming to her rescue, but her field of vision came up blank.

"Um . . . may I offer you something cold to drink?" she asked, hoping to change the subject. "I have apple juice and water, all on ice."

"Oh, no, thank you," Ida answered, her smile firmly back in place once again as she laid her hand on Norm's arm. "We have lunch waiting for us back at our spot, but we just wanted to stop by and say hello while we had the chance." She paused then, as her face lit up with what appeared to be a new idea. "But maybe you'd like to come over and join us at our table. We have it set up over in the far corner, and we have plenty of room. It would be lovely to catch up, especially after you being gone so many years."

There it was, that inference to her skipping out on Bloomfield. Her heart missed a beat as she scrambled for the right answer. The last thing she wanted to do was offend any of the town's residents, but join them? At their picnic table? Now? For some reason the proposition didn't appeal to her at all, particularly when she considered what all that "catching up" might entail.

"That is so sweet of you," she said, smiling as warmly and sincerely as possible. "I'd love to, but . . . actually, I think I'll stay right here and wait for Rachel to come back. Plus . . ." She glanced down at Beasley. "Well, I have Beasley to consider. It's best to keep him here in a quiet, shady spot. You understand."

Ida peered down at the dog and nodded. "Of course I do. We have pets too—though, of course, we don't bring them along to church functions." She glanced back up at Lynn. "Well then, we'd better be going. I do hope you'll stop by and say hello before you leave town. For dinner maybe? You could bring Rachel. I'd love to spend some time getting to know her."

"Dinner? Well, we'll see how things go. We won't be here long, but . . . that would be lovely, Ida. Thank you."

"Perfect! I'll call you."

And with that, she turned and led her husband back the way they'd come. Lynn breathed a sigh of relief when she realized Ida hadn't thought to ask for her number. Maybe it was just as well—though she didn't remember until they were gone that she'd planned to ask around about the man named Last Chance Justice. Dismissing the thought, she settled in beside Beasley and closed her eyes, enjoying the perfect weather and peaceful surroundings.

# Chapter 9

"SO . . . WHAT DID YOU THINK OF YOUR FIRST BLOOMFIELD CHURCH picnic?"

Lynn watched her daughter's face turned straight ahead and peering out the windshield as she drove. The tinge of pink that rose to Rachel's cheeks was slight, but enough to let Lynn know the girl's reply would be measured and reserved.

"It was nice. Great people, perfect weather, good food. What's not to like?"

She flashed her mother a smile and then looked back at the road, as if that were the end of the conversation.

"Good point," Lynn said. "I think even Beasley had a good time."

Rachel didn't answer.

Lynn decided to try again. "I couldn't help but notice that John and Hayden seemed quite . . . attentive to you." She'd resisted the temptation to use the word smitten and watched for a response.

Rachel blinked. "I . . . suppose. They're both very nice."

"Handsome, too."

Rachel blinked again before turning to Lynn with a sigh. "All right, Mom. Fine. Let's talk about the elephant in the room." She returned her attention to driving. "Hayden and John are both good-looking, both very nice and both . . . available. And for whatever reason, both paid a lot of attention to me today."

"For whatever reason? Rachel, don't you realize how beautiful you are? You're also a charming, intelligent young woman. I can't think of any good reason why they wouldn't be attracted to you."

Rachel chuckled. "That's because you're my mom. You're just a bit prejudiced, you know."

"Maybe," Lynn admitted. "But that doesn't change the fact that any man with half a brain would be captivated with you."

She glanced at Lynn, one eyebrow cocked. "Meaning someone with a fully functional brain wouldn't be?"

Lynn laughed and shook her head. "You know what I mean, young lady. Stop trying to change the subject. I think you've got the makings of a love triangle going on."

"A love triangle!" Rachel's mouth dropped open and she slapped the steering wheel with one hand. "Mom, are you serious? I just met these guys. We're friends, that's all. How could we be anything else? We hardly even know each other."

"I didn't say it was a love triangle already. I said you have the makings of one."

Rachel shook her head, though her smile belied her scolding tone. "Leave it alone, Mom. Don't try to make it into something it's not. Besides, if they are attracted to me, it's just because I'm the new girl in town, one they haven't known all their lives. There's nothing more to it than that."

"Maybe. Maybe not."

Rachel turned the car into the driveway and pulled up in front of the house. Shutting off the engine, she turned in the

seat and fixed her green eyes on Lynn in exactly the same way
Daniel had done when he determined to make a point. "I'll tell
you the maybe. They are two very nice young men, and *maybe*
I'll see them again, *maybe* I won't. But we're not going to make
this a point of conversation and speculation, all right? Seriously,
Mom. I mean it."

Lynn tried to swallow her grin, but it didn't work. "Whatever
you say, sweetheart." She opened the door and stepped outside,
then reached for the back door to let Beasley out. "Whatever
you say."

By evening the women were back in Myron's library, reading
through the remaining journals and trying not to become discouraged about their lack of discoveries that shed any more light
on the situation with Last Chance Justice.

"If this thing with Last Chance was such a big deal to Uncle
Myron," Rachel commented, "you'd think he'd talk about it
more. But nothing. Absolutely nothing! He writes about the
weather, about what he had for lunch, about who he saw when
he ventured into town to pick up supplies. It's a bit like reading
someone's tweets or Facebook posts. Stuff that doesn't matter
and nobody cares about, you know what I mean?"

Lynn smiled. She knew exactly what Rachel meant. She'd
been thinking pretty much the same thing—minus the tweet
and Facebook references, of course, since Lynn had never
bothered to get involved in such Internet nonsense. Rachel and
Daniel had both tried to get her going with e-mail—"so you
can stay in touch with people you care about," they explained.
But she'd argued that she had a telephone for that very purpose,

and she would much rather hear someone's voice than read their "tweet" or e-mail, and that had been the end of it.

She looked up from the journal she held in her lap, eyeing her daughter who sat sprawled on the brown leather couch against the far wall, just under the window. The sun had started its descent on the western side of the house, causing bright rays to dance across Rachel's dark hair. With her head bent over the journal she held in her lap, she was oblivious to her mother's gaze.

A sense of love and pride swept over Lynn as she studied her only child. Though she had always loved Rachel with a maternal passion that knew no bounds, she had only lately come to realize how much she liked and admired the woman her daughter had become. When had it happened? How had the little girl with the gangly arms and legs and a smattering of freckles across the bridge of her nose turned into such a delightful young woman? How could she have missed it? Was it because Rachel had been away at college for much of the past four years?

Lynn sighed. She supposed that was a big part of it. She also imagined that all parents woke up one day and realized their children were no longer babies. The thought made her smile, and yet her heart ached at the same time.

The sound of chimes interrupted her thoughts, and Lynn frowned, even as Rachel looked up from her reading.

"Someone's at the front door," Rachel commented, setting her journal down and standing to her feet. "I wonder who it could be."

"I can't imagine, but let's go find out together, shall we?"

When they reached the front door, Lynn stood back and allowed Rachel to open it. There, on the front porch, stood Hayden Blackstone, his dark hair damp and freshly combed.

He had dressed up a bit since they'd seen him in his jeans and T-shirt at the picnic.

"Hi," he said sheepishly. "I'm sorry I didn't call before I came, but I didn't think to get your cell number while we were at the picnic."

Lynn opened her mouth to respond, but Rachel beat her to it. "No problem," she said, motioning him inside. "Come on in."

Hayden hesitated. "Well, actually, I . . . I really came to see if you've had dinner yet. I mean, I know we ate at the picnic, but . . . well, I thought you might want to go out and grab a quick bite somewhere . . . or something."

Lynn knew she should intervene to ease the poor man's discomfort, but part of her enjoyed watching him squirm. She couldn't help but think he was being a bit pushy, dropping by unannounced and inviting Rachel to dinner when they'd just met a matter of hours earlier. Still, he had a perfectly reasonable explanation for not having called first—come to think of it, the same reason given by everyone else who had just dropped by without calling first.

Rachel turned to her mother. "What do you think, Mom? Do we have anything planned? I hadn't even thought about it, but I am getting a little hungry. How about you?"

Lynn noticed Hayden's face fall slightly, but he didn't let his disappointment become obvious. "Yes, I hoped all three of us could go out. My treat, of course."

Lynn smiled. "Thank you, Hayden. That's very thoughtful of you. But to be honest, I'm not hungry at all. In fact, I'm feeling a little tired. I think I'll just stay here and relax a bit, maybe finish up a little reading and go on to bed." She looked from Hayden to Rachel and back again. "I assume you won't be late, will you?"

"Oh, not at all," Hayden assured her. "We'll just go to a fast-food place somewhere and get a burger or something. I'll have her home in a couple of hours, if not sooner."

Lynn looked at Rachel and raised an inquisitive eyebrow. Responding to her signal, Rachel nodded. "Absolutely, Mom. An hour or two at the most. Do you want us to bring you something?"

"No thanks, honey. I think I'll just fix a cup of tea and maybe a piece of toast or something. You two go on, and I'll see you later."

In moments the two young people were out the door, chattering to one another as if they'd been friends for years. Lynn stood in the entryway and listened to their voices fade away as they climbed into Hayden's car.

She turned toward the kitchen, deciding that cup of tea sounded pretty good, though she'd wait on the toast. Maybe, after she'd finished her tea and the last few pages of the journal she'd been reading before Hayden arrived, she'd go soak in the old claw-foot bathtub. She and Rachel had been using the bathroom's shower since they arrived, but Lynn had been eyeing that tub and thinking how luxurious it would feel to sink down in some warm, bubbly water and just drift away for a while. Since she now had the house to herself, tonight seemed the perfect time to indulge.

Rachel breathed deeply, determined not to let her nerves betray her. How long had it been since she'd been on a date, even an informal one with a guy she barely knew on her way to grab a burger at some nondescript fast-food joint? Longer than she wanted to admit.

Not that she hadn't had a ton of invitations, especially during her four years at Bible college. But she'd been determined to stay focused on her studies. She always kept in mind how her mom had missed out on a college education so she could marry her dad—not that Rachel wasn't glad she did, since she would no doubt never have been born otherwise—but she had decided early on not to follow in her mother's footsteps.

With college behind her now, she was no closer to knowing what she wanted to do with the rest of her life than she had been the day she first packed up and moved into a dorm room at the age of eighteen. Why was that? Other students, even her roommate at college, seemed to find their life direction with ease, while she continued to drift. Some days she thought she wanted to be a missionary in some exotic, faraway land; other times she felt more drawn to work with the elderly or with children, and to teach, right here on the home front. She'd spent the last four years of her life begging God for an answer—loud and clear—but none had come.

And now here she was, in Bloomfield with her mother, feeling an inexplicable pull to stay in this quaint, somewhat behind-the-times town. It made no sense.

"A penny for your thoughts."

The voice seemed to come out of nowhere, jarring her back to the present. She blinked and turned toward the tall, dark-haired man in the driver's seat. He had braked his nearly new black sedan at one of the few stoplights in town and now sat grinning at her.

Embarrassed, she smiled back. "It'll take more than a penny to worm anything out of me," she said, hoping her tone came across as light as she intended. "I don't give up information easily—or cheaply, for that matter."

Hayden laughed. "Why am I not surprised?" He nodded.

"You strike me as a strong woman who knows what she wants in life and goes after it with gusto."

Wow, Rachel thought. *How absolutely wrong can a guy be?* But she wasn't about to let him know what an indecisive flake she was.

She shrugged. "I guess. Nothing wrong with a little gusto now and then."

The light changed and Hayden turned his attention back to driving. "So, are you okay with a burger? I mean, if you'd rather have something else—maybe something a little nicer—our town does have a few decent places to eat. You know, places where you can actually sit down at a table, study a menu, and give your order to a waitress."

Rachel laughed. "No, I don't think I'm up to that tonight. Let's stick with a burger. I've got my mouth all set for one—with lots of drippy cheese, of course. And fries."

"Of course. What's the point of a burger without cheese or fries?"

"No point at all."

They laughed together as Hayden pulled into a parking spot in the lot next to Burger Heaven. "How's this?" he asked, turning in his seat after shutting off the ignition.

Rachel read the sign. "Works for me. And the name seems appropriate for a Sunday too."

Hayden smiled. "I hadn't thought of that, but you're right. So, let's go get those drippy cheeseburgers and greasy fries. I just might order a giant milkshake to top if off."

Rachel felt her eyes widen. Did she dare? Sure, why not? Though Hayden didn't know it, she hadn't been out on a date in ages, so why not splurge and go all out?

"I'm up for that," she said, reaching for the door handle. "And the sooner, the better."

 Chapter 10

WITH NO NEW REVELATIONS COMING FROM MYRON'S JOURNAL, Lynn had finished her tea and headed upstairs to run a bath. The very thought of luxuriating in the warm water sounded almost decadent, particularly since she'd packed some strawberry scented three-in-one shampoo, body wash, and bubble bath before she left home. How was that for great planning?

She smiled as she stepped into the nearly hot water and lowered herself all the way to her neckline. This was going to be fun. And if the water cooled off before she wanted to get out, she'd just drain it and add more.

Lynn closed her eyes and leaned back against the cold porcelain edge, shivering at the sensation. After a few moments, her skin temperature adjusted, and she sighed. Maybe having the house to herself for an evening wasn't such a bad thing after all— though she couldn't help but wonder how Rachel and Hayden were getting along.

Just the evening before, Lynn had been so certain that John Currey had snagged Rachel's attention—and he no doubt had.

But now he had competition with the tall, handsome, recently divorced accountant.

Divorced. Not so sure I like that for Rachel. Even though it was a brief marriage and there were no children involved, it was still a very serious relationship that just didn't work out. True, I've heard it was Hayden's wife who ended it—ran off with someone else, which must have been devastating for him. But who knows what might have precipitated such a decision? Is he really faultless in all this? If nothing else, it doesn't speak very highly of his choice of a life partner.

A crunching sound from outside caught her attention, and she opened her eyes. Was someone walking around out there? Had Hayden and Rachel returned? She hadn't heard a car come up the driveway, and it had only been an hour or so since they left. Lynn really didn't expect them for a while yet. But if not them, then who was it?

She heard the noise again, more than once actually. Yes, someone was definitely outside. It had to be Jason . . . didn't it? Who else could it be?

"Beasley?" she called. "Come here, boy."

Her faithful dog, who had been snoozing on the bench at the foot of the king-sized bed, took his sweet time responding. By the time he finally sauntered into the bathroom and offered her a sleepy but quizzical look, she had begun to wonder if he'd even heard her.

"A fine watchdog you are," she scolded. "Didn't you hear that noise? Aren't you supposed to bark and alert me when someone's around?"

Beasley yawned and sat down, watching her with his warm brown eyes. She didn't doubt his loyalty, but his worth as a protector had definitely come into question.

"Never mind," she said, waving him away. "Go on back to bed. There's nothing you can do anyway."

As if he'd understood her dismissal, he stood and turned back toward the bedroom. Certain he'd fallen asleep again before she even climbed out of the tub, Lynn grabbed a clean towel to dry herself.

"So much for a nice, leisurely soak," she grumbled. "Even though I know it's only Jason out there, skulking around as he always does, there's no way I'm going to relax now. Might as well put on a warm robe and go back downstairs to wait for Rachel."

She talked to herself often these days, particularly since Daniel died. She'd caught herself many times and even considered directing her comments toward her dead husband, as if she were talking to him, but she knew that wasn't a scriptural response.

"I should use these times for prayer," she said aloud. "After all, Lord, I know You're listening. Besides, You know who's out there, and You're the only One who can really protect me anyway—if I need protecting, that is. I suppose old Jason is harmless, as Myron always said, but . . . well, sometimes I wonder."

She cinched her robe with a tie belt and ran a comb through her hair before sliding her feet into slippers and exiting the bathroom. Sure enough, Beasley lay snoozing on the bench. Lynn shook her head and made her way out of the bedroom and down the stairs. Maybe she'd put the kettle on and fix another cup of tea, along with a piece of toast this time. Rachel should be back soon, and perhaps she'd join her for a cup while she told her about her evening out with Hayden. Lynn had missed hearing about Rachel's social life while she was away at college. During her daughter's high school years, Lynn had relished Rachel's updates. It would be fun to hear them again . . . though she had to admit she would have preferred the update to be about an evening out with John rather than Hayden. Was it just because Hayden was divorced . . . or could it have something to do with the fact that John was a pastor? A youth pastor, to be sure, but a pastor nonetheless, and Lynn had always dreamed of Rachel marrying someone in full-time ministry, someone who would draw her into ministry right alongside him. And with her fresh-from-Bible-college diploma tucked away in her personal belongings, she'd be the perfect pastor's wife.

Enough of that, Lynn Myers. You're meddling and match-making, instead of leaving things in God's hands—quite capable hands, mind you. Now leave it alone, will you?

With no more sounds coming from outside, Lynn turned the fire on under the kettle, plopped a tea bag in a mug, and sat down at the table to wait.

Rachel's stomach was pleasantly full, though she hadn't quite been able to finish the last of her fries. The quarter-pound burger, loaded with cheese and tomatoes, had been delicious, but it was the chocolate shake that had undone her.

Half a chocolate shake, she reminded herself as Hayden steered his sedan down Cemetery Road. It was the first time she'd shared a shake with anyone in ages, but when the waitress brought the mammoth drink in two vessels—one a decorative glass with a straw and spoon, the other a half-full metal container, cold to the touch, she'd looked at Hayden imploringly.

"There is no way in the world I can drink all this," she'd said. "Not with a burger and fries too. You should have warned me."

He'd laughed and reached out to take the portion of the shake in the tall metal cup. "Don't worry. I hoped you'd say that because I love chocolate shakes and have no problem helping you drink one."

And so they had shared the drink, talking and laughing throughout the meal until at last Rachel glanced at her watch and said, "I hate to do this, but we'd better get back. I don't like leaving Mom alone in that big old house at night."

Hayden said he understood and quickly paid the bill before escorting her back to his vehicle and opening the passenger side door. It wasn't the first thing he'd done that night that impressed Rachel with his manners. It seemed Hayden Blackstone was not only handsome and successful, but polite as well.

Now, as Hayden parked the car just yards from the front porch, Rachel watched him turn off the ignition and pivot toward her. The night was dark, with only the faintest light coming from the stars and a sliver of moon. But Rachel could see his features, including his smile, as he gazed at her.

"That was fun. I hope you had a good time."

"Absolutely," Rachel answered, "despite the five-gallon chocolate shake."

Hayden chuckled. "They don't skimp on portions there, that's for sure."

He paused, and Rachel felt her stomach clench. Surely he wouldn't try to kiss her, not after only one date—which wasn't even really a date, she reminded herself. It was just a shared meal with a new acquaintance, and that certainly did not warrant a good-night kiss.

"I . . . hope you'll consider doing this again sometime," he said, raising his eyebrows. "Would you? We could even go somewhere nicer—the Fancy Schmantzy, maybe."

Rachel grinned. She knew about Bloomfield's only upscale restaurant, and she wouldn't mind going there at all. Still, if she accepted Hayden's invitation now, then she really had to count it as a date . . . didn't she? Especially if they went to such a nice place.

She shrugged. "Sure, we can do this again sometime, though I'm not sure I brought anything nice enough for the Fancy Schmantzy. Seriously, anywhere is fine with me. Personally, I love Bert's Barbecue."

Hayden laughed. "A girl after my own heart. I'd rather eat at Bert's than just about anywhere. Okay, Bert's it is. When?"

She frowned. "What do you mean?"

"I mean, when should we go? Tomorrow night? The next night? You name it, I'll pick you up."

Rachel hesitated. Unless her mom suddenly came around to Rachel's way of thinking, their stay in Bloomfield was temporary at best, so she really couldn't put him off too long. Still, tomorrow night was a bit soon. And besides, she had to consider her mom.

"To be honest," she said, "I really don't feel right leaving Mom alone again so soon. Maybe we should wait a few days."

"Why not bring her with us? I'd love a chance to get to know her better."

Rachel cocked her head. This guy really did know how to get to her. "I'd like that. Tell you what. Let me talk to Mom and see what she says about the three of us going out to eat together—maybe in a couple of days. I can let you know tomorrow. Would that be all right?"

"That would be great. Sure."

With that settled, Hayden exited his side of the car and hurried around to open the door for her and offer his hand as she stepped out.

This chivalrous stuff could grow on a girl, Rachel thought.

By the time he walked her to the door, she determined to say a quick good night and get inside before he got any crazy ideas. He probably knew better than to try to kiss her yet, but she wasn't taking any chances.

"Good night, Hayden," she said, snagging her key from her purse and shoving it into the lock. "Now that you have my cell number, why don't you call me tomorrow and we'll see what we can work out about the three of us going out to eat soon?"

With that, she stepped inside, turning to watch Hayden as he said good night and headed back down the porch steps. It had been a nice evening, but she was nowhere ready to let a brand new friendship morph into anything more serious.

Lynn resisted the impulse to jump to her feet and hurry to the front door to welcome Rachel home. She'd heard the car drive up, the crunch of footsteps to the front door, and the quick good night the two had uttered before Rachel closed the door behind her. Lynn's patience was fraying by the time her daughter finally stepped into the kitchen.

"Hey, Mom," she said, "I saw the light and figured you were in here waiting for me."

Lynn felt her cheeks warm. "What makes you think I was waiting? Maybe I was just sitting here having a cup of tea."

Rachel chuckled. "You were having a cup of tea while you waited. I know you, Mom." She eyed the kettle on the stove. "Is the water still hot?"

Lynn nodded. "It should be. I just turned off the burner a few minutes ago."

"Good. I'm full, but I think I have room for tea."

In a few moments Rachel had joined her mother at the table, her own mug of tea in front of her. "So how was your evening?"

Lynn raised her eyebrows. "My evening? Who cares about my evening? I want to know about yours."

"Aha! I knew it. You were waiting for me."

Lynn sighed. "Okay, I was waiting. Now reward me. How did it go? What do you think of this guy, Hayden? Are you going to see him again?"

"Wow, are you full of questions!" Rachel sipped her tea before continuing. "It went well. We pigged out on major burgers, with drippy cheese and greasy fries and a mega-shake, which we shared. I'm thinking we each ingested something like ten thousand calories, at least."

"I don't know how you do it," Lynn said, shaking her head. "If I ate half as much as you, I wouldn't fit through the front door."

"Come on, Mom, how many times have you told me you used to be just like me when you were young? Ate all day long, anything you wanted and as much as you wanted, and never gained an ounce."

Lynn groaned. "Yeah, well, those days are long gone. Now I just look at food and gain weight."

Rachel smiled. "I suppose I'll be that way some day, but for now I'm going to enjoy myself."

"So . . . did you? Enjoy yourself, I mean?"

"I did. Hayden's a nice guy—polite too. We talked and laughed and had a good time."

"Did he ask you out again?"

Rachel set her cup down and raised her eyebrows. "As a matter of fact, he did. And he wants you to come with us. I told him how much I like Bert's, and it turns out that's his favorite place too. So he offered to take us both. What do you think? I told him I'd let him know tomorrow, and then we'll pick a day and time."

Lynn shook her head. "That's really sweet of both of you, but you don't need your mother trailing along on your dates. You two go and have fun. I'll pass."

"Oh, no, you don't. To be honest, not only do I want you to come along because I enjoy your company and want to give Hayden a chance to get to know you, but I also want you there for the very reason that it will make it seem like less of a real date." She paused and reached her hand across the table, laying it on Lynn's arm. "Mom, I'm not ready for a serious relationship, and going out on dates is a sure way to risk having one. But if it's just a three-way dinner at Bert's, it's safe. So you see? You have to come." She grinned. "It's your duty as a mom—to protect your daughter."

Lynn laughed. How could she resist such logic? "Okay, fine. I'll come with you. But just this once. I can't see us ending up as some sort of ongoing threesome."

"Perfect," Rachel said, withdrawing her hand and picking up her tea. "I'll tell him tomorrow." She took a couple of sips and then said, "So, you never did tell me about your evening. You're in your robe. Does that mean you soaked in the tub like you said you might do?"

"I did. And I highly recommend it. That tub is heavenly—not to mention huge. Fill that thing up with warm water and bubbles, and you can get lost in there."

Rachel laughed. "You're tempting me. I just might have to give it a try before we go to bed." She glanced at Lynn's nearly empty cup. "Can I get you a refill?"

Lynn shook her head. "No, thanks, honey. This is my second cup. If I drink anymore I'll be up all night."

"Yeah, me too," Rachel said, setting her own cup down. "So what about the journals? Find out anything else about Last Chance?"

"I'm afraid not. To be honest, I didn't really try that hard after you left. That tub was calling me. But I plan to get back to it tomorrow."

"And if you don't find anything? Then what?"

"I've been thinking about that. I had meant to ask around at the picnic, but the opportunity just didn't present itself. Still, if anyone in town would know anything about this Last Chance Justice guy, it would be Homer Tatum or Jolene Trump. Those two have been around for as long as anyone can remember—especially Homer. At least, I guess he's still around. Mom always said he was the closest thing to a town historian that Bloomfield had. I'd better check and make sure he hasn't already passed away or something. Last I heard he was living at the retirement village, but he's got to be in his nineties by now, so if he's still alive he might be in a nursing home or something. I'll ask around. It shouldn't be that hard to find out where he is. One of those two Bloomfield old-timers just might be able to shed a little light on this so-called mystery that my brother was so determined to solve."

"Maybe. But if not, there's always Jason. Why don't you just sit down and talk to him about it?"

Lynn suppressed a shiver. It wasn't like she hadn't already asked herself that very question—more than once. But each time she came up against it, she pushed it back. Surely there had to be another way. Jason was just too strange. Besides, how reliable would he be? Most people in town questioned whether or not the old guy's elevator went all the way to the top, not to mention the way he snuck around, giving everyone the creeps. Like tonight while she was in the bathtub . . .

"I'll keep Jason as a last resort," she said. "First, I'm going to try Jolene and Homer. We'll see what we can find out that way. Surely someone in this town knows what this is all about. And if they don't, then it's probably the first time anyone in Bloomfield has ever kept a secret successfully."

# Chapter 11

JOHN CURREY WAS A NERVOUS WRECK. HE FELT MORE LIKE ONE of the inexperienced high school students in his youth group than a grown man. Then again, inexperienced described him when it came to matters of the heart. Other than a couple of inconsequential crushes during his teens, he'd never had a real relationship with a girl. He'd always been happy to hang out with his church friends and the guys on the basketball team, where he was a star point guard. But from the moment he laid eyes on Rachel, his priorities had changed.

He drove his twelve-year-old Ford Taurus up the driveway toward the two-story house at the end of Cemetery Drive. Who chose to live in a place like that? Rachel's uncle, that's who—and everyone in town knew what a strange bird he had been.

Strange, but kind, he reminded himself, thinking back to the handful of times he'd met Myron Cofield at Sunday morning church services. The man wasn't much for getting involved in any of the social activities at the church, but he never missed Sunday morning.

John turned off the engine and stared up at the quiet, sprawling house. What would Rachel and her mother do with it now that Myron was gone? Would they consider moving here? A faint flicker of hope flamed in John's heart, but he knew the chances were slim. Who in their right mind would want to move to a place like this—right next to the cemetery, of all places? And then there was the matter of old Jason . . .

He shook his head. He'd better stop speculating and get out of the car before someone spotted him and thought he was the strange one. He pocketed his keys and climbed out onto the gravel driveway. *What used to be a gravel driveway,* he thought as he approached the house. *Looks like it could use a new layer, that's for sure. What's left is pretty sparse and scattered, and nearly overgrown with weeds.*

As he pressed the doorbell and listened to the somewhat eerie chimes that responded, he tried to quell the mob of flighty moths swirling around in his stomach. What made him think that anyone as beautiful as Rachel Myers would be interested in him, especially when Hayden Blackstone had already honed in on her and gotten a head start? John had heard from three different people how Rachel and Hayden had been seen eating together at Burger Heaven, talking and laughing like long-lost friends. How could John compete with something like that?

He'd nearly convinced himself to turn around and leave when the door opened, and he found himself gazing into those wide green eyes that had mesmerized him from the moment he'd met her in this very place on Friday. Could she be any more beautiful?

She flashed him a brilliant smile, and he had his answer. Yes, when she smiled, she could. And she was. Stunningly more beautiful. Breathtakingly so. And he couldn't think of a thing to say.

"John, what a nice surprise. How are you?"

He swallowed, knowing his cheeks were flaming and hoping she didn't think he was a complete idiot. "I'm . . . fine," he managed to say. "I didn't get your number yesterday at the picnic, so I just took a chance and dropped by. I . . . hope that's all right."

She laughed, and he wondered how laughter could sound so musical. "Of course it is. It seems to be a common problem lately. Hayden did the same thing."

The level of heat in John's cheeks rose a notch, but he determined to ignore it. So that was how the guy wangled a burger date with her the previous evening. He took a deep breath and smiled. "It's just that . . . well, I have Mondays off, and I thought maybe we could go out for lunch . . . or something. I mean, if you don't already have plans."

Rachel shook her head. "Not at all," she said, glancing at her watch. "Though Mom and I were just talking about fixing something to eat." Her smile brightened as she opened the door wider. "I have a great idea," she said, just as Beasley came up behind her, spotted John, and wriggled to his side, welcoming John's touch. "Why don't you come in and have lunch with us? Mom and I made a quick grocery run this morning, so I can throw together some sandwiches and a salad. The three of us can get to know each other better. Wouldn't that be fun?"

John swallowed the lump in his throat and nodded. "Sure. I mean, if it wouldn't be too much trouble. I'd be glad to help."

She motioned him inside, and he followed her lead. As they stepped into the kitchen doorway she announced, "Mom, John Currey is here. He's staying for lunch. Isn't that nice?"

Within moments, the friendly atmosphere helped John to relax. Rachel put him in charge of fixing the sandwiches while she made the salad, and Lynn took care of the drinks. As their conversation took on a more natural bent, John found himself feeling a lot better about his decision to drop in unannounced. Maybe this day would work out all right after all.

As they sat down around the kitchen table, Rachel fixed her eyes on his and asked, "John, would you mind offering the blessing?"

John had prayed in public many times over the years, and without the least bit of discomfort. Suddenly, all that confidence melted away, and he found himself once again at a loss for words.

Are you grateful for the food I've provided you with—and the ones who will share it with you?

The familiar voice came from the depths of his heart, and John smiled. Reaching out to take their hands, he opened his mouth and prayed with familiarity and gratitude. How did he keep forgetting the simplicity of speaking to the One who knew him better than anyone else—and still loved him beyond John's wildest imaginings?

As they settled in around the table, John caught Rachel's warm smile and he couldn't help but wonder if it had something to do with his prayer. He returned the gesture and eyed the sandwiches he'd made. He was relatively sure he'd remembered to include everything Rachel had given him, but they were a bit crooked. Oh well, he never claimed to be a deli pro.

Lynn passed him the large salad bowl, and he used the plastic tongs to maneuver a serving of greens onto his plate. He hadn't realized he was hungry until now, and he decided that was a good sign. Obviously, his nerves had settled down a bit, and maybe he had a chance of making a favorable impression on Rachel and her mother.

"Ranch or Italian?" Lynn asked, catching his attention.

He looked up and raised his eyebrows. What had she just asked him?

Lynn smiled and held up a bottle of dressing in each hand. "Ranch or Italian?"

Relieved, John opted for the Italian and poured a generous amount on his salad and then waited until the ladies took their first forkfuls to do the same. He told himself to keep in mind that this was a three-way conversation so he wouldn't end up staring at Rachel throughout the meal, but it wouldn't be easy to keep his focus.

They were still discussing the perfect weather they'd experienced at the picnic the previous day when a classical tune interrupted them. Rachel's cheeks flushed as she dug her cell phone from her pocket and glanced at the number. "Hayden," she said, looking up and smiling. "I'll call him back. Now where were we?"

Suddenly the pieces of lettuce and cucumber in John's mouth seemed to turn to sawdust. Hayden had her number now? Great. Who was John kidding if he thought he had a chance with Rachel? She was beautiful and intelligent and sweet; she probably wouldn't be in Bloomfield much longer—and Hayden Blackstone was already making headway in pursuing her. John couldn't help but wonder if he was wasting his time even trying to compete with a successful CPA, but he wasn't anywhere near ready to give up.

As the conversation continued, John felt his smile growing more wooden by the moment. He had to make it through lunch as graciously as possible, but then he was going to excuse himself and beat a hasty exit, stage left. If there was one thing he'd learned playing basketball, it was to recognize when you were out of your league. And this appeared to be one of those times, though John was determined not to admit defeat.

"That John Currey is certainly a nice boy, isn't he?" Lynn asked after they'd waved him off and closed the front door. "Handsome, too. I'm surprised he left so quickly."

Rachel squirmed, certain that it was her fault he was gone. She hadn't meant to announce that it was Hayden who'd called while they were having lunch. It had just popped out, and she knew it had made John uncomfortable. She hadn't dated much, but she knew enough not to play games when it came to matters of the heart. Both John and Hayden were fine, respectable young men, and they deserved better. She would make a point to treat them both with respect, though she doubted she'd have much more interaction with them if her mother followed through on leaving Bloomfield soon.

Rachel realized her mother still watched her, no doubt waiting for a response. She smiled and nodded. "Yes, he's very nice. I'm glad he dropped by."

Lynn raised her eyebrows as if to imply Rachel hadn't answered the entire question, but she didn't pursue the subject. "So, shall we go back to the last of the journals? We don't have any dishes to do, since John insisted on helping us clean up. We may as well spend our afternoon doing something constructive."

Constructive? Rachel doubted that reading through old journals in an effort to solve a seven-dollar mystery qualified as constructive, but it was as good a way to use the time as anything else. Still, she did owe Hayden a phone call . . . didn't she? At the very least she should check his message.

"I'll be right there," she said. "Just give me a minute."

Beasley trotted after Lynn toward the library, and Rachel

returned to the kitchen where she dialed her voice mail. Hayden's upbeat greeting brought a smile to her lips.

"Hi, Rachel. I told you I was going to call, so here I am, a man of my word. Are you up for going out tonight? We can bring your mom if you want. Or if tonight doesn't work, how about tomorrow? Whatever works best for you. Give me a call when you can. If I don't answer, I'm with a client, but you can leave a message. Talk to you soon."

Goodness, going from dateless to having two men wanting to take her out and feed her was quite an adjustment. Still, how could anything come of either relationship when she and her mom were only here for a few more days? Should she take advantage of all the attention, or would it be unfair to Hayden and John? Then again, it wasn't as if they didn't know she was only here temporarily . . . right?

She sighed. Rachel didn't even have to ask her mom which man she preferred; it was John, hands-down. John was a young, never-married, no doubt poverty-stricken youth pastor; Hayden, though established in a lucrative profession, was divorced. The vote was already in, and Hayden didn't have a chance.

But was this really about her mother? Of course not. Rachel was an adult now, and perfectly capable of making up her own mind. Or was she? If so, why was her stomach in knots and her head beginning to ache? And why did she still regret that John left so soon? Was it possible her mother's preference was hers as well?

She shook her head. No, there was only one way to handle this. She and her mom would have dinner by themselves tonight. She'd leave Hayden a message that she'd have to pass on his invitation tonight but would get with him about tomorrow. That would give her a little time to pray and clear her head. This was no time to make decisions under pressure.

With that resolved, she dialed Hayden's number and breathed a sigh of relief when she got his voice mail. She left her pre-planned message, and then hung up to go into the library and join her mother as they delved through the last of the musty old journals.

Lynn sighed. They'd spent the better part of the afternoon, ever since John left, leafing through books that produced no more information than they'd had before they started. Now what?

"Are you really surprised, Mom?" Rachel asked, eyeing Lynn from her favorite spot on the couch, just under the window. Beasley lay curled up at her feet, snoring softly. "If the answer you were looking for was in these journals, Uncle Myron would have solved this problem years ago. But from his last entry, that doesn't appear to be the case."

Lynn shrugged. "I know. You're right, and I suppose I suspected that all along, but I thought he might have mentioned something about the incident somewhere along the line, something that would at least point us in the right direction."

Rachel set the journal down on her lap. "Mom, you already know the right direction. You need to sit down and talk with Jason. No one spent more time with Uncle Myron than he did. Why are you so opposed to doing the obvious?"

It wasn't often that Rachel confronted Lynn and made her uncomfortable, but right now that was exactly what Lynn felt. Logically, she knew her daughter was right, but she simply did not want to go there.

"I told you I'd talk to Jason if and when I couldn't find anything in these journals or by talking to other people. My next stop is Jolene Trump, and if she doesn't work, then Homer Tatum. They've been around Bloomfield forever, and nothing much gets past them. One of them is bound to have something they can tell me about this Last Chance man and the missing seven dollars and fourteen cents."

Rachel frowned. "Seriously? You'd rather try to worm information out of Jolene Trump or Homer Tatum than just go out back and ask Jason? Or maybe I should go ask him."

Lynn held up her hand. "Stay right where you are. Neither one of us is going to go outside and confront Jason—at least not until we've exhausted all other possibilities."

Rachel shook her head. "Fine. I suppose Mrs. Trump might be able to help you, but . . . Homer Tatum? Are you kidding me? From what you said, the man's ancient. Did you even find out if he's still around?"

Lynn shook her head. "Not yet, but I will—if we don't get the information we need from Jolene, that is."

"Wait a minute," Rachel said, sitting up straight and startling Beasley in the process. "Does that mean we can go to Bert's for dinner tonight? Maybe you can ask Mrs. Trump while we're there."

Lynn smiled. "I don't see why not. Might as well kill two birds with one stone, as my dad always liked to say."

Rachel laughed and stood to her feet. "Excellent. Suddenly your idea sounds like a good one after all, even if it is just because that's still my favorite place in Bloomfield to eat. Let's go. I'm starved!"

Lynn laughed and shook her head. "I think you were born starved," she said, getting up to follow her daughter out of the room. "Let me grab my purse and I'll be right with you. But this time we're leaving Beasley here to hold down the fort."

 Chapter 12

JOLENE HAD BEEN BUSTLING JUST ABOUT AS MUCH AS SOMEONE her age could bustle—and then some. Lynn marveled at the woman's energy and endurance, but despaired of getting much time to talk with her, as crowded as Bert's was that evening. She and Rachel had waited nearly fifteen minutes for a place to sit and eat, something nearly unheard of in Bloomfield.

She and Rachel sipped their water while they perused the menus, waiting for Jolene to return and take their orders. When another voice—only vaguely familiar—interrupted Lynn's concentration, she frowned and glanced up to find Kathy Wilson standing beside their booth.

"Lynn Cofield, is that you?" she nearly squealed, reminding Lynn of their high school days. Kathy had been a year behind Lynn, and though they hadn't been close, they'd at least known one another and had crossed paths a couple of times when Lynn came home to visit. It appeared, for the most part, that the years had been good to Kathy. Her hair wasn't gray yet, and she carried only a few more pounds than the last time Lynn had seen her.

Kathy Wilson, Lynn thought. *Of all people! A nice person, but definitely not known as a secret-keeper. Still, if I can remember her married name, you'd think she could remember mine.*

She smiled. "Myers," she said. "It's Lynn Myers now, remember? How are you, Kathy?"

Kathy scarcely missed a beat. "Myers, of course. You'd think I'd have that straight after all these years, wouldn't you?" She shrugged. "It must be something about seeing a face from the past that transports me back to those wild, crazy high school years, including our maiden names."

Wild and crazy? Lynn wondered for a moment if she and Kathy had indeed attended the same high school. But before she could think of an appropriate comment, Kathy had already turned her attention to Rachel.

"Hello, Rachel," she said, grinning. "It's so good to see you again. You were quite a bit younger the last time you were in Bloomfield, but look at you now. All grown up and absolutely beautiful."

Rachel smiled up at her. "Thank you so much, Mrs. . . . ?"

"Wilson. Kathy Wilson. I'm Stan's mother. He owns the local auto shop, you know."

Lynn was certain that Rachel did not know, nor did she particularly care, but her gracious daughter continued to smile up at their visitor. "How nice," she said, offering her hand.

Seemingly surprised, Kathy took it and gave it a quick pump before letting go. "Your mother and I have known each other for years. Decades, actually. It's always so nice to see her back home in Bloomfield, where she belongs."

Home? Where I belong? Lynn bit her tongue to keep from correcting her former high school chum. Why did everyone insist on trying to reconnect her to Bloomfield? This is where she grew up, not where she lived now, and certainly not where she'd spent the happiest years of her life. Those years would always belong to her memory of Daniel and all they shared together—no matter what the residents of Bloomfield thought about her leaving.

"As a matter of fact," Kathy went on, still directing her comments to Rachel, "I heard you and your mom were in town when one of my friends from the garden club told me she spotted you at Burger Heaven with Hayden Blackstone. How exciting! We all just love Hayden—he's my son's best friend, you know—and we were just heartbroken over what happened with his marriage."

Rachel's eyebrows lifted, and she flashed a quick SOS at Lynn with her eyes. Lynn dove right in.

"Yes, well, Hayden does seem like a nice young man, though he and Rachel just met and went out for a quick burger. It's nothing, just . . . just a casual friendship, very much like her new acquaintance with John Currey. Nothing serious, nothing exclusive, just . . . friends."

This time it was Kathy who raised her eyebrows and widened her eyes as she gave her entire attention to Lynn. "John Currey? The youth pastor at Bloomfield Community? He and Rachel are also seeing each other? Well, that certainly is something new, isn't it?"

Lynn could have kicked herself. In trying to diffuse a potential gossip situation, she'd just added fuel to the proverbial fire—and the so-called "news" would no doubt spread through town accordingly.

She sighed. Was there any point in trying to tamp down the wildfire now, or would any further attempts simply exacerbate the problem?

"Well," Kathy said, her voice warm as she shot a quick parting glance at Lynn and Rachel, "Frank's waiting for me in our booth. I told him I'd just be a minute, but I had to pop over and say hello. It's so good to see you—both of you." She turned to leave, but then quickly looked back. "Oh, one more thing," she said, smiling down at Lynn. "If you're going to be here for any length of time at all, I'd love to have you come to a garden club meeting as my guest. We've grown a bit since you lived here, and we so miss your mom's presence. She was quite a gardener, wasn't she? Well, as I said, I'd better go. I'm so glad we ran into each other. See you soon!"

And with that she swished away, flitting back to her husband who sat quietly, waiting for her.

Lynn sighed again. "I'm so sorry, honey. Kathy Wilson is a lovely woman, and she means well. It's just . . . well . . ."

Rachel leaned close and whispered, "She's a gossip, right?"

"Let's just say she has loose lips."

"And you know what they say about loose lips," Rachel added.

Lynn nodded. "Unfortunately, I do. Let's just hope we're not one of the ships that her loose lips sink."

Rachel laughed and sat back. "I don't know how we could be. If the most exciting thing anyone can find to say about us is that I shared a burger and fries with Haydon Blackstone at Burger Heaven, that hardly qualifies as a torpedo, does it?"

Lynn relaxed. Rachel was right. So what if Kathy told people that not only had Rachel gone out to eat with Hayden but that she might also have something brewing with John Currey? Rachel was young and single and available, and so were John and Hayden. No one was doing anything wrong, so how much gossip could such information generate?

She nearly laughed out loud. In a town the size of Bloomfield? Quite a bit. But it was harmless, as was Kathy Wilson. Actually, Lynn had always liked Kathy, though she scarcely knew her husband, Frank. The two seemed happy, though, so Lynn imagined he must be a decent man.

"You two ready to order?"

Lynn jerked her head up to find Jolene standing above them, pencil and order pad in hand, her blue-gray perm slightly askew and her ever-present yellow apron mussed. Otherwise she looked about as fresh as someone her age possibly could.

"Um, sure," Lynn said. "I believe I'll just have the tuna salad—a half order—and some iced tea."

Jolene scribbled on her pad and then looked to Rachel, who ordered her favorite pulled pork sandwich and fries. As Jolene stuffed the order pad back in her apron pocket and turned to leave, Lynn decided to take her chance while she had it. "Jolene, have you got a minute? I need to ask you something."

Jolene turned back, a slight frown marking her forehead. "I suppose. But I am kind of busy right now."

Lynn nodded. "This won't take long. It's just that you've been in town longer than nearly everyone else, and I'm wondering if you might be able to help me with some information." She paused but then decided to press ahead before Jolene took the opportunity to escape. "My brother kept journals through the years, and it appears that at the end he was quite interested in clearing the name of a former Bloomfield resident. This was so important to him that he requested he be buried beside the man."

Jolene's invisible brows rose a fraction. "Last Chance Justice?" She nodded. "Yeah, I heard about that. Can't imagine why Myron would want to do something like that. I mean, it's not like they were close or anything."

"I wondered that too," Lynn admitted. "But Myron apparently admired the man, even though they only met a time or two when Myron was a boy. But I found something in my brother's journal about an incident involving Last Chance and a missing seven dollars and fourteen cents. Do you know anything about that?"

Jolene's frown wrinkles deepened. "I'm afraid I don't, though now that you mention it, I do remember hearing about that missing money somewhere along the line. The subject comes up now and then, I suppose, but it hardly seems a big enough deal to worry about. Never really gave it much thought, to tell you the truth."

"So you don't know anything about how it went missing or who it belonged to—anything at all?"

Jolene shook her head. "Sure don't. And to be honest, I don't care. Why does it matter? Listen, I need to get back to work, but if you really want to know, there are two people in this town who might just have the answers you're looking for—Homer Tatum and old Jason, out there by your brother's place. He's a strange one, that Jason, but he spent more time with Myron than anyone. Why not start with him? He's right there, after all." She leaned down and lowered her voice. "Of course, there's always Miss Pearl, but from what I've heard, she's not talking."

It was Lynn's turn to frown. "Miss Pearl? Who's that?"

She straightened up, her eyes still fixed on Lynn. "She's the only one left of the Justice family," she said. "One of Last Chance's sisters. But anyone who's ever tried to ask her about Last Chance and the missing money nearly got run off with a shotgun." And with that, she laughed and hurried off.

Rachel and Lynn exchanged wide-eyed glances. A shotgun? Surely Jolene was joking . . . wasn't she? But she'd also suggested Lynn start with Jason, an idea Lynn knew her daughter would support.

Before Rachel could say anything, Lynn shook her head. "No shotguns," she said, "and no Jason until I try Homer Tatum first. He might be nearly deaf and blind, but he sounds like the best chance we've got at this point."

Rachel opened her mouth, paused, and closed it again. "Fine," she said at last. "But even if you bypass Last Chance's gun-wielding sister—which, by the way, I wholeheartedly encourage you to do—chances are you're going to end up talking to Jason about it sooner or later, or just forget the whole thing. And come to think of it, that wouldn't be a half-bad idea. I mean, seven dollars and fourteen cents, Mom. This is not prime-time TV stuff here."

Lynn knew her daughter was right, but her curiosity about what had now been confirmed as missing money was driven by her brother's apparent obsession with it. Why had it been so important to him? Why did it matter at all? This Last Chance Justice guy was dead and buried—as was Myron—so if she had any sense, she'd let it go. But for some reason, she knew she couldn't.

"I need to at least try," she said, hoping Rachel would understand. "I may not find out anything, but for Myron's sake—"

"I know," Rachel interrupted. "For Uncle Myron's sake, you have to give it the old college try." She smiled. "Fine. I'll help you if I can."

"I appreciate that, sweetheart."

Rachel's expression changed then, and her eyes squinted together as she leaned forward. "Mom, I've been thinking about

Mrs. Wilson. When she mentioned the garden club, you seemed to tense up. Was that my imagination, or is there something going on that I don't know about?"

Lynn's first reaction was to deny the fact that she'd grown tense over Kathy's mention of the garden club, but even now that tension had returned, squeezing her stomach into knots that made no sense at all. She shook her head. "I'm not sure I have an answer for you. Really, honey, I'm not trying to be vague. It's just that . . . I really don't know why talking about the garden club bothers me. Your grandmother was one of its star members, and if I hadn't moved away to marry your father, I no doubt would have been sucked into it too." She shrugged. "But I did move away, and the garden club never became a part of my life, so who knows?"

Rachel continued to study her mother, and Lynn felt herself beginning to squirm. A wave of relief washed over her as Jolene arrived with their orders, and she turned her attention to her tuna salad. It looked delicious, and she knew she could count on Rachel to drop the subject of the garden club so she could dive into her own meal.

Saved by the bell, Lynn thought, stifling a smile. *The dinner bell, that is. Perfect timing, Jolene.*

Lynn was absolutely content to let her daughter drive home, and she relaxed in the passenger seat. There were certainly some distinct advantages to having an adult child, particularly when that child was near enough to share responsibilities. Lynn glanced at Rachel in the near darkness of the car's front seat and smiled. She could get used to this—not simply being chauffeured around, but having her daughter close by. The last few years had been tough with Rachel away at Bible college, but at least in the beginning Lynn had been blessed to have Daniel by her side. They'd done nearly everything together; when he died, Rachel's absence had seemed even more pronounced. The house that had once been filled with love and laughter suddenly felt devoid of all emotion except sadness. Only Beasley had stayed at her side, faithfully and continually, offering his unconditional love and comfort.

But Beasley isn't enough, Lord. You know that. Is that why You brought Rachel home when You did? You know how much I'd love it if she stayed, at least for a while.

Though no answer came, Lynn couldn't help but think God had orchestrated the timing of Rachel's arrival and their subsequent visit to Bloomfield. Lynn couldn't imagine coming back to her hometown and dealing with everything on her own.

"What are you thinking about, Mom?"

Lynn turned and studied her daughter, whose face still pointed straight at the windshield. "Oh, nothing in particular. Just letting my mind drift a bit, I suppose. Though I must admit I was expressing my gratitude to God for bringing you home when He did. Coming back to Bloomfield to settle your uncle's estate isn't exactly something I would have wanted to do alone."

Rachel nodded. "I've thought the same thing. God always has His reasons, doesn't He? And His perfect timing too."

Lynn's heart soared. Was there anything better than knowing your child had accepted her parents' faith as her own? There was no doubt in Lynn's mind that Rachel had done just that, and Lynn was so grateful, particularly when she thought of the many parents she'd known through the years who had despaired of their children ever coming into a personal, meaningful relationship with God. Oh, the tears Lynn had seen her friends shed as they prayed for their prodigal children to return to the fold! Lynn and Daniel had talked often about how very blessed they were never to have experienced that with their only child.

But what now? Rachel had completed Bible college. How would she apply her education? The thought that she might choose to go into mission service overseas somewhere struck a chord of ice in Lynn's heart, though she knew she'd have to release Rachel to whatever God had planned for her. But oh, how Lynn prayed the Lord's plans wouldn't take Rachel away from her, at least not for a while.

"Here we are," Rachel said, turning into the driveway. "And it looks like we have company."

Alarmed, Lynn spotted a lone figure on their front porch, slowly making his way down the steps. *Jason. What is he doing here? Why is he always sneaking around, as if he owned the place? Why can't he just stay in his own little spot and leave us alone?*

"Should I stop him so we can talk to him?" Rachel asked, shutting off the motor.

Lynn's answer came quickly. "No," she snapped. "Let him go. We don't need to talk to him about anything."

"Not even the missing money?" Rachel turned in her seat and faced her mother. "Even Mrs. Trump said Jason was the obvious person to ask about it."

"I told you," Lynn said, "I'm going to talk to Homer Tatum first. Jason is my last resort."

Rachel sighed and shrugged her shoulders. "Fine. We'll do it your way."

She opened the door and stepped out, heading for the now vacated porch with Lynn close behind. Why couldn't Rachel understand her reluctance to get chummy with Jason? It was bad enough that Myron had written him into the will and they were stuck with him on the property; that didn't mean they had to spend time socializing together, did it?

Rachel had the front door unlocked by then, and Lynn stepped inside with relief.

The two women had no sooner bestowed their obligatory greetings on an excited Beasley and gone into the kitchen to put the kettle on for a cup of evening tea than Rachel's cell phone rang out with its classical tone. Lynn watched her daughter peek at the incoming number.

Her cheeks flushed slightly and she answered, "Hello?"

Lynn was relatively certain of the caller's identity, even before she heard Rachel speak Hayden's name. Well, at least Lynn could be grateful he hadn't called earlier and interrupted their dinner. As much as she knew about Hayden, she liked him, but the divorce issue—despite the fact that everyone agreed it had not been Hayden's fault and that he had, in fact, been terribly hurt by his wife's betrayal—definitely bothered Lynn. Rachel was young and vulnerable, and certainly pure. It was obvious her heart was to serve God, and though Hayden was most likely a dedicated Christian, Lynn couldn't help but envision Rachel with someone more like John Currey.

John.

Lynn plopped tea bags into mugs and waited for the kettle to whistle, picturing the pleasant young man who had shared lunch with them in this very kitchen. The good-looking youth pastor would no doubt be a dedicated and loving husband, whoever he married. How she wanted that for Rachel; an honest, hard-working, deeply committed man of faith—like her own Daniel had been.

She sighed and snatched the kettle from the stove before it could whistle and interrupt Rachel's conversation. Pouring the boiling water into the mugs, she allowed her thoughts to linger on the man who had loved her so completely for so many years.

But not long enough. Never long enough. If we'd had twice as many years together, it wouldn't have been enough. I was so blessed to have such a wonderful husband, Lord.

Lynn blinked away her tears and reached into the cupboard for the partially full bag of cookies. She wasn't especially hungry, but she knew her daughter would never turn down dessert, even though she'd sworn she didn't have room after they completed their meals at Bert's. By now, Rachel was bound to have enough empty space for a cookie or two.

The table was set with two steaming mugs and a small plate of cookies by the time Rachel flipped her phone shut.

"Sorry about that. I didn't mean to leave you with all the work, but I left a message with Hayden earlier, and he was returning my call." She sat down at the table, joining her mother, and then continued. "Of course, I was just returning his call first. Seems we've been playing phone tag, so I didn't want to miss him again when he called just now. I know we'd been talking about the three of us going out to dinner one evening soon—and we still may do that—but now he wants to take me on a picnic tomorrow."

"That sounds lovely," Lynn said. "And you don't have to explain yourself, sweetheart."

Rachel glanced at her and smiled. "Thanks. I guess in some way I thought I did."

Lynn shook her head and laid her hand on Rachel's. "Well, you don't. And forgive me for making you feel that way. You're a mature young woman, a grown-up now, with a good head on your shoulders and a solid faith in your heart. I'm very proud of you, Rachel, and I don't ever want to try to control you with my emotions. Forgive me if I do."

Rachel nodded, and Lynn's heart squeezed when she saw the hint of tears in her daughter's eyes.

"Anyway," Lynn went on, "I just want what's best for you—God's best. You understand that, don't you?"

Rachel nodded again. "Sure I do, Mom. That's what I want too."

Lynn smiled and withdrew her hand. "Well then, I believe we can trust God to bring that about, can't we?"

"We sure can," Rachel agreed. "In both of our lives."

Lynn lifted her head and caught her daughter's meaningful glance before they returned to their tea and cookies—and to discussing the possibility of the two of them joining Hayden for dinner one evening soon.

 # Chapter 13

TUESDAY DAWNED WARM AND SUNNY, AND BY THE TIME RACHEL opened her eyes, the other side of her bed was empty. Not too surprising, since her mother often got up ahead of her, but Rachel determined not to waste the morning sleeping.

She rolled to her side and sat up on the edge of the bed. No response from Beasley told her the dog had followed his mistress downstairs and was no doubt already gobbling up his morning offering. Rachel knew her mother tried to keep Beasley healthy by not allowing him to eat people food or to overindulge in his own canine meals, but she also knew her mom occasionally caved in to the canine's big brown eyes and gave him a treat— healthy or otherwise.

Rachel smiled at the thought as she padded to the bathroom. Beasley was a faithful companion to her mom, especially after her dad died. Rachel could only begin to imagine her mother's pain at losing her life partner. Throughout Rachel's growing-up years, her parents' relationship had been her model, not only for marriage but for friendship. They'd set the bar high, and her mom didn't need to worry that Rachel would compromise or settle for anything less.

Still, she thought as she tested the water temp in the shower, *that doesn't mean I can't go out for a simple lunch or dinner with a friend—male or female. And that's all this so-called date is today with Hayden. He wants to take me on a picnic. What can that hurt? He's even taking a couple hours off work to do it, which is very thoughtful of him. But . . . I can't help but wonder if I'd like it better if it were John and not Hayden picking me up at noon.*

By the time she showered and had her slightly damp hair pulled back in a ponytail, it was nearly nine o'clock. She took the stairs two at a time as she headed down to the kitchen, her mouth already watering at the smell of fresh coffee. Nobody made coffee like her mom, and no one appreciated it more than Rachel.

Beasley spotted her first, abandoning his spot under the table next to Lynn's feet to bound over toward Rachel and give her a sloppy, wet welcome when she bent down to hug him. Rachel laughed and played with him for several minutes before going to the counter to pour a mug of hot brew.

"This smells wonderful," she said, inhaling the steam as she held it up to her nose. "Did you just make it?"

"As soon as I heard you in the shower," Lynn answered. "Are you hungry? How about some eggs? We've got bacon too."

Rachel smiled. "I think I'll just have toast for now. Hayden's picking me up at noon and we're going on a picnic, remember? He insisted I'm not supposed to bring anything, says he has it covered, so we'll see what that means. But I don't want to fill up too much before we go."

Lynn's smile faded only slightly as she listened to Rachel's words, but she nodded. "That's right. I'd forgotten. Did he say where you'll be going for this picnic?"

"Nope. I'm thinking the park downtown where we had the church picnic on Sunday, but I could be wrong."

"That would be my first guess too, although there are several nice picnic spots outside of town."

Rachel turned back toward the counter, anxious to change the subject. She snagged the whole wheat bread and plopped a couple of pieces into the toaster, then rummaged in the refrigerator for some strawberry jam. "So what are you going to do all day while I'm gone?" she asked, pushing down a slight twinge of guilt for leaving her mother alone.

"Oh, I don't know. There are a few spots—okay, lots of them, really—out in front of the porch that need some serious attention. I think there were actually flowers there at some point, but they're fairly overgrown with weeds now. Not that I've got much of a green thumb, as you know, but I think I can at least identify weeds when I see them. I'll get them pulled and water what's left." She laughed, and Rachel thought she heard a nervous lilt to the sound. "At least then if any of the garden club members drop by, they won't be greeted by an army of weeds. After that, I just might try to track down Homer Tatum and set up an appointment to go see him tomorrow. If I do, will you come with me?"

"Absolutely. I've heard so much about this crusty old guy that I wouldn't dream of missing out on a chance to meet him."

Lynn smiled. "Great. I'll see what I can do to find his number and give him a call. Hopefully, I'll have that settled by the time you get home this afternoon."

Hayden splashed on just a tad more men's cologne before leaving his office in the capable hands of his administrative assistant,

Belinda, and heading out for his picnic with Rachel. He was excited and hopeful, sensing he had made progress this week. He now had Rachel's cell number programmed into his own phone, and this would be their second date. The first one might not count as an actual date, since they hadn't planned ahead, but today's outing did, at least as far as he saw it, and maybe that gave more credibility to their first meal together as well.

Either way, Hayden was pleased. He thought about the youth pastor, John Currey, as he made his way to his car and climbed inside. John was a great guy, but Hayden was determined not to get squeezed out of another relationship. He'd already lost Amber to his best friend, Stan—which was only right, he reminded himself, since the two of them had known one another forever and just hadn't figured out until recently that they were meant to be together—but this was different. Rachel was new in town, and Hayden figured he had just as much right to pursue a relationship with her as John or anyone else. And if she and her mother left in a few days, he'd crank it up a notch and establish a long-distance relationship, driving up to see her every chance he got. After all, there were only so many attractive young single women in Bloomfield, and so far he was striking out with most of them. Maybe it was time he extended his reach a bit.

It didn't take long to arrive at Cemetery Drive, and in moments he pulled into the driveway that led up to Rachel's uncle's house. Hayden shook his head as he parked his sedan and opened the door. This house was a real monstrosity. He couldn't imagine staying in such a creepy place, let alone living there. He wondered why Rachel and her mother didn't get a room at the bed and breakfast, but maybe they had things they needed to do right here in the house in order to settle the estate. Still, he suppressed a shudder as he mounted the front porch steps, glad he didn't see the old groundskeeper lurking about.

He pressed the bell and listened to the chimes, accompanied by barking on the other side of the door. He hoped Rachel hadn't decided to invite her mother—or even the dog—to accompany them. He liked dogs, and he liked Rachel's mother too, but he really wanted to spend the afternoon alone with this beautiful young Bible school graduate. Still, he hadn't forgotten that he and Rachel had discussed the possibility of taking her mother out to dinner one evening soon, and he filed that thought away for future reference.

When the door opened and he saw Rachel standing there dressed in calf-length jeans and a pink sleeveless top, his heart jumped. He was about to speak when the dog burst past her and scurried up to him, silently begging to be petted. Hayden readily obliged, glad for the diversion. Maybe taking the dog along wouldn't be such a bad idea after all.

"I just need to tell Mom we're going," Rachel said. "Are you sure I can't bring something? I feel terrible not contributing to this picnic."

Hayden smiled, the dog forgotten as he refocused on Rachel. "Like I said, I've got it all covered. When I told my mom what I had planned and that I was going to stop by the deli to pick up some sandwiches, she wouldn't hear of it. She said she'd fix everything, and boy, did she! We have fried chicken and potato salad, fresh fruit, a thermos of lemonade, and warm sugar cookies fresh from the oven." He shook his head. "I think we have enough food for an army. I hope you're hungry."

Rachel laughed. "Count on it! And everything sounds delicious. I'll be right back."

As she turned to find her mother and tell her they were leaving, Hayden took a couple of deep breaths in an effort to settle his emotions. Just seeing Rachel's eyes sparkle and hearing her laugh had nearly sent him over the edge. He just hoped he didn't make a complete fool of himself before the afternoon was over.

Rachel had no sooner closed the door and driven off with Hayden than Lynn heard the familiar crunch of gravel under tires.

What did she forget? Lynn frowned and went to the front door to wait for her daughter and find out what she needed. But when she opened the door, it wasn't Hayden's sleek sedan that pulled up in front of the house, but Bailey McCullough's dark SUV.

Well, this is quite a surprise. Seeing her reminds me that I should have called to thank her for doing such a good job on the piece she wrote about our visit, though I still find it amazing that it would be considered newsworthy.

She stepped out onto the porch with Beasley at her side and watched Bailey climb out of the vehicle. She returned the young woman's wave when their eyes connected. Bailey wasn't carrying the case with her laptop and other equipment this time, so Lynn relaxed, knowing she wasn't here for another interview.

"Hello," Bailey called as she climbed the steps, stopping to pet Beasley before greeting Lynn. "I hope you don't mind that I dropped by unannounced. I hadn't really planned to come over, but I was coming back from an assignment when I realized I had extra copies of the paper with your article in it, and I wanted to make sure you got them, so I thought I'd swing by." She grinned. "It's not like anything in Bloomfield is really out of the way, you know."

Lynn chuckled. "True. And of course I don't mind. In fact,

if you have a moment, why don't you come inside for a glass of sun tea? I just made a fresh jug of it this morning. Or if you'd rather, we can sit out here on the porch and drink it."

"That sounds perfect. It's beautiful out today—as usual."

In moments, they settled into the rocking chairs, with the pitcher of tea on the table between them and two icy glasses full of the delicious liquid in their hands. Lynn couldn't help but think Bailey's timing was perfect. The last thing Lynn wanted to be was a possessive mother, but she did get a bit lonely in that big old house when Rachel was gone.

"You know," Lynn said, setting her glass down, "I meant to call and thank you for the great job you did on the article. I really appreciate it, and I must admit I was a bit apprehensive before I saw it."

Bailey smiled. "I understand. It doesn't take more than a couple of purposely or even inadvertently misplaced words to change the twist of an entire piece, does it? I may just be the society reporter around here, but I'm determined to write with accuracy and integrity."

"Good for you. If more reporters shared your convictions, we might be able to trust the news."

Bailey smiled and nodded. "So where's Rachel?" she asked, taking another sip of her drink.

Lynn hesitated but decided she might as well answer. After all, in Bloomfield everyone would know about Rachel's whereabouts before the day was over.

"She's gone on a picnic with Hayden Blackstone," she said, watching Bailey for a reaction.

"Ah. Nice guy. Good-looking too. And successful. Too bad he got burned so badly by his ex-wife. I didn't know her well, but I understand she was quite a piece of work." She flitted her eyes toward Lynn. "Sorry. I shouldn't say something like that about her. Like I said, I didn't really know her."

"So . . . it really is as people say? She left Hayden for another man?"

"That's the story. In fact, I heard she and the other guy already have a baby, so they didn't waste any time."

Lynn raised her eyebrows. That part of the story was news to her. Poor Hayden! Still, the fact that he was the obvious innocent party in the breakup didn't ease Lynn's concerns for her daughter.

"Well," Bailey said, taking the last swig from her glass and depositing it on the table, "I really need to get back to the office and tie up some loose ends before the close of the day." She smiled. "Thanks for the nice break, not to mention the great tea. And I'm glad you liked the article."

"I did. And I appreciate the extra copies. It isn't often my daughter and I take a little trip together and end up in the newspaper."

Bailey laughed as she stood up and fished her keys from her purse. "Only in Bloomfield," she said. "Only in Bloomfield."

Lynn watched as Bailey descended the porch steps, then caught her breath as a thought occurred to her. "Bailey," she called, stopping the woman mid-stride. "Have you got just a couple more minutes? I have a question for you."

Bailey turned, her eyebrows arched curiously. "Sure. Fire away."

"Are you by any chance familiar with the Last Chance Justice story? About the missing money from when he was a young boy?"

Bailey's face went from curious to recognition as she nodded. "Vaguely. I've heard mention of it anyway. Why do you ask?"

"It seems my brother was determined to solve the mystery and clear Last Chance's name but didn't live long enough to do so. I'm trying to see if I can find out anything about it. So far, I've talked to Jolene Trump, who referred me to Homer Tatum. I plan to talk with him, of course. But I also understand that Last Chance has a living relative in the area—a Miss Pearl, his sister, I believe. Do you know anything about her?"

Bailey chuckled. "Only that she's quite a character. Lives pretty much like a hermit. Friendly for the most part, but definitely not open to discussing the situation with her late brother and the missing money. Several people have tried to talk to her about it over the years, and not one has made any headway." She frowned. "But why are you talking to Jolene or Homer about it, or even considering Miss Pearl, when you've got Jason right here? Anything your brother knew or discovered about Last Chance, he probably shared with Jason. If I were you, I'd invest my time picking his brain. Bound to be something in there that could shed some new light on the subject, don't you think?"

Lynn forced a smile. Back to Jason again. Why did everyone seem determined to force her into conversation with the man?

"I suppose you're right," she said. "Thanks for the suggestion. Anyway, I didn't mean to keep you. I know you need to get back to work. Have a great day, and thanks again for stopping by with the extra papers."

"My pleasure." Bailey smiled and turned back toward her SUV. Lynn watched her leave as she stood on the porch and wondered if she'd ever be able to unearth any new information about Last Chance and the missing money.

 # Chapter 14

THE PICNIC HAD BEEN LOVELY, AND RACHEL WAS IMPRESSED WITH the spot Hayden had chosen, next to a small stream in an open meadow. She hadn't even realized there was such a place so close to Bloomfield, but they'd driven only fifteen minutes outside of town to get there. Now, full of fried chicken and some of the best potato salad she'd ever tasted—though she probably wouldn't say that to her mom, who was quite proud of her own potato salad—Rachel and Hayden munched soft sugar cookies as they headed back into town.

"That was absolutely wonderful," Rachel said, smiling at Hayden as he took his eyes off the road just long enough to glance in her direction. "Not just the food, which was fantastic, but the entire afternoon. I loved it, and I can't thank you enough for taking me there. I can't wait to show that place to Mom, although I'm sure she's already been there somewhere along the line."

Hayden laughed. "No doubt about it. If she grew up in Bloomfield, she's been to that spot—and several others like it.

There are tons of nice places scattered in and around here, just waiting to be explored." He glanced at her again. "And there's nothing I'd like better than the chance to take you out to see as many of them as possible."

Rachel felt the flush creep up her neck and into her cheeks. Why did she feel as if Hayden had just ruined their perfect day? She'd had a great time, and he hadn't tried anything to make her uncomfortable. She was so appreciative of that, but now she felt painted into a corner. Hayden was a nice guy—a good-looking, successful guy—and maybe if she had a better sense of who she was and what she planned to do with her life beyond the next few days in Bloomfield, she might be inclined to let him get a little closer and maybe even cultivate a relationship. But under the circumstances . . .

"I'm pushing too hard, aren't I?" The question came as Hayden turned back to look at the road. "I'm sorry. I didn't mean to, really. It's just that . . . I so enjoy being with you, and I really don't want this day to end. I'd like to . . . to see you again."

Rachel hesitated. "I know," she said softly. "I enjoyed being with you too, and I see no reason why we can't see each other again before my mom and I leave town. Maybe the three of us will even go out for that meal we talked about. But . . . I just don't want to give you any false expectations. Hayden, I'm not even close to being ready for a relationship right now. A friend-ship? Sure. But nothing more. It's nothing personal, but . . . I hope you understand."

She saw his jaw twitch before he nodded. "Of course I do," he said, his voice husky. "And I'll honor that, I promise."

Rachel breathed a sigh of relief. "Thank you." She resisted the impulse to reach over and lay a hand on his arm. There was no sense sending mixed signals, so she kept her hands in her lap

as they continued down the road. They had just turned onto
Main Street when a familiar old Taurus rattled past them. She
glanced at the driver just in time to see John Currey's surprised
expression as their eyes met.

Her heart sank. She told herself it didn't matter that John
had seen her with Hayden, but after she'd received a phone call
from Hayden while she was with John, she couldn't help but
wonder what John must think. Though it seemed she'd suc-
ceeded in establishing the boundaries of her relationship with
Hayden, she may also have succeeded in misrepresenting them
to John. And for whatever reason, that truly bothered her.

Lynn was upstairs folding a load of freshly washed towels and
wondering how long the ancient washer and dryer on the back
porch would hold up when she heard the gravel crunch and then
the front door open, followed by Beasley's excited yips. Rachel
was home. Pleased, Lynn abandoned the last of the towels on the
bed and hurried downstairs to greet her daughter.

"How was it?" she asked, finding Rachel in the kitchen
drinking a glass of water.

"Beautiful. We drove to a fantastic place just outside of town
about fifteen minutes, an open space next to a little creek. It was
gorgeous! And the weather couldn't have been better. Sunny and
warm, with just a light breeze. Hayden said he was sure you'd
been there at one time or another."

"He's probably right. I can think of a couple of places
around here that fit that description."

Rachel set her empty glass down on the counter and grinned.
"Maybe we'll go by there one of these days before we leave and

I'll show you where it is. Anyway, Hayden's mom made fried chicken and potato salad and lemonade and cookies. Everything was wonderful, but now I am *so* stuffed."

"Now," Lynn teased. "But what about by suppertime?"

Rachel laughed. "Okay, maybe by then I'll be able to eat again. So what have you been up to while I was gone? Were you able to track down Mr. Tatum?"

"Believe it or not, I was. And let me tell you, it was no small feat to get him to understand what I wanted. I told you he's nearly deaf, didn't I? Anyway, he lives in the assisted living section out at Lake Bliss Retirement Village, and I finally got one of the aides to help me communicate with him. With her help, we convinced him to meet with us tomorrow morning at ten. What do you think of that?"

"I think that sounds fine. Though I can't imagine how much information we'll get from someone in his condition. How old did you say he is?"

"He's in his nineties. And we'll just do our best. If anybody knows about that missing money and what Last Chance Justice had to do with it, I would imagine it's Homer Tatum. He's a walking encyclopedia when it comes to the history of Bloomfield. Besides, he might be hard of hearing but I'm told he's still sharp as a tack mentally. I sure hope that's true. Personally, I can't wait to talk to him."

"If you say so," Rachel said, grinning.

"Oh, and by the way, Bailey McCullough stopped by and left us a handful of extra papers with our article in it. She thought we might want them for a keepsake. Isn't that nice?"

"It sure is. Where are they? I know I already read the article when we picked up a copy the other day, but I'd like to see it again."

"I put them in your uncle's library. Come on, let's go take another look."

They traipsed out of the kitchen together, arm in arm, chattering like two school chums, and Lynn thought she hadn't been this happy since . . . since before Daniel died. Maybe being here in Myron's old house with Rachel wasn't such a bad idea after all—at least for a little while.

John's fingers twitched each time he thought of his cell phone, stuffed into his jeans pocket. Tuesday was one of the few evenings he wasn't busy doing something at the church, but he almost wished he were. At least when he was busy he didn't have so much time to think. Right now, with his feet propped up on his ratty old footstool and the rest of him firmly ensconced in the only real chair in his little bachelor pad, he knew he should be studying for the next night's youth service but all he could think of was how much he wanted to call Rachel.

At least I have her number now, he reminded himself, as he once again resisted the impulse to call her, *even if I did have to ask for it twice while I was at her house for lunch the other day. Apparently, Hayden got it, no problem.*

John sighed. Why not just accept it? Hayden had moved in ahead of him, fast and smooth, leaving no room for competition—at least not from the likes of him. He might as well just focus on his lesson for the kids, not to mention his weekly visit to the shut-ins at Lake Bliss Retirement Village the following day.

Funny. I'm batting zero when it comes to establishing a relationship with anyone close to my own age, other than shooting hoops or watching a football game with the guys once in awhile. But I seem to be doing fine with everyone at opposite ends of the age differential. The young people at church love me, and apparently so do the old ones, since I keep getting invited back to the retirement village. Of course, that might have something to do with the fact that some of the oldest residents can't get out to go anywhere and seldom have any visitors. Maybe I'm not just the best game in town for them, but the only one. He shrugged. *Oh well, at least they're happy to see me.*

He grinned and opened his Bible, determined to prepare for the next evening's lesson—and to keep his mind off Rachel Myers, at least for the time being.

Chapter 15

LYNN DID HER BEST TO REMAIN HOPEFUL AS THEY DROVE INTO the parking lot at Lake Bliss Retirement Village, though she realized it wasn't likely she would get much useful information from Homer Tatum, regardless of how much Bloomfield history he had stored away in his ancient memory banks. She pushed the thought away and glanced around as they stepped from the car. The retirement center was a lovely facility, with two stories of townhomes backed up against a common area with a fountain and garden. Though Lynn wasn't even close to considering a move to such a place, she had to admit there were worse places for the elderly to spend their final years on earth.

"Do you know which place is Mr. Tatum's?" Rachel asked as they stood beside the car. Once again Rachel had offered to drive, and Lynn had readily agreed. She missed the days when Daniel drove her wherever she needed to go, and it was comfortable to be back in the passenger side again.

"He's actually over in that one-story section toward the back," Lynn said, gesturing in the right direction. "It's their assisted living facility for the residents who are no longer able to care for themselves, almost more like a nursing home, from what I understand. I called ahead and found out the procedure for getting in to see him. We have to stop in at the main office and sign in first. Then they'll call the back and let them know we're coming and who we want to visit."

Rachel nodded. "Sounds efficient—safe too. I think it's great that residents don't necessarily have to move from here when their health and care levels need a change."

Lynn had thought the same thing when she learned of the extent of Lake Bliss's care and facilities, and she imagined someone Homer's age, with his obvious physical challenges, needed someone to watch over him. She just hoped he wasn't so far gone that they couldn't have a conversation with him.

In moments, they found themselves checked in and directed to the back facility, adjacent to the gardens. "It's really lovely out here, isn't it?" Rachel commented as they approached the full-care building. A handful of wheelchair-bound residents sat in the midmorning sun, enjoying the view and eyeing the two women as they walked by. A couple of them looked hopeful, but their expressions fell as Rachel and Lynn passed on without stopping. Lynn's heart ached to think how lonely it must be to sit around all day and wait for a visitor who, most likely, would never show up.

They stepped through the front door into the cozy, cool lobby, and paused to let their eyes adjust to the lack of sunlight. Almost immediately, they were greeted by a pleasant young woman in a flowery smock and padded white shoes.

"I'm Josie," she said, "Mr. Tatum's primary caregiver. He's expecting you, but I'm not sure he's too happy about it or that he quite understands who you are."

Lynn nodded. It was about what she expected, though she still hoped to come away with some sort of useful information.

Josie led the way down the pine-scented hallway to the third door on the right. Like the other doors, it stood open. A blaring TV set was mounted on the wall in front of the hospital-style bed where a surprisingly large man with a full shock of white hair was propped up, eyeing them as they entered. A bed stand and a small dresser covered with pictures of adults and children of all ages—no doubt the old man's family members—completed the room's furnishings except for two folding chairs, which Lynn imagined had been brought in for the visit. She took a deep breath and was about to step forward and introduce herself when Josie intervened.

"Homer, your company's here," she announced, her voice surprisingly loud and clear, reminding Lynn that she too would have to speak at such a volume during her conversation with the elderly gentleman. "This is Lynn Myers and her daughter, Rachel. They've come to talk with you."

The old man's eyes narrowed. "About what?" he demanded.

Josie looked at Lynn and raised her eyebrows, as if to say, "Your turn."

Lynn smiled and consciously raised her voice as she answered. "About a man who used to live in Bloomfield. His name was Last Chance Justice."

A flicker of recognition passed across Homer's face as he snagged his remote and turned off the television. "What if I don't want to talk about him?" he asked, his jaw setting into a strong line.

"You . . . you certainly don't have to," Lynn answered, encouraged that he'd turned off the TV, "but I surely would appreciate it if you would."

The words hung in the air for a moment until Homer finally nodded. "Sit," he ordered. "I'll tell you what I know, but it isn't much. And if it takes past lunchtime, I quit. Got it? I never miss my lunch."

Lynn felt her eyes widen, and she wrestled with a grin. "Got it," she said, pulling one of the two folding chairs a bit closer to the head of Mr. Tatum's bed. Out of the corner of her eye, she noticed Rachel sit down beside her as Josie excused herself.

Homer Tatum's eyes were a faded blue and rheumy from age, but Lynn had the feeling he saw her face just fine.

"It's nice to meet you, Mr. Tatum," she said. "I've heard you know more about this town and its former residents than just about anyone else in Bloomfield."

"That's because I'm older than just about anyone else in Bloomfield," he answered, "except a couple of people around here who are nearly a hundred. But they don't even remember their own names, let alone anybody else's, so I guess I'm the best chance you've got."

The guy had certainly earned his reputation as crusty and cantankerous, Lynn thought, but she liked him nonetheless. His feistiness was refreshing. Now to see if he could shed light on the missing money.

"I don't doubt you are," Lynn said, "so I'm assuming you knew my brother, Myron Cofield. He lived in the big house by the cemetery."

"Of course I knew Myron. I'd have to be deaf, blind, and stupid not to—and stupid I'm not. Come to think of it, I heard old Myron passed on not long ago. That so?"

Unexpected tears stung Lynn's eyes as she nodded. "Yes," she said, her voice just above a whisper. "Just last month."

"What?" Homer demanded. "Speak up, will you? I can't hear you when you mumble."

Lynn raised her head and sat up straight, taking a deep breath. "Yes," she said, louder this time. "Myron died. That's why my daughter and I came to Bloomfield—to settle his estate."

Homer nodded. "That's better. My ears aren't what they used to be, you know. Why, when I was young I could hear a mosquito buzz in the next county. Now I can barely hear myself breathe. Sometimes I wonder if I'll know when I stop." He chuckled at his own joke before his face went back to serious. "So what's Myron's death got to do with Last Chance? And why does it matter to you?"

"It matters to me because apparently it mattered to my brother. For one thing, he specifically requested that he be buried next to Mr. Justice, in the older part of the cemetery. And then I found an entry at the end of his most recent journal, mentioning his desire to solve the mystery that surrounded him. Apparently it involved a missing seven dollars and fourteen cents, and in my brother's words, it 'besmirched' the man's reputation. Does that make any sense to you?"

Homer snorted. "Sense? Not at all, but that don't mean I don't remember it. It didn't make sense then, and it don't make sense now. But I can tell you this. Last Chance Justice was one of the most honest men who ever set foot in this town, and it's a crying shame that something like a missing seven bucks and fourteen cents in Sunday school donations could taint a man's reputation for the rest of his life." He shook his head. "Seems Last Chance was in charge of taking the donation from the rooms out back behind the church where the under-twelve classes met at the time and delivering it to the office in front. Somewhere along the way—which wasn't more than thirty yards, mind you—he lost it. Said he looked everywhere for it but never found it. Most people wanted to believe him, but it just didn't make sense. How could anyone lose a handkerchief full of change walking from one spot to another, especially when it was so close by and he swore he couldn't remember what happened to it? It's been a mystery that never got solved and one that haunted the poor kid for the rest of his days."

Lynn frowned. Homer's story confirmed and even added a bit to what she knew so far, but the situation itself really didn't add up. As honest as Homer swore Last Chance Justice was, she could still see how some people might suspect him of lying about the money.

Rachel's voice cut into her thoughts, her decibel level surprisingly loud. "May I ask you a question, Mr. Tatum?"

The old man veered his eyes toward Rachel and squinted them up, as if trying to decide what his answer would be. "I suppose so," he said at last, "but only because you're so pretty." He grinned then. "I'm not as blind as everybody thinks, you know."

Rachel laughed. "Why, thank you, Mr. Tatum. I'm flattered." She took a deep breath before plunging forward. "I have two questions, actually. First, why was the money in a handkerchief? And second, where did Mr. Justice get such a strange name?"

"Come to think of it, I'm not sure," Homer answered with a shrug. "If I remember correctly, in those days the classes just gathered up whatever change the children had for the offering and delivered it whatever way was handiest. Seems a handkerchief worked fairly well, I suppose. And as for Last Chance and his name? Now that's a story."

When he paused, Lynn found herself scooting toward the edge of her seat. Surely he wasn't going to stop now. Did she dare prod him . . . or should she wait a bit? Opting for the latter, she tried not to hold her breath. Apparently, Rachel had come to the same decision, and they both sat quietly, staring at Homer Tatum.

At last, he opened his mouth, and the story began to spill out. "Last Chance Justice came into this world on May 17, 1935, the very same day his mother made her exit. His father and six sisters were there when he was born, and they were there when his mother passed." He shook his head before continuing. "There was never any question about naming the baby. Months earlier, when his mother found out another child was on the way, she declared, 'Our last chance for a boy! Surely the good Lord will grant us a son at long last.' Story has it that she smiled then and announced, 'Yes, I believe He will. And in gratitude, we will name him Last Chance.'"

Despite her earlier determination not to hold her breath, Lynn found herself doing just that. What an amazing story! But what happened after that?

"Her words proved true," Homer continued. "At the age of forty-three, Mary Nell Justice gave birth to a son while she lay in her bed in their tiny little home on the outskirts of Bloomfield. She held on until she heard her baby cry, and then she breathed her last, leaving little Last Chance to be raised by his father, John William Justice, and his six older sisters." His eyes twinkled for a brief moment as he added, "And let me tell you, everyone said those six sisters pampered and catered to that boy for twenty-three years. And then he died. Doctor said he never was very strong and just slipped away one night, right into the arms of Jesus. Some folks said he died of a broken heart because he never did get over losing that money and knowing he was suspected of being a thief and a liar. Don't suppose the mystery of why he died so young or what happened to that money will ever be solved, leastwise not in this world."

Lynn's heart constricted at the realization of how young Last Chance had been when he died, and she scolded herself for not paying more attention to the headstone next to her brother's.

"The funeral was well attended," Homer said, regaining Lynn's attention. "Although many in Bloomfield still suspected Last Chance of taking the money, the Justice family itself was respected in the community, even though they were one of the few black families around in those days. I always wondered if being black had anything to do with poor Last Chance being suspected of stealing that money, but I really don't think so, not in Bloomfield anyway." He shrugged. "And that's the end of the story, at least as far as I recollect. Most everyone who was around in those days is gone now. I'm one of the few still hanging around, I guess. Didn't know Last Chance well, and I don't think your brother could have known him well at all, since he died when Myron was still a kid. But I imagine they crossed paths a few times before that, and for some reason Myron must have taken an interest in the missing-money part of his story and set out to solve it. Too bad he wasn't able to do it."

Lynn nodded. Yes, it was too bad. Now Myron was gone too, and unless she could figure out how to pick up where her brother left off, she imagined no one would ever find a way to exonerate poor Last Chance.

Or to prove his guilt. What if he really did take that money? After all, how does someone lose a handkerchief full of coins on a thirty-yard walk?

"Mr. Tatum," she said, determined to try to dig another nugget or two from his memory, "I understand Last Chance has a sister still living in the Bloomfield area, a Miss Pearl. Do you know anything about her? Would it do any good to try to talk to her about the situation?"

The old man's bushy brows drew together, and he glared at her a moment before answering. "Forget it," he said. "Miss Pearl would as soon skin you alive as talk about the accusations against her brother. There's no way you're getting any information from her, even if she has any, which I doubt."

Lynn sighed and nodded. Quite obviously Miss Pearl was not an option. Still . . .

"Are . . . are you sure you don't remember anything else, Mr. Tatum?" she asked. "Anything at all? Maybe—"

She was interrupted by the rattle of what sounded like a food cart making its way down the hall. Homer held up his hand. "Sorry, but even with my bad ears I can hear lunch coming. You're just going to have to leave now so I can eat. I don't have many pleasures left at this stage of life, but food is one of them." He directed a wink at Rachel and added, "And I don't miss that for anything, not even a pretty girl."

Lynn chuckled despite the dismissal, and she and Rachel stood up to make room for Homer Tatum's lunch tray. "Enjoy your meal," she said, patting the old man's age-spotted arm. "Maybe we'll come back to visit you another time."

"Maybe," he said. "And maybe not. Just make sure you work around my meal schedule, will you?"

Lynn and Rachel exited the room as the food cart arrived at the doorway. The aroma of what Lynn imagined to be some sort of casserole teased her nostrils, and she nodded at the aide preparing to carry the covered dish into Homer's room. The two women hadn't made it to the end of the hallway before a male voice stopped them in their tracks.

"Rachel? Mrs. Myers?"

Lynn stopped, as did her daughter, and they turned around to find themselves standing nearly face-to-face with John Currey, a Bible in his right hand and a surprised expression on his face. "What are you two doing here?"

"We were visiting Mr. Tatum," Lynn said. "And you?"

John's face flushed slightly, and Lynn wished she hadn't been so abrupt. She really liked the young man and wanted to put him at ease.

"I . . . I come here every Wednesday morning," he said, "to visit the shut-ins. I pray with them and read Scriptures to them. Sometimes I serve them communion."

"I think that's wonderful," Rachel said.

Lynn cut her eyes toward her daughter, who beamed.

"I've always wanted to do something like that," Rachel went on. "I love working with older people—children, too. I volunteered with both while I was in Bible college."

John smiled, his discomfort seeming to dissipate. "Really? That's great. Do you think you'd like to help out in some of those areas? I mean, we could really use a volunteer with the kids, and here at this facility too. It wouldn't take much time, but it's so rewarding."

The two of them had obviously forgotten her by now, and Lynn smiled. Timing was everything, and she couldn't help but think God's hand was in this little hallway meeting. She watched them proceed toward the exit, chattering all the way, while she followed along behind.

This was turning out to be a better day than she could ever have imagined.

Abandoned. Well, why not?

Lynn smiled. So her daughter had thrown her over to ride back to the church with John and discuss how she might help with either the children or the seniors. The fact that she would be leaving town in a matter of days hadn't even seemed to cross the girl's mind, or John's for that matter, and Lynn wasn't about to bring it up. After all, Lynn might need to head back home shortly, but there wasn't really any pressing reason for Rachel to do so. Lynn couldn't help but wonder if God wasn't up to something here.

She smiled as she drove in the direction of Cemetery Drive. She may not have come away with any clear-cut answers to what happened to the money, but at least she knew a bit more about Mr. Last Chance Justice.

A sad life, she reflected. *His poor mother died before he even had a chance to get to know her, and then to die so young himself, after spending most of his brief existence under a cloud of suspicion. Tragic. No wonder Myron was so determined to clear the man's name. Now it seems the task has fallen to me, but . . . is it even possible?*

The problem, she decided, was that Last Chance might very well have been guilty. True, it wasn't a major crime, but for a child to steal a Sunday school offering didn't speak very highly of his character. After the little she'd heard from Homer Tatum about Last Chance and his family, however, she had a hard time believing the young boy took the money.

But what else could have happened to it?

She shook her head. If she'd hoped for an easy answer, she knew now it was not forthcoming. Obviously, Miss Pearl didn't seem to be an option, so did this mean she would finally be forced to talk to Jason about it? And if she did, could she get a straight answer from him? Did he even have one to offer?

She turned into the driveway just in time to spot the old groundskeeper hoeing weeds in the cemetery—his "garden," as he called it. Was this God's way of telling her to walk right up to him and ask about Last Chance? She would certainly rather have done so with Rachel by her side, but now she'd have to settle for Beasley, who she knew waited anxiously inside to greet her.

All right, then, Beasley, she thought, shutting off the engine. *Here I come . . . and then we'll confront Jason together and see what we can find out.*

 Chapter 16

IT HADN'T HIT RACHEL UNTIL SHE AND JOHN PULLED INTO the church parking lot that she had not only left her mother behind but had accompanied John to the church to talk about getting involved in either youth or senior ministry. She was relatively confident that her mom was fine with Rachel's actions, particularly since it was obvious she preferred John to Hayden, but the ministry thing was a different story. What had she been thinking? She and her mother would be leaving Bloomfield soon . . . wouldn't they? So what was the point of even considering volunteering for anything?

Oh well, we're here now, she thought as John parked his old Taurus and turned the key to the off position. Simultaneously, they opened the doors and climbed out, stepping into the warm sunshine that now beamed down on them from directly overhead.

John hurried around to Rachel's side of the car. "I just realized it's lunchtime. I should have offered to get you something on the way over."

Her stomach had already started to rumble, but she shrugged it off. "No problem. I'm fine."

John grinned. "From the sounds of things, I'd say you're nearly as hungry as I am. How about we pick up a few things about the different ministries and then take them with us? We can go get a sandwich or something and talk about the possibilities over lunch."

"That would be nice," Rachel said, surprised at just how much she really meant the words she spoke. She had enjoyed her times with Hayden, but there was something about John Currey that stirred her emotions at an entirely different level. Both men were good-looking, with good reputations and seemingly level heads on their shoulders. And yet . . .

Was it the fact that John was in full-time ministry that drew her? It was too soon to be certain, but Rachel imagined that had at least something to do with her attraction to him. She hadn't spent all those years in Bible college for nothing, after all, and her dream had always been to become involved in some sort of ministry, either locally or overseas. Could meeting John have something to do with God's direction for her life?

They turned toward the church building and circumvented the main entrance, heading out toward the back and walking along the brick fence line. A couple of ancient outbuildings jogged her memory of Homer Tatum's story about Last Chance Justice. Could one of those buildings be the place where the Sunday school classrooms had met those many years ago? Was the grassy space she viewed now, bordered by the long brick fence and sporting a couple of swing sets and a large sandbox, the very spot he had crossed on his way to deliver that handkerchief full of the offering? If so, how in the world could it have been lost between there and the back entrance to the church building? It didn't make sense. No wonder he had lived and died under a cloud of suspicion.

"Here we go," John said, holding the door open for her.

She stepped inside, blinking her eyes to adjust to the lack of sunlight. The temperature had just dropped about ten degrees, but it was a refreshing change as she walked at John's side toward a door on the right marked JOHN CURREY, YOUTH PASTOR. He pushed it open and waited until she was inside before following her, leaving the door open.

"Let me grab some folders and brochures," he said. "Nothing fancy or formal, but enough to give you an idea of what we're doing here with these two ministries. Then we're outta here and off to eat, I promise."

Her stomach chose that particular moment to growl again, and they both laughed. "And none too soon," Rachel said.

In moments, they were back in John's car, backing out of the parking space as he asked, "So where to? Any preference?"

She shook her head. "Surprise me. I've done Bert's a couple of times since I've been here—and love it, of course. Also done Burger Heaven, which is fantastic. But if you know somewhere different, I'm always open to trying something new."

John laughed. "Don't know how new or different anything is in Bloomfield, but since you don't live here, that gives me a few more options. There's a deli down on Main Street that has some excellent sandwiches, but I'll warn you, they're huge and delicious. What do you think?"

"Right now huge and delicious sounds perfect. Let's do it."

John nodded and pointed his car toward the main drag as Rachel relaxed, anticipating her meal and getting to know John Currey a little better.

Beasley's greeting was enthusiastic when Lynn opened the front door, but it didn't do anything to make her feel more optimistic about going back outside and around to the cemetery to try to talk with Jason. Still, she knew she'd put it off as long as she could and had seemingly exhausted all her other possibilities. Unless she was willing to drop the Last Chance missing-money mystery, she had no other choice.

Gulping down a cool drink of water while she gathered her courage, she considered how best to approach the eccentric caretaker.

Surely that's all he is. He's eccentric, nothing more. Not dangerous, or Myron would never have made the provision for him in the will . . . would he?

She shook her head. Of course not. She was just being silly and paranoid.

"And procrastinating," she said out loud, causing Beasley to tilt his head as if trying to figure out the meaning of her remark. She smiled down at her faithful pet. "Come on, Beasley. Let's go get this over with, shall we?"

If dogs could smile, she imagined he had as he gazed up at her with his warm brown eyes and did his best to wag his stub of a tail. Lynn knew he'd follow her anywhere, so she placed her now-empty glass in the sink, turned on her heel, and nearly marched toward the front door, confident that Beasley was right behind her.

Once out the door, the dog walked at her side, though she knew he itched to break away and run. She also knew he wouldn't do so without her permission, so the two of them approached the nearest gate to the cemetery together. Sure enough, Jason still hoed the weeds, though he'd made a bit of progress since she spotted him a few moments earlier.

"Hello," she called, standing just inside the gate, several rows away from him.

He lifted his head and squinted into the noonday sun. "Mrs. Myers," he said, nodding a brief greeting before returning to his work.

Frustrating man. Isn't it obvious that I came to talk with him?

She cleared her throat. "Excuse me, Jason. I know you're busy, but I wondered if I could interrupt you for just a minute. I . . . have a question I'd like to ask you, something I think you might be able to help me with."

He looked up again, his brows drawn together in a frown this time. Even from a slight distance, she could tell he studied her, and he appeared none too pleased. At last he shrugged. "Sure. Why not?"

He carefully propped his hoe against the fence before taking a few slow, deliberate steps in her direction. By the time he got to within a couple feet of her, she'd wished she'd remembered to test the breeze first and made sure not to stand downwind. Did the man ever bathe or change his clothes?

He stopped in front of her and fixed his eyes on hers. That's when she realized the ball was back in her court.

"I . . ." She hesitated. Where did she start? *The journals,* she decided. Jason was the one who originally mentioned them to her, so that would be the logical place.

"I found my brother's journals in the library, and I've been reading through them, just as you suggested. His final entry was about the man named Last Chance Justice." She glanced toward the spot where the two headstones lay next to one another, then pulled her eyes away and looked back at Jason. "I couldn't find out much else about him, even though my daughter and I searched through all Myron's journals. I've asked around town and got a few basic facts about Last Chance's story—the missing money and all that—but those facts don't do anything to clear the man's name. If that's what Myron was trying to do, and it appears he was, and if he wanted me to pick up where he left off, then I need more information. I don't even have a starting place. Where do I look? Who do I talk to? And how can I possibly figure out something that no one else in Bloomfield ever could?"

"Maybe no one else in Bloomfield figured it out because no one ever tried hard enough," Jason answered. "It was easier to bury a seven-dollar mystery with the man whose name was ruined by it. But Myron knew better. Told me many times that a man like that, from such a respected family, just couldn't have flat-out taken that money and lied about it for the rest of his short life. What happened to the money, who knows? But there's got to be an answer buried somewhere."

Buried. Why did everything that had to do with her brother's life, death, and even his estate, somehow have to tie in with being buried? The thought made her want to shiver, even in the warm sunshine.

Okay, so she'd forced herself to talk to Jason about Last Chance Justice. And where had it gotten her? She knew no more now than she had a few minutes ago before she asked him. Why had she even bothered? Maybe she'd have to face facts and give up this pointless quest. After all, it's not like she ever knew Last Chance, or anyone in his family for that matter. What did she owe any of them?

She sighed. No sense spending any more time out here in the sun talking to Jason. This was going nowhere fast.

"All right, thanks," she said, turning to leave. "I appreciate it, and I'll follow up if I can figure out what to do next." She stepped outside the cemetery, turning one last time to call out, "Thanks again."

For nothing, she added silently, heading back toward the house with Beasley padding along at her side.

That's it, God. I've done what I can do. I've read through the journals, talked to anyone who might possibly be able to give me a clue, and I've got nothing. If You want me to pursue this, You're just going to have to show me somehow, because otherwise I'm done with it.

With that she threw open the front door and made a beeline for the kitchen, ready to rummage in the refrigerator and make a sandwich.

Lynn had just sat down at the kitchen table with her grilled ham and cheese sandwich when her cell phone jingled. She glanced around the room, annoyed that she hadn't thought to keep it handy. Rachel was so good at that, but Lynn still thought in terms of a landline, tethered to the wall where she couldn't lose it. The cell phone had too many possibilities of being misplaced.

Hopping up from her chair, she followed the continued ringing from the kitchen back to the entryway and spotted her purse lying on the small table by the door. Of course. She'd never taken it out when she got home.

Thinking the call must be from Rachel, since she couldn't imagine who else would be calling her, she dug through the bottom of her handbag until she found her phone and snatched it out.

"Hello?" she said, pressing it up against her ear. "Rachel, is that you?"

A familiar laugh rang in her ear. "No, Lynn, it's not Rachel. It's me, Kathy." When Lynn didn't answer right away, the voice said, "Kathy Wilson."

The light came on and Lynn blinked, as if trying to clear her mind. Why in the world would Kathy Wilson be calling her? And how had she gotten her number? Lynn didn't remember giving it to her, but then she had to admit that ever since Daniel died she found herself forgetting more details than she wanted to admit. Was it on purpose, a determined effort to block out painful memories? She shook off the thought and forced herself to answer.

"Yes, Kathy, of course," she said, carrying the phone back to the kitchen and re-situating herself in her chair as she stared at her cooling sandwich with its congealing cheese. "How are you?"

"I'm just fine. The question is, how are you? You sounded a bit flustered when you answered. Obviously, you were expecting Rachel. You're not concerned that she's out having lunch with John Currey, are you?"

Lynn felt her eyes widen. Rachel and John had gone out to lunch? She thought they were at the church, discussing various ministries. Then again, it was lunchtime, and why shouldn't they go out to grab a bite to eat? But even if they had, how did Kathy Wilson know about it? Is that why she'd called, to report on Rachel's whereabouts?

"I . . . knew she was with John," Lynn said, "but I didn't realize they'd gone out to lunch. How did you know about it?"

Kathy laughed again. "Oh, you know me, Lynn. I have my ways. Not much gets past me in this town. Seriously, I was at the deli with some of the girls from the garden club when in walked your daughter with that handsome youth pastor. My first thought was that they make such an attractive couple. But . . ." She paused, and Lynn held her breath, wondering what was coming. "But isn't she already seeing Hayden Blackstone? Or did I misunderstand?"

The question hung in the air while Lynn thought about how best to answer it. *Truthfully,* she reminded herself. *It's not like we've got anything to hide or that Rachel's doing anything wrong.*

"She's not actually seeing either one of them," Lynn said, careful to keep her voice pleasant but firm. "We're only in town for a few days, and both Hayden and John have been kind enough to befriend Rachel while she's here. If she has an occasional meal with them during that time, I don't think that actually constitutes a relationship."

Kathy sounded a bit chagrined when she answered. "I'm sorry. You're right, of course. I didn't mean to imply there was anything serious going on with Rachel and either of the young men—and fine young men they are too, I might add. Hayden, as you know, is my son's best friend."

Lynn sighed. Yes, she did know that, which only added to her conviction that despite the fact that Kathy meant no harm, the news of Rachel's multiple meal partners would soon be buzzing all around town—if it wasn't already.

"Anyway," Kathy went on, "that's not why I called. Actually, I got to thinking about how important the garden club was to your dear mother—she loved it, as you know. And now that you're back in town, even if it's just for a little while, I thought you might want to reconnect with some of the women who were so important to your mom. That's why I got your phone number from Rachel when I saw her at the deli. We're having a gathering at my place on Friday at noon, an informal potluck luncheon, and it's one of the few times we can invite nonmembers to join us. I thought it would be perfect if you could come. You'll still be here, won't you?"

Lynn caught herself. She wanted desperately to say no, that she and Rachel would be gone by then, but she knew that wasn't true. At this point, she figured they'd be here at least through the weekend, longer if she left it up to Rachel. So how did she gracefully decline?

"I, well . . . yes," she said. "We'll still be here, but—"

"Wonderful," Kathy exclaimed. "The girls will be thrilled. And you're welcome to bring Rachel along—unless, of course, she's out with Hayden or John. And I'll put you down to bring a dessert. How about your mom's famous flat apple pie? That was always such a hit, and it would be a lovely tribute to her memory if you'd do that. Can I count on you?"

Lynn found herself wishing she'd left her phone in the bottom of the purse and let Kathy's call go to voice mail where she could ignore or delete it or . . . anything but answer it. But now she was stuck. Not only would she have to spend the afternoon with people who would rave about her mother's green thumb as well as her cooking, but she would have to produce a flat apple pie on a par with the ones her mom used to make.

No small order. I haven't made one of those in years. I'm not even sure I remember how. I know I have the recipe somewhere at home, but . . .

"Lynn? Are you there?"

She swallowed and took a deep, shaky breath. "Yes, of course, I'm here, and . . . sure, I can bring a flat apple pie. I'm . . . looking forward to it."

"Wonderful! Then it's settled. I'm so glad I ran into Rachel while I was with the garden club ladies. Wasn't that perfect timing?"

"Perfect," Lynn mumbled, her eyes falling on her uneaten lunch. She pushed it away as she said goodbye and closed her phone. "Just perfect. Oh, Beasley," she said, glancing down at the snoozing animal who lay at her feet, oblivious to her dilemma, "what have I gotten myself into now?"

 Chapter 17

BY THE TIME JOHN DROPPED RACHEL OFF IN FRONT OF THE OLD house at the end of Cemetery Drive, the two of them talked and laughed as if they'd known one another forever. Rachel exited the car and nearly skipped up the steps to the front porch. She waved one last goodbye before John backed out of the driveway then watched him disappear down the road before she turned and let herself inside.

She was immediately greeted not only by an excited, wiggling, yapping cocker spaniel, but also by the delicious aroma of apples and cinnamon. What was going on in the kitchen?

"Mom?"

She followed her nose and stopped just feet from her mother. Lynn's normally loose-hanging, shoulder-length hair was clipped up with a barrette, her flushed cheeks and forehead were streaked with what appeared to be flour, and she actually wore an apron—something Rachel hadn't seen her do in a very long time.

"Wow," Rachel said, exhaling as she took in the telling scene. "You've been baking."

"Brilliant deduction," Lynn said, grinning. "How could you tell?"

"Seriously, Mom, this is the last thing I expected to come home and find you doing. Although I must admit, if running off and leaving you alone for a couple of hours will cause you to do more of it, I'm happy to oblige."

"No, thanks," Lynn answered, pulling out a chair and nearly flopping into it. "I'm ready for a break. I'd forgotten how much trouble it is to make one of these flat apple pies."

"A flat apple pie? From Grandma's recipe?"

When Lynn nodded, Rachel quickly pulled out another chair and sat down beside her. "I haven't tasted one of those in years. Not since . . . well, since before Grandma died, I don't think. I didn't even know you knew how to make one."

Lynn's expression betrayed only a slight offense. "I can do a lot of things you don't know about. And baking flat apple pies is one of them. Your grandmother taught me years ago, when I was still in school. I even have the recipe somewhere, though I'm not sure where. I really need to find it so I can pass it on to you. Don't want that little family secret to get lost in future generations."

"Oh, great," Rachel said. "No pressure there. Now it's up to me to preserve the family tradition and honor. You know I don't cook—other than an occasional something in the microwave."

"Well, then, it's time you changed your ways, young lady," Lynn teased. "And once you bite into that pie and remember how good it is, you'll be begging me for the recipe."

Rachel shook her head. "I wouldn't count on it, Mom. But I have to admit, I'm looking forward to having some. John and

I grabbed a sandwich earlier, but we didn't have time to hang around for dessert. He had to get back to the church office."

Lynn nodded. "Yes, I heard the two of you went out for lunch."

"Are you kidding me? Those ladies called and told you already? John warned me that word travels fast in this town and that Kathy Wilson's tongue can out tap-dance a Western Union telegraph machine, but this is ridiculous." She glanced at her watch. "We just saw them a couple of hours ago."

"That's all it takes. Now, let's check that pie, shall we? I don't want to risk burning that flaky crust."

The minute Lynn pulled the oven door open, the already delicious aroma that permeated the house increased, causing Rachel's mouth to water. "How much longer?"

Lynn closed the oven. "I'd say another ten or fifteen minutes, but then it has to cool awhile. You don't want to burn your tongue."

"Yes, I do," Rachel insisted. "Who cares how hot it is? It smells delicious."

"And it will be," Lynn agreed, "in due time. Now sit down and tell me about your lunch with John."

Rachel recounted their quick stop by the church before heading to the deli, how they ran into Kathy Wilson and her friends, and the ministry opportunities John had told her about. "Of course, I explained to him that I didn't see how I could commit to anything long-term at this point, but he said for as long as we're in town, I can help him with the youth group on Wednesday nights and go with him when he visits over at Lake Bliss. Isn't that cool? That means my first night helping out is tonight. Why don't you come with me and go to the service?"

Lynn hesitated. "I might. I still have to clean up." She looked around the room. "As you can see, I made quite a mess."

Rachel laughed. "Oh, Mom, it's not bad at all. Tell you what. When the pie is done, I'll clean up in here. That'll free you up to do whatever else you need to do before we go to church tonight. What do you say?"

Lynn raised one eyebrow. "Can I trust you to leave the pie alone while it cools?

"Who, me?" Rachel grinned. "Why would you even ask?"

At last, Lynn nodded. "All right, you've got a deal. I have some clothes to fold and a couple other odds and ends to tend to. And now, with that luncheon looming on Friday . . ."

Lynn's voice trailed off and a tinge of pink rose to her cheeks. Rachel knew the look. Her mother had just said something she wished she hadn't.

"What luncheon would that be, Mom?"

"The one at . . . Kathy Wilson's on Friday. It's mostly the garden club ladies, but Kathy said it's one of the few events where they can invite guests. So . . . she invited me. And she wants me to bring your grandma's flat apple pie."

"Aha. Now all this makes sense." Rachel laid a hand on her mother's arm. "It still matters to you what Kathy and the others think of you, doesn't it? Peer pressure, even after all these years. That's why you're practicing with the pie now."

"That's not it at all. Well, not really. I just . . . I just want to do a good job honoring your grandmother, that's all."

Rachel nodded. "Sure, Mom. If you say so."

Lynn stood up. "Well, I do say so, and that's that. Now let me check that pie again. If it's ready, I'll take it out and head upstairs." She turned back as she reached the oven. "Just remember to let it cool before you start sampling it."

By the time the pie had cooled, Lynn had finished her tasks upstairs and Rachel had cleaned up the kitchen, and they were both ready to dive into the tantalizing dessert for a sample. Lynn was pleasantly surprised at the results, though she was nearly certain she'd forgotten one tiny ingredient.

"Your grandmother's was better," she said, laying her fork down on her plate. "I'm missing something."

Rachel's green eyes widened. "Better than this?" She shook her head. "Impossible. Mom, this is incredible. Amazing! I could eat the whole thing."

Lynn laughed. "I wouldn't advise it. Did you notice it's the size of an entire cookie sheet? That's a lot of flat apple pie, even for you."

Rachel laughed. "I know. And I had a big lunch besides. Okay, here's the deal. I'll skip dinner so I can have another piece. This is just too delicious. It's going to be a serious hit at Kathy Wilson's luncheon on Friday."

"Do you really think so?"

Rachel rolled her eyes. "I know so. Those women will forget there's anything else there. This pie will disappear in seconds."

Lynn shook her head. "I hope you're right. I just wish I knew what I've forgotten. It must be a pinch of something or—"

"Mom, stop it." Rachel interrupted her mother by laying her hand on her arm. "If this pie were any better, I'd die and go to heaven the minute I ate it. Now leave it alone, will you?"

"You're right, sweetheart. I know you are. It's just . . ."

"It's just that it matters to you what those women think of you. Admit it, Mom. You're intimidated by peer pressure."

Lynn was glad she didn't have a bite of pie in her mouth at the moment or she probably would have choked. Intimidated by peer pressure? At her age? Ridiculous. Or was it?

She sighed. "I really don't want to talk about this right now. You may be right, and if you are, I know how silly it is. But whether I am or not, I need to stop worrying about this pie, don't I? Not to mention the luncheon on Friday." She smiled. "Let's change the subject. It sounds as if you had a nice time with John today."

Rachel nodded. "I did. He's a great guy, Mom. I love his heart for working with young people and seniors too. You know they've both been ministry passions of mine."

"Yes, I do know that. Since you were a little girl."

"And what about you?" Rachel asked. "I felt bad leaving you at the retirement center and running off with John. Did you come straight home and start baking?"

"Not really. I came straight home, sure, but then . . ." She took a deep breath. "You'd be proud of me, Rachel. I went out to talk to Jason. I saw him hoeing weeds in the cemetery when I drove up, and I decided to get it over with. So I asked him about Last Chance."

"And? Did he fill you in?"

"I'm afraid not. He actually didn't seem to know much more than I did." She shrugged. "So for now, that's about all I've got to go on. If something else doesn't turn up soon, we're going to have to leave Bloomfield with its seven-dollar-and-fourteen-cent mystery still unsolved."

"You may be right," Rachel said. She smiled and pointed at Lynn's plate. "You going to finish that?"

Lynn glanced down at her half-eaten slice of pie. "I don't

think so," she answered, looking up at her daughter. "Are you offering to help me?"

Rachel grinned. "Glad to do it . . . if you're sure you don't want it."

"Be my guest," she said, shoving the plate across the table. "And there's plenty more where that came from."

"You could always take some to Jason," Rachel suggested.

Lynn raised her eyebrows. She supposed that would be the neighborly thing to do—the right thing. But two encounters with Jason in one day? She wasn't sure she was up to it.

"Tell you what," Rachel said before shoveling a bite into her mouth, "you cut some and put it on a plate, and I'll take it out to him. Deal?"

Lynn smiled with relief. "Deal. And then, yes, I'll plan on getting ready and riding over to the church with you this evening. Thanks for suggesting it."

The two women said goodbye to Beasley and headed out to the car for the short drive to church. A voice from near the side of the house interrupted them. They turned to see Jason watching them.

"Thanks for the pie," he called. "Not the best I've ever had, but not the worst either." With that, he turned and proceeded back toward his shack.

Lynn's stunned amazement quickly gave way to irritation. "Well, he's got his nerve," she declared. "Not the best indeed! I doubt he's ever had flat apple pie in his entire life until today."

Rachel grinned. "Don't worry about it, Mom. Coming from Jason, that's probably a compliment. At least he acknowledged it."

"I suppose," Lynn grumbled. "Or else I really did miss an important ingredient when I put it together. I sure hope I can remember what it was before I make the one for the luncheon on Friday."

Rachel laid her hand on her mother's shoulder. "Mom, stop obsessing. It was delicious, I promise you, and everyone at Kathy Wilson's place is going to love it. Now come on, I don't want to be late for my meeting with John. I told him I'd show up a little early so he can run through a few things with me before the youth service starts."

Thoughts of Jason's remark and Kathy's luncheon flitted from Lynn's head as she turned her attention to her daughter. Smiling, she accompanied Rachel to the Corolla, easily falling into the habit of climbing in on the passenger side.

"So," she said, still smiling as Rachel started the car, "you're looking forward to your time with John, aren't you?"

Rachel's cheeks colored slightly. "If you mean I'm looking forward to helping out with the youth group, yes, I am. Even if it's just very temporary, it should be fun."

Lynn nodded. *Temporary.* The way Rachel spoke the word told Lynn her daughter would like to at least extend their stay in Bloomfield, maybe even make it permanent. Should she consider it, despite the fact that it made no sense whatsoever?

Against the advice of most folks in Bloomfield, she had left the quaint little burg behind more than three decades ago and gone out to make a very nice life for herself. Just because Daniel was gone now, did that mean she had to return? On the other hand, was she being selfish and stubborn not to at least consider it? And why did it seem to mean so much to Rachel? She'd never lived there, so she had no real roots in Bloomfield, yet she seemed drawn to the simple ways of the little town, which Lynn sometimes thought of as a town caught in a time warp.

Except if that were true, my parents and brother would still be here. They're not, and there really is nothing else to hold me here . . . is there?

As they turned from Cemetery Drive onto Main Street, Lynn gazed out the window, amazed at the strong sense of familiarity and belonging she felt. She'd spent far less than half her life there, and yet there were moments like this when it felt as if she'd never left.

She sighed. They were nearly at the church, the familiar grounds where she'd spent so many hours as a child. She knew nearly every nook and cranny of the place by heart since it had changed so little over the years. Maybe it was that very sense of belonging that drew her back and also wooed Rachel, or maybe it was something stronger. Whatever the reason, she realized suddenly that her daughter wasn't the only one looking for reasons to extend their visit awhile longer.

 Chapter 18

LYNN HADN'T BEEN TO A WEDNESDAY NIGHT SERVICE SINCE before Daniel died. The two of them had always attended together, but Lynn preferred not to drive at night, so staying home in the evenings had become a simple habit to adopt. Now, as she waved goodbye to Rachel, who headed down the hallway toward John's little office, she found herself drawn to the warm, lively music drifting outward from the sanctuary. Almost as if they had a mind of their own, her feet took her through the open doors and down the middle aisle toward some empty seats in the front rows.

She and Rachel had arrived a bit early, so few people were there yet. That suited Lynn just fine. She was there to worship and study, not to socialize. And she knew firsthand how important socializing was in Bloomfield.

Lynn had just settled into a seat next to the aisle and opened her Bible when she felt a hand on her shoulder. Startled, she looked up to find Ida Blackstone, Hayden's mother, smiling down at her.

"I thought that was you," she said. Without waiting for Lynn to scoot over so she could join her, she pushed right past Lynn's now-scrunched knees to sit on her other side. "I'm so glad I spotted you," she went on, settling her purse and Bible on the empty space next to her. "Norm isn't feeling too well this evening, so he decided to stay home and I'm here all by myself. But now I can sit with you." She beamed as if she'd accomplished a great coup, and Lynn scrambled to find an appropriate response.

"That's . . . wonderful," she said, feeling a bit flustered. "Not that Norm isn't feeling well, of course, but that you saw me and we can sit together." She flashed what she hoped was a convincing smile and plowed ahead with the first thought that popped into her mind. "I haven't been here on a Wednesday night since I can't remember when, but Rachel convinced me to come along. She's going to be helping John with the youth group tonight."

Ida's smile faded. "I see. So Rachel and John are seeing each other, are they?"

Lynn realized she'd taken the conversation in an awkward direction and hoped she could get it back on track.

"Oh, no, not really," she answered quickly. "It's just . . . well, they have similar ministry interests. Rachel just graduated Bible college, you see, and she's looking for direction about where to get involved. Her two primary ministry focuses have always been working with the elderly and with youth, and since John does that too, well, it just seemed natural . . ."

She let her voice drift off then, knowing she was probably making the situation worse. With Ida's son, Hayden, already vying with John for Rachel's attentions, Lynn had no doubt complicated things.

"Anyway," she said, hoping to change the subject, "I had a call from Kathy Wilson about the garden club luncheon at her place on Friday. She graciously invited me to come as a guest. Will you be there?"

The frown lines in Ida's forehead smoothed out a bit, and a hint of her former smile returned. "I wouldn't miss it. I love being part of the garden club. You've seen my yard, haven't you?"

Lynn hesitated. She probably had at some point, but she couldn't remember anything special about it. "Of course," she said, smiling, hoping Ida wouldn't press her for details.

"Then you know I love gardening. I even won the award one year and got to have Gnorman in my yard the entire season."

"Norman?"

Ida's smile widened. "The garden gnome. Gnorman, with a G. He's our little plastic gnome who holds the trophy and stands in the yard of the annual garden club prize winner each year." She leaned toward her and whispered. "We had quite an adventure with him being gnome-napped not long ago. Remind me to tell you the story." She chuckled. "You'll get a kick out of it."

Only in Bloomfield, Lynn thought, her curiosity piqued, *could a gnome-napping be considered a "big adventure."* She made a note to ask about it when they had time to chat.

More people drifted in by then, and the front rows began to fill up. Lynn was glad, more than ready to let this conversation drop and get on with the worship and study. As the canned music that had been playing over the loudspeakers shut down and the team of song leaders took over, Lynn relaxed. This was why she'd come tonight—not to chitchat with Ida Blackstone. Still, she couldn't help but wonder how things were going with Rachel and John as they prepared for the youth service.

"I'm a little nervous," Rachel admitted as she and John made their way downstairs to the large open room where the junior and senior high youth group gathered. "I don't know why. I mean, I love working with this age group, and it hasn't been that long since I was one of them. But for some reason, I feel intimidated."

John smiled as they continued to descend the stairs. "I won't tell you not to be. There's no reason to be, of course, but I know from experience that just telling someone not to be nervous doesn't change the butterflies-in-the-stomach feeling."

Rachel laughed, impressed by someone of the male gender who actually seemed to "get it" when it came to feelings. "Thanks for that. I appreciate the honesty. There's nothing worse than having someone tell you not to feel what you already feel."

They'd nearly reached the bottom of the stairs when John said, "By the way, tomorrow's my day to go visit a couple senior citizens who don't live at Lake Bliss, and I thought you might like to come along. One of the ladies I visit each week lives with her family and doesn't remember much anymore—probably won't have a clue who we are or even that we're there—but the other one is a real character. I think you'll like her. She lives alone in an old cabin outside of town. Very independent, and she keeps to herself most of the time. But boy, can she tell some great stories about the old days in Bloomfield."

Rachel paused and looked at John. "I'd love that. Should I meet you here at the church in the morning?"

"You could, or I can just swing by and pick you up. How about at nine?"

Rachel smiled. "It's a date," she said, and then nearly bit her tongue, wondering why she'd used that word. It wasn't a date at all; they were simply going to visit a couple of elderly people together. She sure hoped she hadn't given John the wrong impression.

Before she could dwell on the issue, John steered her toward the front of the room where they looked out on an assembled group of about forty teenagers. It didn't take long for the chatter and laughter to die down as the group became aware of John and Rachel's arrival. As all eyes settled on her, Rachel told herself to relax. This was a great ministry opportunity, something she'd trained and studied for during the last four years. Most important, God was in charge. What happened here was up to Him, not to her, or even John. With that thought, she allowed a smile to spread across her face, relieved to realize it was genuine.

Rachel was not only awake ahead of her mother, but showered and dressed before Lynn had even stirred. Shushing Beasley, Rachel escorted him down the stairs and into the kitchen. She was busy getting the coffee made when Lynn walked in. Yawning and stretching, she eyed Rachel warily.

"You're up early. Something going on this morning that I don't know about?"

"Maybe," Rachel answered. She shrugged and grinned. "Maybe not."

"All right, that's it. Spit it out."

"You could at least have waited until I finished making the coffee," Rachel teased, setting the table with mugs and spoons. "How about some eggs and toast, or cereal and fruit?"

Lynn shook her head. "Maybe later," she said, plopping
down in a chair and leaning an elbow on the table while she
studied Rachel. "First I want to hear what you've got planned
for today. It must be something good to get you to roll out of
bed this early."

Rachel smiled down at her. "I'm going with John this morning to visit a couple of elderly people who don't live out at the
retirement home. He invited me to go with him, and I didn't see
any reason not to."

"I think that's great," Lynn said. "But why didn't you mention it last night on the way home from church?"

"Oh, I don't know. You have to admit, I was pretty fired
up about how well things went at the youth service. I basically
talked your ear off about that, and today's plans sort of slipped
to the background."

"Until now."

"Yes, until now." She smiled again. "So, now you know
what's going on with me today. What about you?"

Lynn yawned again. "Nothing that I know of, though
Myron's lawyer might call. If so, I may go in to meet with him.
Will you be taking the car today?"

Rachel shook her head. "No, John's picking me up at nine.
The car's all yours."

"Good. Though I may not need it either." She stood up.
"Think I'll go take a quick shower before snagging a cup of that
coffee." She glanced at her watch. "If you leave before I come
back down, when do you plan to be home?"

"I'm not sure," Rachel admitted. "I would think before
lunch, but . . . well, you never know."

Lynn smiled. "Don't rush. If John wants to take you to
lunch again, go for it. I'll be fine. Have a nice day, sweetheart."

John's heart sang as he pulled into the driveway and stopped in front of the house next to the cemetery. He grinned at the thought that it was a good thing his heart could sing because his radio sure didn't work.

Climbing out of the car, he bounded up the front steps and tapped on the door. Rachel answered quickly and invited him in for a cup of coffee.

"I'd better pass," he said. "We're on a pretty tight schedule for these two morning visits. At least one of these ladies is expecting us—and she doesn't like it one bit if I'm late."

Rachel offered him one of her head-swimming smiles, and John's heart went off on another rhapsody trill. Would he ever stop feeling blown away by this woman's beauty? He just hoped he would have the chance to find out.

As they drove down Main Street to the opposite end of Bloomfield, he explained a bit about their first visit. "Mrs. Majors is nearly a hundred years old. She's been living with her daughter and son-in-law for several years now. I never know how much of what I say gets through, but I always read a chapter or two of the Scriptures to her, and then pray with her before I leave. Her daughter says she seems happy and peaceful for quite a while afterward."

The visit went as expected, and Rachel and John were back in his old Taurus in less than an hour, heading down a winding dirt and gravel road, thick stands of pine trees on both sides.

"I didn't realize anyone lived this far out," Rachel commented. "It seems really isolated."

"It is. But she's lived here her entire life, which the best anyone can figure is some eighty-plus years. Could even be ninety, but no one knows for sure."

"She's been here her whole life? Even as a child?"

John nodded. "Born and raised here, along with her five sisters and one little brother." He chuckled. "The boy's name was Last Chance, apparently because his parents had always wanted a boy but got six girls instead. They thought he was their last chance at a son because of their advancing age, but it turned out his mother died giving birth to him, so Last Chance just seemed to fit him." He stopped when he heard Rachel gasp and turned to see her staring at him, her mouth hanging open.

"Last Chance Justice?"

"Sure. Why? Have you heard his story already?"

"I sure have. Mom and I have been trying to find out as much about him as we could. Old Jason, the caretaker, told us my uncle was trying to solve a mystery that involved Last Chance and some missing money. We even read through all of my uncle's journals but couldn't find anything. That's what we were doing at the retirement center when we ran into you. We stopped to talk to Homer Tatum to see if he could give us any clues about it."

"And did he?"

Rachel shook her head. "No. He filled us in on a few little things, but nothing much. And Mom tried to get a bit more out of Jason too, but . . ." Her eyes grew wide again. "I can't believe we're going to go talk to his sister. Miss Pearl, right? Do you think she knows anything? I heard that if she does, she's not talking."

John shrugged. "I have no idea. I know about the rumors, of course, but I've never brought up the subject with her. She's a talker about other things, though—so long as you approach her right. Miss Pearl is very protective of her brother, even after all these years, so we need to make sure we don't appear to be attacking his reputation in any way."

"Absolutely," Rachel agreed. "I'll let you take the lead. But it sure would be great if she could shed some light on what happened. My mom seems to have picked up the cause where my uncle left off, but she's about to give up, I think. We just didn't know where else to turn or who to ask. Maybe Miss Pearl will end up being the key."

"She might," John said, though deep down he doubted it. He too had heard that talk of Last Chance and the missing money was an off-limits subject with Miss Pearl. Besides, if the woman knew something that would clear her little brother's reputation, surely she would have told someone years ago.

Then again, his dad used to say that life was full of surprises, and today's visit just might turn out to be one of them.

# Chapter 19

JOHN SLOWED HIS FORD TAURUS TO A CRAWL AS THEY PULLED UP in front of the rickety old cabin, but their arrival still kicked up a swirl of dust. When he shut off the engine and they opened the doors, the only sound they heard was the distant cawing of a couple of crows, no doubt hiding somewhere in the thick stand of trees behind the house. But before they could step outside of the car, an angry-looking dog that Rachel imagined must be half wolf came roaring off the porch and straight for them. Rachel was back inside the vehicle with the door shut before she could catch her breath.

John's chuckle startled her almost as much as the dog's menacing appearance. Daring to look toward the driver's side of the car, she was stunned to see that John hadn't rejoined her inside but rather bent over to welcome the dark, shaggy creature with a hug and a greeting.

"Hey there, Bear."

Bear? Why wasn't she surprised? The name fit the ferocious creature, though he and John were obviously old friends.

"It's safe to get out," John called to her. "Bear's all bark and only a little bite."

"A little? Why would I feel better if you'd said 'no bite'?"

John laughed. "Don't get me wrong. Bear's the best watchdog around, and no one gets past him and near Miss Pearl unless she tells him it's okay. But Bear knows me now, and since you're with me, he'll accept you too."

Rachel swallowed. She sure hoped John knew what he was talking about. Cautiously, she reopened her door and stepped outside. "Should I . . . wait here," she asked, "or come over there?"

"Come on over. I'll keep Bear here with me."

Doing her best to block out the admonition she'd heard somewhere along the line about how animals can smell fear, she approached slowly. Bear eyed her every step of the way as John stood at his side, his voice soothing.

"There you go, Bear. That's my friend Rachel. You'll like Rachel. She came with me to visit Miss Pearl. Isn't that nice? Good boy, Bear."

The dog sniffed her then, and within moments he licked her hand. She felt her shoulders relax. Apparently, he had accepted her. She couldn't imagine anyone approaching this remote place—and living to tell about it—if Bear decided otherwise.

"That you, John? Who you got with you?"

The seemingly ancient voice carried from the direction of the porch, and Rachel turned her gaze toward the sound. There, in the doorway, holding the screen door open with one hand and leaning on a cane with the other, stood a woman the color of dark, rich coffee, her white, wiry hair pulled back in a bun at the nape of her neck. She was dressed in a flowered housedress that hung nearly to her ankles. On her feet, she wore solid black shoes with white socks. Her face was lined and yet strangely smooth, her eyes appeared strained to focus on the new arrivals, and her smile was as warm as the sunshine overhead. The image of the elderly woman brandishing a shotgun flashed through her mind, but Rachel dismissed it as absurd, just another exaggeration that had cropped up in Bloomfield somewhere along the way. Rachel knew immediately that she was going to like Miss Pearl. She just hoped the feeling was mutual.

"Yes, it's John all right," he answered. "And this is Rachel Myers. Myron Cofield was her uncle. You remember Myron, don't you? Lived out there by the cemetery until he passed away recently. Rachel and her mom are here for a few days to settle Myron's estate, so I thought I'd bring her out to meet you."

"Well, bring her on in here," Miss Pearl called. "No sense standing out there in the heat. I got some nice cool strawberry tea I made fresh this morning. Come on in and have some. You know how much I like company."

John and Rachel hurried up the steps, leaving Bear to plop down in what appeared to be his favorite spot on the porch, right under the shade by the door. Rachel entered the small home, surprised at how cool it felt inside, considering she didn't hear an air conditioner, or even fans humming. The fresh smell of lemons and strawberries teased her nose, and Miss Pearl invited them to sit at the small wooden table in the corner next to the stove and a small refrigerator.

"This here's my kitchen," she explained, "and over there is the rest of my house."

Rachel followed Miss Pearl's direction and spotted a rocking chair and a small sofa in the opposite corner. Their host explained that the two small doors led to bedrooms. "One was my parents' room, and the other was for us six girls. When Last

Chance was born and Mama died, Daddy took Last Chance into his room. Sometimes we kids thought things were a bit crowded around here, but now that it's just me, I wouldn't mind a little bit of a crowd now and then."

She laughed before leaning her cane against the table and opening the refrigerator to pull out a pitcher of tea. Rachel was about to jump up and offer to help when she caught John's eye. He shook his head, and she recognized his effort to tell her that Miss Pearl preferred to do things on her own.

In moments, they all sipped cold tea and munched on the most delicious molasses cookies Rachel had ever tasted. How did a woman the age of Miss Pearl live out here all alone and do such a great job of taking care of herself—and even providing for occasional guests? She was an amazing woman, Rachel decided, who no doubt had a generous number of fascinating stories to tell.

But did she have any about her brother, Last Chance, that might help solve the mystery of the missing money? And if she did, would she share them?

Within moments, Rachel had her answer. The charming Miss Pearl regaled them with stories of her long life in Bloomfield, but each time either John or Rachel tried to steer the conversation in the direction of Last Chance, Miss Pearl threw up a roadblock and immediately changed the subject. It didn't take long for Rachel to realize that everything she and her mother had heard about Miss Pearl's refusal to discuss her brother and the missing money was absolutely true. So she gave up the attempt and settled in to enjoy the rest of their visit.

"So what did you think of Miss Pearl?"

Rachel smiled. She hadn't stopped thinking about Miss Pearl Justice since they left her charming home. "She's a character. And I mean that in a very good way. I like her a lot. I'd love to go back and see her again . . . if I'm still here the next time you visit, that is."

She cut her eyes sideways toward John and caught him looking at her before he turned back to the road. Had she imagined it, or did he appear saddened by her comment? Strangely, she felt a bit sad herself, but she brushed it away and returned to the topic at hand.

"How long have you been visiting Miss Pearl, anyway?" she asked, grateful to see his expression relax as they veered away from the subject of her leaving.

"Just since I've been on staff at the church, about a year."

Rachel nodded. Her mother had told her a few days earlier that she vaguely remembered the Justice family from when she was young, since they attended the same church. But she hadn't really known them well and didn't remember any details about them, though Lynn said she'd imagined her parents would have at least heard about the cloud that hung over Last Chance's head throughout his brief life. For whatever reason, they'd never mentioned it to Lynn.

"She's a fascinating woman," Rachel mused, "even though we didn't really come away with any new or useful information since she absolutely refused to talk about the missing money. Still, it was a great visit, and I hope I'm here long enough to go back with you again—if I'm still invited."

John glanced at her, his smile wide. "Consider it an open invitation—anytime."

The warmth of his gaze washed over her, and she forgot her disappointment at not getting any insight regarding Last Chance as they pulled into her driveway. Her eyes widened at the sight of the dark sedan parked there, and her heart skipped a beat when she realized John had already spotted it as well. No doubt they both recognized whose car it was, and both realized the driver was there to see Rachel.

Now I know why I didn't date during college, Rachel thought. *Technically, I'm not really dating Hayden or John now, but already life is so much more complicated.*

With the first sign of awkwardness between them, Rachel and John said goodbye and she got out of the car, wondering what the remainder of the day might bring.

Hayden's smile seemed a bit sheepish as Rachel walked into the kitchen and found him sitting at the table with her mom, sipping sun tea. Beasley jumped up from his spot under the table and ran to her the moment she stepped into the room, giving her the diversion she needed to turn away from Hayden's inquiring gaze.

"Rachel," Lynn said, her cheeks flushing a light pink, "you're back. Look who just stopped by."

Rachel knew her mother was trying to imply that Hayden had arrived only moments ahead of her, but she deduced that it must have been slightly longer since both their tea glasses were nearly empty.

She smiled. "What a nice surprise," she said, going to the

cupboard to get herself a glass, and wondering if he'd catch her silent implication that he should have called first. "How are you, Hayden?"

"I'm fine," he answered, "but I was getting a little concerned about you, which is why I decided to drop by. I tried to call you a couple of times earlier, but my calls went straight to voice mail."

Rachel stopped midway through pouring tea over the ice in her glass and turned toward Hayden. She must have been out of cell phone range while she was at Miss Pearl's house, and she hadn't thought to check messages later—highly unusual for her.

"Oh, I'm sorry," she said, glancing back and forth between her mother and Hayden. "I hope I didn't miss anything urgent."

"Not from me," Hayden said, grinning. "Unless you consider missing my dinner invitation urgent."

Rachel raised her eyebrows. "Dinner? Oh, well, I . . ."

Lynn's eyebrows raised as well, but she made no move to jump in and bail her out.

"I actually had a late lunch," Rachel said. "I doubt I'll be very hungry this evening, but . . ."

Hayden's eyes telegraphed his disappointment, obviously trying to hold his smile.

"But I'd be happy to take a rain check," she added. "Tomorrow, for lunch, maybe? You've got something going on during the day tomorrow anyway, don't you, Mom?"

Lynn smiled. "The garden club luncheon at Kathy's, yes."

Hayden redirected his smile toward Lynn. "Ah, so they roped you into that event, did they? I know my mom's planning to be there. She's been talking about it for days."

Lynn chuckled. "Well, I know how important this is to the members. And, yes, I'm going—as a guest, of course."

"So that's lunch, not dinner," Hayden said, turning back to Rachel. "How about if we make it another picnic? We could go back to that spot we went to the other day, or try a new one if you prefer. There are lots of them around here."

Rachel found herself slightly relieved at the thought of an informal picnic rather than dinner, which seemed that much more like an actual date, particularly since Hayden hadn't mentioned including her mother in his original dinner invitation.

Rachel nodded. "Sure, a picnic tomorrow would be great. And the same spot is fine. I loved it there. But this time you've got to let me fix the food. Your mom will have enough to do getting ready to go to the shindig at Kathy's house. I know my mom is going to be baking up a storm so she can take my grandma's flat apple pie with her."

Hayden's eyes widened. "Oh, now that sounds delicious. Almost makes me want to go to that thing myself."

Rachel laughed. "No need. Mom did a practice run yesterday and we have plenty left. How about a piece to go with that sun tea?"

"Sounds like a plan . . . if I can get a refill on the tea."

"Coming up," Rachel assured him.

Chapter 20

LYNN FELT FLUSTERED AND SHE HADN'T EVEN LEFT YET. THE luncheon would start in an hour, and she was determined to race upstairs and take a quick shower before throwing on a cool dress and heading out. Rachel had just gone off on her picnic with Hayden, and the kitchen was still warm from all the baking and food preparation that had gone on throughout the morning. At least Rachel had taken care of the cleanup work before leaving.

With Beasley hot on her heels, Lynn hurried upstairs and rummaged through the meager selection of clothes she'd brought with her. The sleeveless pink cotton would have to work. She could always accessorize it a bit.

Beasley had already settled onto the bench at the foot of the bed, snoozing happily by the time Lynn finished her shower. She glanced at her watch. Thirty minutes left. Thankfully, there wasn't much traffic in Bloomfield to worry about—rush hour meant waiting for three cars to pass, rather than one—so she should be fine.

The flat apple pie was cool enough to carry by the time she hit the kitchen, so she grabbed her purse and the dessert and headed out the door, leaving Beasley in charge. Lynn wondered whether she or Rachel would get home first.

All depends on how the picnic goes with Hayden—not to mention the luncheon.

She did her best to tame the butterflies kicking up a fuss in her stomach as she started the car and backed out of the driveway. She'd attended a couple of garden club meetings with her mother when she was young—before she'd committed the cardinal sin of marrying a stranger and abandoning Bloomfield—and knew well how important the gatherings were to the tight-knit community.

Practically the end-all of social activities in this town. I just pray my pie passes muster.

As she turned from Cemetery Drive onto Main Street, she suddenly felt ridiculous for her concerns. *Why does this matter so much? Why do I care what the garden club thinks of my pie—or of me, for that matter? I don't even live here! I left this town behind thirty-five years ago to marry the man I loved, and I shouldn't have to make excuses for that, not to the garden club or anyone else.*

And yet, as ridiculous as it seemed, she realized the club's opinion did matter, maybe even more so than the opinions of other Bloomfield residents.

Rachel was right, she thought with disgust. *Peer pressure, at my age! You'd think I'd have outgrown that long ago. How old does one have to be to get over such silly feelings?*

The thought of Jolene Trump and Homer Tatum flitted through her mind, and she decided that surely they had reached that stage.

Her hands were damp as she pulled up in front of the Wilsons' modest but perfectly-manicured home. Several cars already filled the driveway and a section of the street, so Lynn found an empty space half a block away and maneuvered her Corolla into it. Balancing her nearly cool pie, she breathed deeply while making her way back toward Kathy's place. She was about to head for the front door when she noticed two other arrivals, chattering as they carried their culinary offerings and making their way straight down the driveway toward the backyard. Obviously, that was where the action was, so Lynn followed them.

The heady aroma of roses in full bloom greeted her before she even stepped foot through the gate. She glanced around. If there had ever been a weed in this yard, it had long since run for its life. A white canvas canopy covered the middle of the yard, providing shade for the two tables, already laden with food. Soft music played in the background, and at least thirty women, interspersed with a couple of brave men, were scattered around the yard, sitting on benches or folding chairs or just standing in pairs or groups, talking and laughing. If ever Lynn had felt out of place, it was now. What had she been thinking to accept Kathy's invitation?

She'd just about convinced herself she could sneak back out the way she'd come when Kathy's voice greeted her from behind. "Lynn, you're here! Oh, I'm so glad."

Lynn turned, making sure her smile was in place and that she didn't drop her dessert in the process.

"Oh," Kathy exclaimed, her face lighting up as she spoke, "and you brought your mother's flat apple pie, just like you promised. I can't wait to taste it. No one made flat apple pie like your mom. No one."

Including me, Lynn thought. *I just know I forgot an ingredient, and if anyone notices, it'll be Kathy.*

"Here, let me take that for you," Kathy offered, holding out her hands. "We'll set it over there on one of those tables—if we can find some room—and then we'll get you a nice cold drink. I want you to have a chance to meet some of our members, and maybe even get reacquainted with the ones you may have known in the past."

With the apple pie safely squeezed between a lemon meringue and a chocolate cream, Lynn followed Kathy around as her gracious hostess introduced her to the board members first, and then to as many others as possible. Lynn remembered some of the ladies and did her best to absorb the names of the ones she didn't, but she knew she'd be doing well to keep track of a tenth of them.

Waylaid with a mini-emergency in the kitchen, Kathy soon took off, leaving Lynn with the opportunity to sink down onto a folding chair in a corner. Sipping her now lukewarm punch, she glanced at her watch and wondered how long she should stay. Kathy had said they would start eating in a few minutes, so maybe an hour, or . . . ?

"Hey, Lynn, how are you?"

Lynn glanced up to see Bailey McCullough headed her way, her ever-present briefcase slung over her shoulder and her digital camera in hand. Lynn smiled with relief at the genuinely friendly face.

"Bailey," she said, "I should have known you'd be here."

Bailey laughed as she pulled a vacant chair over beside Lynn's. "Are you kidding? As society page editor, I nearly live at garden club events. If I missed one, I'd probably lose my job."

Lynn chuckled. "I'm sure you're right. I'd nearly forgotten what a big deal this is."

"You can say that again. I've been jotting notes and clicking pictures for two hours already, and lunch hasn't even started." She glanced at the crowded food tables. "I'm starved," she whispered. "Can't wait to dig in. The food is what makes these events worth attending, believe me." She paused and looked around. "Didn't Rachel come with you?"

"No, she had other plans," Lynn said, reluctant to specify what they were. She didn't want to add fuel to the gossip fires that were no doubt already raging in Bloomfield, particularly with members of the garden club. Somehow she didn't see Bailey being a part of that gossip ring, but who knew who might overhear their conversation?

"Probably a smart decision," Bailey said. "Listen, I have to go snap a couple more pictures of the food tables before we start annihilating them. Would you mind saving my spot? Once I have my plate, I can take a little break and sit down and eat with you—unless you'd rather sit somewhere else."

Lynn shook her head. "Absolutely not. This is perfect. I'd love to share lunch with you right here."

"Good. I'm off to take pictures, and I'll be back as soon as I can snag some grub."

Lynn smiled. The day had just taken a definite turn for the better, and she decided she might have an enjoyable lunch after all. She only hoped Rachel was doing the same.

John had tried to expunge the memory of Hayden's sedan sitting in the driveway when he dropped Rachel off the day before, but he hadn't been very successful. He'd gotten through the remainder of the day at work yesterday, tossed and turned through the night, and ran bleary-eyed through his tasks that morning. Now, as he snatched his brown paper sack with its meager offering of a peanut butter sandwich and a banana and headed out behind the church to find a quiet place to eat, he couldn't help but think of the nice lunch he'd shared with Rachel the day before.

Before I took her home and found my competition waiting for her, he thought, dropping down under a shade tree in the corner and leaning against its rough trunk. He stared at his sandwich, disgusted with himself for his thoughts. *She's not some kind of prize, Currey. What's wrong with you? Hayden isn't your competition; he's your friend, not to mention your brother in Christ. So get over yourself, will you?*

As he did his best to focus on his lunch, as dull as it was, and to maintain a good attitude, he noticed a couple of familiar kids zigzagging across the church yard, heading straight for the fence. He knew exactly what the two elementary-aged boys would do even before they jumped up on the old brick structure and sat down, their legs swinging in front of them. It seemed children, especially boys, could not go past that fence without climbing or walking or at least sitting on it. He didn't blame them; he'd been a fence climber when he was young too. But he knew the senior pastor discouraged children from doing anything on the church grounds that might endanger them in any way, so he figured he might as well shoo them off before something happened.

"Hey, guys," he said, leaving his lunch behind and sauntering over to where they sat, sharing a couple pieces of red licorice, "how are you?"

The boys, who regularly attended church and Sunday school

there, smiled up at him. "Good, Pastor John," the oldest one answered. "We're just resting."

"I see that." John smiled. "Looks like you're enjoying a good snack too."

They nodded in unison.

"Tell you what," John said. "How about if you get down and come over and sit with me under that tree for a few minutes? It's really not a good idea to climb on the fence, you know."

The older boy dropped his eyes for a moment and shrugged. "I know. Our Sunday school teacher tells us that all the time."

John laughed. "Well, then, let's pay attention to your Sunday school teacher and go sit on the grass, okay?"

The boys climbed down and followed John back to where his lunch sat waiting for him. "I guess I just like sitting on fences," the younger boy said as they plunked down beside him.

"Me too," said the older boy.

John's eyes widened. *Sitting on fences . . .*

He glanced back at the brick fence and studied it for a moment, searching his memory for the approximate date he'd heard the fence was built. Was it possible . . . or was his imagination running away with him?

Snatching his cell phone from his pocket, he said, "Excuse me, boys. I have to make a quick call."

* * *

Rachel thought she'd never seen a more picture-perfect day. The early afternoon sun was warm but not so much so that she felt uncomfortable. With the shade tree above them and the light breeze tossing their hair, they sprawled on their blanket, talking and laughing and devouring the ham and cheese sandwiches

Rachel had made, along with leftover flat apple pie and ice cold sun tea. Despite her misgivings about seeing Hayden again, Rachel had to admit she was enjoying the day immensely.

"Thank you so much for suggesting this," she said, setting the last of her sandwich down on a paper plate. "With Mom gone, I probably would have spent the day hanging out with Beasley. It's not that I don't love that old dog, because I do. But still, this is much nicer."

Hayden's eyes lit up even before the smile touched his lips. "I'm glad," he said, his voice slightly husky. "I'm enjoying it too. But then, between this perfect picnic spot, the excellent food and great weather—not to mention getting to spend time with you—how could I not enjoy it?"

Rachel's cheeks warmed as she realized Hayden had taken her comments farther than she'd intended. Though she appreciated their outing, she knew deep down he hoped for more than a picnic or two before she left Bloomfield behind. But even if she were interested in pursuing a relationship with him—which she wasn't, she reminded herself—how could she even consider it, knowing she would be gone in a matter of days?

She opened her mouth to respond but stopped again. What could she say besides reminding him of her very temporary status? It wasn't as if he didn't already know that. And to say anything more would be unnecessary, at least at this point.

"It's all right," Hayden said. "I'm sorry if I made you uncomfortable with what I said. You were just being honest about the nice time we're having, and I had no right to try to turn it into something else."

Rachel gazed into his dark eyes and blinked tears from her own. Hayden Blackstone was a very nice man, and he had already experienced great pain in his life. She certainly didn't want to be the cause of more. And yet . . .

"Friends," Hayden said. "That's what you want to be, isn't it?"

Rachel nodded. "I . . . Yes, it is. I'm just not looking for anything else in my life right now. I'm trying to stay focused and hear from God about what He has planned for me now that I've finished Bible college. I just can't let myself get distracted by anything else."

"That's one of the reasons I like you so much," Hayden said, his smile tinged with sadness. "You're not just beautiful—though you certainly are that—but you're kind and sweet, and you have a really good head on your shoulders. Whatever God has in mind for you, you'll do well."

Before Rachel could come up with an appropriate response, her cell phone played its classical ringtone. Relieved and imagining it to be a call from her mom, she rummaged in her purse and pulled it out, glancing immediately at caller ID.

John Currey, it said, and her eyes widened. Once again her life had become a bit more complicated. She considered letting the message go to voice mail, but Hayden spoke up before she could.

"Go ahead and answer that. I'll just gather up a few things and put them in the basket. I really should be getting back to work anyway. I left Belinda in charge of the office, and I don't want to take advantage."

Rachel nodded and pressed the phone to her ear.

"Hello?"

"Rachel, it's John. Any chance you can drop by the church this afternoon? I have an idea—a harebrained one, most likely—but I'd like to tell you about it in person."

Rachel raised her eyes and spotted Hayden near his car, loading a few odds and ends into the trunk. "Sure. I suppose I can come over. But Mom has the car, and I don't know what time she'll be back."

"I can swing by and pick you up."

"Umm . . . that won't be necessary. I'm not home right now anyway, but I think I can get a ride to the church. Give me half an hour or so, will you?"

"Sure, no problem. See you then. Thanks."

Rachel was about to disconnect the call when John added, "Uh, Rachel, I hope you won't think I'm crazy. Like I said, it's a harebrained idea, at best."

She smiled. "I've always been partial to harebrained ideas. See you soon."

Chapter 21

HAYDEN HADN'T BLINKED AN EYE WHEN RACHEL ASKED HIM TO drop her at the church rather than home after their picnic, but he obviously knew she went there to see John. How had she let herself get involved in such an awkward situation? As she watched Hayden pull out of the church parking lot, she knew she had to set things right, once and for all, the very next time she saw him. Though a future relationship with John was still nothing more than a vague possibility, she sensed in her heart that it was never going to happen with Hayden, so she might as well make that clear to him now.

She turned away from watching the departing sedan and approached the church, wondering exactly what making it right or clear with Hayden might entail. It wasn't as if she'd implied she had a romantic interest in him . . . had she? No, she was certain she had not. Hayden had even admitted that he knew she wanted only to be friends. Still, she knew he hoped for more and, therefore, interpreted her words and actions accordingly. Most likely, he now understood the situation clearly, but if he called her or stopped by the house again, she would confirm the situation just in case.

And what about John? She approached the door to his tiny office and let herself wonder if maybe she did have at least a little personal or even romantic interest in this handsome youth pastor. Was it his position that intrigued her? No doubt Hayden made ten times the money John did, but that was irrelevant to Rachel. The call of full-time ministry is what wooed her, and she'd known for years that if she ever married, it would be to someone who shared that call.

The door was ajar, and Rachel let herself in. John sat behind his desk, winding up a phone call, and he motioned her inside. A small oscillating fan whirred in the corner, stirring up the warm, stuffy air. The walls were relatively bare, except for John's diploma from Bible college and his ordination papers. One large poster of a lion and a lamb adorned the spot behind his desk, and that was it. Rachel smiled. She liked the simplicity and focus on the eternal.

John hung up and smiled, leaning forward and clasping his hands together. "I'm glad you came, though I have to tell you, I'm a bit embarrassed at how farfetched my idea is."

Rachel raised her eyebrows. "Oh, so now it's farfetched, is it? On the phone you said it was harebrained."

He laughed. "Yeah, well, it's that too. Harebrained and far-fetched, at best. Still, I figured I couldn't let it go by without at least mentioning it to you. If you laugh it off and say forget it, then I will. What do you think?"

"I think I don't have a clue what you're talking about." She grinned. "But I'm intrigued, and I'd really like to know what it is."

"Great," he said, getting up from his chair. "Follow me."

Rachel stood to her feet. "Where are we going?"

"Out back. Behind the church."

Rachel frowned but let curiosity lead her on. When they exited the building and stood overlooking the large grassy area behind the church, he pointed toward the brick fence. "It's that fence. It runs the full length from those old out buildings where they used to hold the Sunday school classes for kids years ago to the main church building itself. See it?"

She nodded. Of course she saw it, and she'd seen it before. This idea of his was definitely not becoming any clearer. "Okay. And?"

"And," he said, walking toward the fence and beckoning her to follow, "I did some checking, and just as I suspected, this fence was built in the early 1940s."

"I'm not surprised," Rachel said as they stopped in front of the brick structure. "But what's that got to do with anything?"

John turned to her, his eyes sparkling. "That's just about the time Last Chance was a boy, attending Sunday school here—the same time he was charged with taking the Sunday school classes' offerings to the church office."

Rachel nodded. "Okay."

"Somewhere between those buildings back there . . ." John paused and pointed before redirecting his finger toward the church building ". . . and the office, he lost the money." He then pointed directly at the fence. "No doubt he walked right along this fence line, which may very well have been in the process of being built at the time."

She caught her breath. This was going somewhere, but she was still unsure where. "What are you saying, John? Do you think this fence has something to do with the missing money?" She shook her head. "I don't get it."

"Probably not," John admitted, shrugging. "I don't know if there's a connection or not. But if there is, isn't it worth pursuing?" He leaned closer as he spoke, his excitement level rising. "I was sitting out here having lunch today when a couple of boys came into the yard and climbed on the fence. I told them to get down because we're always concerned about anyone, especially kids, getting injured on church property. While I was talking to them, I remembered how much I liked to climb and sit on fences when I was a kid, and they said the same thing." He gently laid his hand on Rachel's arm, and she didn't pull away. "What if—and I'm just speculating here, of course—but what if Last Chance couldn't resist either? What if he was walking along beside that fence and decided to climb it or sit on it for a while? Boys do that, right? Maybe girls too, I don't know. But anyway, what if he did? If the fence was still being built, there may have been places where that handkerchief full of money could have slid down inside without him even noticing it. He may not have realized the money was missing until he got to the office, and no one ever thought to check the fence. Once the fence was finished, no one would ever find it. Rachel, for all we know, that missing seven dollars and change could be buried inside that fence somewhere."

Rachel's eyes widened. It was so ridiculous—yes, so far-fetched and harebrained—that it just might be true. But even if it were, what were they to do about it? They couldn't exactly tear down an entire fence on a crazy hunch, and they certainly couldn't justify the expense of doing so on the off-chance of locating such a small amount of money. And yet . . . it wasn't about that small amount of money being recovered; it was about a man's honor being restored.

Rachel thought of Miss Pearl, nearing the end of her years on earth. What would it mean to her to have her baby brother's name exonerated after all these years? Rachel knew at that moment that, if her uncle were still alive, he'd pursue this possibility, regardless of cost.

"I know what you're thinking," Rachel said, "and it's going to be a serious challenge, to say the least."

"I love challenges. And something tells me you do too."

She grinned. "Let's do it. I haven't a clue where to start, but let's start somewhere."

John nodded. "I think I know exactly where to start—in the senior pastor's office. And let me tell you, if you believe in miracles, you'd better get busy and pray for one right now. Because I don't think he's going to like this idea one bit."

The two of them stood silently in the hallway, staring at the door that read MARTIN BRUNSWICK, SENIOR PASTOR on the smoked glass window pane. They eyed one another warily as John reached out and knocked.

"Pastor?" he called. "It's me, John."

"Come on in," the voice rang out, and Rachel felt her stomach tumble. What in the world were they thinking? How could they even imagine approaching this man with such a bizarre request?

John opened the door and peered in. "Sorry to bother you," he said, holding the door back and motioning Rachel inside. "As you can see, Rachel Myers is with me. We both . . . uh, wanted to see you. To talk to you, actually."

Pastor Brunswick raised his bushy salt-and-pepper eyebrows, which perfectly matched his crew cut. Though he appeared to be a no-nonsense kind of guy, Rachel knew he had a reputation for being a very kind and generous man. Even so, it would take more than kindness and generosity on his part to make this thing happen.

The pastor stood, extending his hand to Rachel. She shook it before she took one of the two seats in front of his desk. John quickly joined her.

"Well, now, this is a surprise," the pastor said, sitting back down. "How are you, Rachel? And how's your mother? Are you two getting things settled with your uncle's estate?"

Rachel glanced at John before answering, but his eyes were fixed on the man across the desk. "I'm . . . fine. Mom's fine too. She's visiting at the garden club luncheon today."

"Aha." Pastor Brunswick smiled. "The garden club luncheon, eh? I imagine that's quite an event. I don't make those meetings often, but when I do, I always come away having eaten some of the best food from anywhere around these parts."

"Mom made one of Grandma's flat apple pies," Rachel said.

The pastor's eyes widened. "Your grandmother was famous for those, wasn't she? I imagine that made quite a hit."

"I'm sure you're right. And as for my uncle's estate, the lawyer says we should be able to wind things up next week."

This time, John threw a quick peek in her direction, and she was certain she saw a hint of disappointment in his eyes. But why? It wasn't as if her statement was unexpected. They'd all known she and her mother were here for a very brief time. Still, why did she feel the same disappointment inside that she'd seen mirrored in John's expression? Shaking away the thought, she returned her attention to the pastor.

"Well, I'm glad you're getting things settled," he said. "I still feel badly that we didn't have a funeral or memorial service for your uncle. He was a long-standing member of this church, you know. But we had to honor his wishes, and that's how he wanted it—quiet and simple, he said. Wrote it in his will, in fact. So that's how it was." He shook his head. "But I sure miss looking out there on Sunday morning and seeing him sitting in his favorite spot, listening and taking notes and nodding his head now and then. He had a way of making me feel validated, I suppose." He chuckled. "At least I knew one person in the congregation was paying attention."

"Oh, I'm sure everyone pays attention to your sermons," Rachel said.

Pastor Brunswick smiled. "Maybe not everyone, but so long as most do, that's all right." He took a deep breath. "Now, what can I do for the two of you? Somehow I don't think you came here to talk about who does and doesn't listen to me on Sunday mornings."

Rachel and John turned toward each other at the exact same moment. John's slight nod let her know that he would jump in first.

"Pastor," he said, "there's something we'd like to talk to you about." He smiled, a bit nervously, Rachel thought. "We've agreed that it's not only a harebrained idea, but a farfetched one too. But . . . we also agreed we had to give it a try."

The pastor's eyebrows lifted again. "Well, I must admit, you've got me intrigued. A harebrained and farfetched idea that you absolutely had to try out. On me, I presume?"

"For starters," John said.

Pastor smiled. "All right then. Let's hear it." He leaned back in his chair and tented his hands in front of him.

"It has to do with a fence . . . and not just any fence."

Rachel heard him take a deep breath, just as the pastor's eyebrows rose inquisitively. She breathed a silent prayer and listened as John explained about the boys and the fence, and the possibility that somewhere, hidden in that brick and mortar, was an old handkerchief filled with seven dollars and fourteen cents.

The story still sounded harebrained and farfetched, but she hoped Pastor Brunswick would at least consider it before giving them an answer.

●　

When John brought Rachel home that evening, she wasn't surprised to see her mother's car waiting in the driveway.

"I imagine Mom will be full of stories about the garden club luncheon," Rachel commented as John shut off the engine and turned in his seat to look at her. "Do you think we should tell her about the fence and Pastor Brunswick's reaction to our idea?"

"We?" John grinned. "Does that mean I'm invited in?"

Rachel laughed. "Of course you are. I might even poke around in the refrigerator and make us something to eat."

"Sounds like a plan to me," he said, opening the car door and stepping out.

"Wait. You didn't answer my question."

John leaned down and peered inside the car. "What question?"

"About whether or not to tell Mom about the fence."

John shrugged. "I'd say, let's play it by ear. Let her tell us about her day, and we'll see what happens." He grinned again. "But I have to say, I can't imagine we'll get through the evening without telling her, can you?"

Rachel returned his smile. "You're right." She picked up her purse from the car floor in front of her and opened her door. "Let's go."

Beasley greeted them at the door, scurrying around them as they made their way toward the kitchen. "Mom," Rachel called, "we're here."

"Well, come on in, you two," Lynn called, turning from the refrigerator where she put away a few groceries, carefully moving them from the neat line where she'd placed them on the counter to an equally appropriate spot in the fridge. "Hayden, I'm surprised you took the entire afternoon off for your picnic with Rachel. You two must have had a nice—"

Her words stopped the moment she laid eyes on John, and her face flushed to the roots of her gray-brown hair. "John," she said. "I . . ." She looked at Rachel, and her brows drew together. "I'm confused. Didn't you go on a picnic with Hayden today?"

It was Rachel's turn to flush then as she realized her mother's obvious assumption. Of course. Rachel had left with Hayden before lunch, and now she returned with John. Her life became more chaotic by the moment. She could only imagine what John must have thought.

Resisting the impulse to check his expression, she kept her eyes fixed on her mother. "Actually, Hayden and I were done with our picnic and about to head back to town when John called and asked if I could drop by the church. So . . . since I knew you had the car, I asked Hayden to leave me off there instead of bringing me home."

"I see," Lynn said, though Rachel knew her explanation was anything but clear.

"Anyway," Rachel said, "John and I have had a very interesting afternoon, and we'll tell you about it later. First, we want to hear all about your time with the garden club." She smiled, hoping to bring a more relaxed atmosphere to the room. "I see you've been grocery shopping."

Lynn glanced at the two bags remaining on the counter. "Oh, yes, I picked up a few things on the way home from Kathy's place."

"Well, you just sit down here with John," Rachel said, pointing her mother toward the table where Beasley sat at John's feet, luxuriating in the youth pastor's attention, "and I'll finish putting these away. Now, how was the luncheon? Did everyone love your pie?"

A visible feeling of relief washed over Lynn's face as she sat down next to John. She smiled as she answered. "As a matter of fact, they did. Would you believe Kathy Wilson said my pie was not only as good as my mother's . . . but better? Kathy said—and publicly, to the entire gathering, I might add—that she'd never thought it possible that anyone could outdo my mom's flat apple pie, but that I had done it. She's been asking me for the secret ingredient ever since." She giggled. "I didn't tell her because I don't know. I didn't bring the recipe with me, so I had to make it from memory. I guess I'll have to wait until we get home to find out what I did differently."

Rachel smiled. It was nice to see her mother in such a good mood. Being here in Bloomfield and reuniting with old friends seemed to agree with her. Though she imagined her mother would continue to grieve her husband's loss for a long time to come, Rachel also sensed that Lynn seemed less depressed and tired than before they came. That had to be a good thing, didn't it? Seeing John sitting next to her mother renewed the inkling Rachel felt to try to prolong their visit for just a little longer. Meanwhile, she'd put groceries away while her mother talked . . . and then she and John would tell her about Last Chance and the old fence behind the church.

Chapter 22

JOHN'S EMOTIONS WERE ON A ROLLER COASTER. HE'D BEEN thrilled that Rachel had agreed to come by the church that afternoon and had even been drawn into his wild suspicions about the fence behind the church. When they approached Pastor Brunswick together, he'd felt as if they worked as a team. On top of that, she'd invited him inside when they got to her place.

And then his heart had taken a plunge when he realized Rachel's mother had expected her to walk in with Hayden. So that's where she'd been when he called her. And yet she'd readily accepted his invitation to meet with him, even asking Hayden to drop her off at his office. No doubt that hadn't thrilled his friend.

I like Hayden, he thought as he drove the short distance home after turning off Cemetery Drive. *I really do. He's a great guy, and he got a raw deal with his marriage. I can't even imagine how that must have hurt, and the last thing I want to do is be even partially responsible for seeing him hurt again. And yet . . . if Rachel's interested in me and not him, is that really an issue?*

He sighed, watching the last rays of sunlight twinkle and fade on the horizon.

Then again, maybe she's not interested in either one of us. It's not like she lives here or anything. She'll be gone in a matter of days . . . and then what? If I had any sense at all, I'd just consider her a nice, temporary friend who brightened up a few summer days for me while we tried to convince the powers-that-be to tear down a perfectly good fence on the slim chance that a handkerchief full of change might be hidden in it somewhere.

John shook his head. When he thought of it that way, he knew he'd never give permission if he were a member of those powers-that-be. *But I'm not,* he reminded himself. *Not by a long shot. I'm just a guy who thinks Rachel Myers is pretty terrific and would like to help her solve this so-called mystery that apparently meant a lot to her late uncle. And I'd also like to help clear Last Chance's name after all these years. Wouldn't Miss Pearl be thrilled if that happened?*

He thought of the kind-hearted woman who lived alone with her dog, Bear, and the many memories of her past—no doubt her younger brother's life and death some of the most vivid, despite the fact that she wasn't willing to talk about them. As he turned onto the street where he lived, he nodded to himself, a fresh sense of resolve welling up in his heart.

This isn't just about some attraction I have to a pretty girl. This is about the possibility of righting a wrong that plagued one of Bloomfield's own throughout his short life. Lord, if You want this to happen, I'm asking You to please step in and open some otherwise impossible doors.

Lynn woke early on Saturday morning and managed to slip out of bed without waking Rachel. She showered and dressed in record time, and then motioned for Beasley to follow her down the stairs, carefully closing the bedroom door behind her. She poured some dry dog food in Beasley's bowl, refilled his water, and put the coffee on. While it dripped, she decided to step outside and enjoy the early morning air.

When she opened the door, she nearly tripped over a copy of the *Gazette*. She frowned. The paper had never turned up on the porch before, so quite obviously someone had placed it there for a specific reason. Bending down to pick it up, she unfolded it and sat down in one of the rockers to see what she could find.

Nothing unusual caught her eye until she got to the society section, where a full two-page spread devoted exclusively to the previous day's garden club luncheon exploded in front of her eyes. More than half of the feature was made up of pictures, including shots of the heavily laden food tables, beautifully manicured shrubs, flowers, and lawns, and of course nicely dressed club members chitchatting with one another. Bailey had even placed a picture of Lynn and Kathy, standing side by side, in the middle of the first page.

"Well," Lynn mumbled, "I'm in the paper again. Twice in just a few days. Who would've thought?"

"Who would've thought what?"

Rachel's voice interrupted Lynn's reading, and she looked up to see her daughter, wrapped in a pink robe and standing on the porch beside the door, her long hair piled on top of her head.

Lynn held up the paper. "I'm in the newspaper again. Look."

Rachel stepped behind her and peered over her mother's shoulder. "Well, don't you look nice? And standing there right next to Kathy Wilson, too. You've only been back in town a short while, and already you're becoming a celebrity, Mom."

Lynn laughed. "I'd hardly go that far, but this is a nice surprise. I imagine Bailey must have dropped it off for us."

"Well, good for her," Rachel said. "I'll pick up an extra copy or two later—if the garden club members haven't already snagged them all." She paused. "I smelled coffee when I walked by the kitchen. Shall I get us some?"

"I'd love it. We can sit out here and enjoy it, along with the beautiful morning sunshine." She sighed. "It's gorgeous, isn't it? Even though this house is right next to the cemetery, it's so peaceful and quiet. I think I'm beginning to understand part of Myron's attraction to this spot."

She looked up at her daughter, who smiled as she turned away. "I knew it would grow on you. I feel exactly the same way."

By midmorning Rachel had decided it was just too nice to drive into town when she could easily walk the few blocks to pick up a few extra copies of the paper. Leaving her mother and Beasley behind, she took off with a water bottle in the purse that she slung over her shoulder, and wearing a floppy hat to protect her head from the sun. There was just enough of a breeze to temper the heat, and she thought the day was about as perfect as it could get.

Though she didn't know many people as she passed them on the street, she realized how much she loved a small town where even strangers nodded or smiled and offered a cheery greeting now and then. She thought of how seldom that happened back home and realized she had become more bonded with Bloomfield than she ever would have imagined possible. Now if she could just convince her I-hate-surprises-or-changes mother . . .

Wait a minute, she thought, stopping in front of the second empty newsstand she had come across so far. *How could staying in the town where she grew up be a surprise? It's not like she doesn't know the town or most of its residents. Coming home, even after several decades, can't possibly be the same as moving somewhere new.*

She sighed and shook her head, wondering if she would find any extra copies of the day's paper. Maybe she'd have to go to the newspaper office itself. Was it open on Saturday? Did she even remember where it was?

She raised her head and glanced up and down Main Street. Now where had she seen the *Gazette* building? Surely it was here on the main drag somewhere.

"Rachel! Rachel, is that you?"

The familiar male voice interrupted her musings, and she turned toward the sound to see Hayden heading her way. She remembered then that his office was nearby, though somehow she'd thought it would be closed today. Was he taking a quick break from work, or did he have the day off?

She smiled in welcome as he approached her. "Hi, Hayden. What are you doing downtown on a Saturday morning?"

He glanced at his watch. "Is it still morning?" He grinned as he looked back at her. "Technically, I guess it is, isn't it? I've been at work, catching up on some things I let go during the week. But I'm done now. I was just running a quick errand when

I spotted you—although with that hat on, I wasn't sure it was you until you looked up. So what's your story? What are you doing here?"

"Looking for newspapers. There's a big write-up on the society page about the garden club luncheon yesterday, and a great picture of Mom with Kathy Wilson, so I decided to take a walk and try to find some extra copies." She shrugged. "So far, I haven't been very successful. All the newsstands seem to be sold out."

Hayden laughed. "I'm not surprised. Anytime the paper runs anything about the garden club—which is fairly often, actually—it sells out right away. Those garden club members all want extra copies. But I'm sure we can get some from the *Gazette* office."

"I was just wondering about that. Is it open today?"

Hayden glanced at his watch again. "Just for another fifteen minutes or so." He reached out and touched her elbow, turning her in the opposite direction. "Come on. It's just around the corner. If we hurry, we can make it."

Before Rachel realized it, she and Hayden were hotfooting it down the sidewalk and into the *Gazette*'s front door. Bailey sat at one of two desks, talking on the phone. She waved them in and motioned for them to sit down.

As they waited, Rachel looked around. Bailey seemed to be the only employee in sight, and even she looked anxious to hang up and get going. No doubt she wanted to get a start on her weekend, and Rachel felt bad about interrupting her.

It won't take long, she reminded herself. *We just need a couple of papers.*

In a few moments, Bailey hung up the phone and got up to fetch the extra copies for them. "I should have left extras this morning, but I only had the one copy with me when I swung by your house." She disappeared into a back room, returning momentarily with extra copies tucked under her arm. After offering a quick thanks and an even quicker goodbye, Rachel and Hayden were out the door, with Bailey locking up behind them.

"Well," Hayden said, "that was quick and easy, wasn't it?"

"I was just thinking that. Ten minutes ago, I was standing on the sidewalk by myself, wondering how I was going to get some copies of the paper, and now here we are, papers in hand and mission accomplished."

Hayden grinned. "Sometimes things just fall into place that way, don't they? Personally, I'd like to think it happened for a reason."

Rachel raised her eyebrows. "Really? And what reason would there be for our getting these papers?"

"I wasn't really thinking so much about the papers. What I meant was there's a reason I spotted you and we connected. That reason would be lunch. It's nearly noon, and I haven't eaten. Have you?"

Rachel immediately thought of her commitment to set things straight with Hayden and not give him any false or misleading signals about their relationship. Maybe this was the obvious time to take care of that, though she didn't exactly look forward to it. Still, better to get it settled sooner rather than later. And since all she'd had this morning was coffee, lunch sounded like a grand idea.

"No, I haven't eaten," she admitted. "Not breakfast or lunch, so maybe that's exactly what we need to do. But this time it's my treat. You don't have to feed me all the time, you know."

"Wait a minute," Hayden countered. "Didn't you bring the sandwiches for the picnic yesterday? Seems to me it's my turn again."

Rachel laughed. "Tell you what. Let's go Dutch. What do you say?"

She could tell by his expression that he would have preferred it if she'd allow him to buy, but knowing what she planned to discuss with him, she felt better about paying her own way. With that settled, they headed back down Main Street toward the deli. It was close enough that they didn't even have to stop and pick up Hayden's car, and Rachel was relieved by that. A Dutch-treat lunch that didn't involve a ride together could certainly not be construed as a date.

 Chapter 23

HAYDEN REALIZED HE WAS KIDDING HIMSELF. FROM THE MOMENT he'd spotted Rachel standing on the street, her hat covering her face as she looked down into the empty newsstand, he'd hoped for a reprieve, but deep down he knew better. Though she'd agreed to have lunch with him, he sensed her pulling back. She was too nice to hit him between the eyes with bad news, but even as they stood in line to order their sandwiches, he felt it coming.

Delivered with a hammer or wrapped in a bow, bad news is bad news, he reminded himself, peering at her out of the corner of his eye. She stared straight ahead, as if fascinated with the menu up on the wall behind the counter. Three more people waited in front of them to place their orders. Hayden imagined Rachel was, to some degree, trying to decide what to order, but also felt relatively certain she avoided eye contact, planning how best to deliver the blow.

It's not like it'll be the first time. It started with Marissa, who promised to stick with me "till death," and then there was

Amber. I thought I had a chance with her, but I should have known better. She and Stan were always meant to be together, period. And he is my best friend, after all.

The man at the counter finished placing his order, and the line moved up a step. Hayden decided to take the opportunity to break the silence. "So what are you going to have?" he asked, watching to see Rachel's reaction to his interruption of her thought process.

She turned slowly, blinking as if surprised to see him standing there. She quickly replaced her slightly confused expression with a warm smile. "I think I'll go with the tuna on rye. There are so many to choose from, but tuna is always good."

Hayden nodded. "Good choice. I've had it here several times. Their macaroni salad is great too. You can get that with it, you know."

"That sounds perfect. I think that's exactly what I'll have. What about you?"

He shrugged. "Got to go with the Reuben. I'm an addict."

Rachel laughed. "Well, then, you definitely need to order that. Don't want you going through any withdrawals or anything."

She turned back toward the counter just as yet another person moved from the order line to the pick-up spot. Now only one person stood ahead of them. Hayden thought he should be grateful, as he really did love Reuben sandwiches, especially the ones they made here, and he'd been quite hungry when he left work and thought about stopping by here to eat. But his appetite had waned since they'd stood in line and he'd thought about his chances with Rachel.

An old saying, "Zero and none," echoed in his mind, though he did his best to shove it away. Was he just being negative . . . or had his track record made him a realist?

It was their turn to order, but before he could try one more time to pay for Rachel's lunch, she made it perfectly clear to the clerk that they would order separately and she would pay for her own meal. Hayden sighed and let her finish ordering, then placed his own before they stepped over into the pick-up line.

"Where should we sit?" Rachel asked, glancing around. The tiny dining area was completely full, but Hayden knew there were often a few empty benches out back. "If you don't mind sitting outside, I think we can find something in the little patio behind the deli."

"Actually, I'd prefer it," she said, smiling again. "It's so gorgeous out today. No sense staying inside if we don't have to. Why don't I go out and see if I can find us a seat, and you can bring the food when it's ready?"

"Works for me."

He watched her walk out the door and pass the window on her way toward the back of the building. So he would have his DEAR JOHN lunch outside in the sunshine.

Dear John? he thought suddenly, suppressing a snort. *How's that for irony? Something tells me it's "dear John" who's at least partially responsible for her decision.*

He sighed, grabbed the baskets full of sandwiches and macaroni salad in one hand and the drinks in the other and headed for the door, ready as he'd ever be to face the firing squad.

When he spotted her at the far table in the corner under the tree, he wondered how a firing squad could look so inviting. Forcing a smile, he straddled the stool across from her and set the food down on the table between them.

"Looks wonderful," she said, her glance moving from Hayden to the food and then back again. "Good choices on our part."

Hayden could feel his smile stiffening as he wondered if there was a double meaning to her comment about choices. Whether or not she had already chosen to pursue a relationship with John, it was obvious she had chosen not to do so with him.

Hoping to ease the tension, he reached for the basket containing his Reuben, but before he could pick it up Rachel laid her hand on his. He lifted his eyes and locked into her gaze, the first time he'd seen it marred with regret.

"We have to talk," she said.

He nodded. He knew what would follow, and he determined to make it as easy on her as possible. Lunch would just have to wait.

Lynn sat on the porch sipping iced tea when she finally saw Rachel heading her way. Though she'd managed to connect with her via their cell phones and had been assured by Rachel that all was well, Lynn was more than slightly curious about why her daughter had been gone for nearly three hours. Surely, she'd done more than pick up extra copies of the paper during that time. Why did Lynn have a sneaking suspicion that Rachel had not only stopped for lunch but that she hadn't eaten alone?

As she watched the graceful young woman make her way down the driveway, Lynn couldn't help but smile. She sometimes wondered if Rachel had any idea how really beautiful she was. Perhaps not . . . and perhaps that was also a good thing. But men were attracted to her like bees to honey, as her father used to say.

"Hey, Mom," Rachel called out, pulling off her hat and

fanning herself with it as she climbed the steps. "Sorry I took so long."

"I assume you stopped for lunch."

"Tuna on rye, at the deli," she said, plopping down in a chair next to her mother. She dug in her oversized purse and pulled out the extra newspaper copies she'd managed to snag at the *Gazette*. "These are from Bailey. The newsstands were all out. We had to go to the office to get them."

"We?"

Rachel turned to her mother and opened her mouth as if to explain. Lynn saw the shift in her daughter's green eyes as Rachel rose to her feet. "I'll tell you all about it in a minute. I need some of that tea first."

She was back in moments with a happy Beasley at her side. He plunked down at her feet the minute Rachel took her seat.

"Actually," she said, "I ended up sharing lunch with Hayden—totally unplanned, of course. We ran into each other on the sidewalk while I was looking for papers. He'd gone into the office to catch up on some work this morning and was about to leave when he spotted me. He walked me to the *Gazette* office to get the papers and then asked me to join him for lunch." She paused and took a long swallow of the ice-cold liquid before setting the glass back down on the wrought iron table. "We went Dutch treat," she added, watching her mother.

Lynn nodded. "I see. At least, I think I do. You're setting some boundaries in your relationship."

Rachel nodded. "I didn't want to be presumptuous, but I honestly believed it was a safe assumption that Hayden wanted more than a casual friendship."

"And you don't?"

"I don't. So as kindly and firmly as possible, I explained that to him."

"Did he take it well?"

Rachel took another drink. "He seemed to." She sighed. "He's such a gentleman. Still, I hate things like that. It's one of the reasons I avoided dating in college."

"You can't avoid it forever, you know."

"I know. But there are some things you just recognize will never be, and I know I'm not going to pursue a relationship with Hayden, so it was best to get that up front now."

"I agree. I'm proud of you."

They sat quietly for a few moments, listening to Beasley snore and the distant sound of an angry crow.

"So what about you?" Rachel asked. "What did you do while I was gone?"

"Not much," Lynn admitted. "I did spot Jason prowling around a couple of times and thought about going out to talk with him, maybe even telling him what you and John are thinking about the old fence behind the church, but I decided against it. There just didn't seem to be much point."

"You're probably right. Especially because the chances of our convincing Pastor Brunswick, not to mention the church board, to tear down an entire fence on the very slim chance of locating a little over seven dollars are not very good."

"True. Unless, of course, we could offer a solution."

Rachel raised her eyebrows. "What do you mean? What sort of solution?"

Lynn smiled. "I may not have accomplished much while you were gone today, but I did do some serious thinking. And I just may have come up with a possibility that will convince the pastor and board members to at least consider tearing down that fence."

Rachel leaned forward, her eyes sparkling. "I'm all ears."

John had spent the afternoon shooting hoops over at the high school with some of the guys from the youth group. Hot, sweaty, and exhausted, he had finally begged off and headed for his car, determined to take a cool shower and get to bed early since he had no prospects for anything other than a quiet Saturday night alone. The teens had teased him about getting old, but he'd laughed it off and refused to take their bait and stay for another game. "Next time," he'd called out, climbing into the Taurus. "See you all in church tomorrow."

He'd scarcely walked in the door, still peeling off his T-shirt and heading for the shower, when his cell phone jingled. Should he answer it? He couldn't imagine it could be important or urgent enough to postpone his much-needed appointment with some soap and water. But then again, it could be the pastor wanting to talk to him about tomorrow's service.

With a sigh, he retrieved the phone from the spot where he'd just dropped it on the rickety wooden table next to the door, the one where he left everything he'd need on the way out. It seemed to be the only way he could keep from losing things in his messy little studio apartment.

He flipped open the phone, and his eyes widened when he saw Rachel's name on the screen. For once, he'd made the right decision about answering. He hit RECEIVE and pressed the phone to his ear.

"Hello?"

"Hi, John," came the reply in a voice that set his sweat glands to pumping harder than they'd done while he ran the basketball court. "It's me, Rachel. Are you busy?"

Busy? Too busy for you? Never happen. "Not really," he said, hoping he sounded at least somewhat casual. "Why? What's up?"

"My mom got an idea today, something to do with the fence at church. Would you have time to swing by so I can tell you about it? I think it just might work—or at least it'll give us a fighting chance."

"Really? No kidding? Sure, I can come by. Just give me a few minutes to run through the shower first. I've been playing basketball with the guys. I'll be over in about an hour, maybe sooner. Will that work?"

"Perfect. And bring your appetite. Mom said she's in the mood to cook."

John laughed. "And I'm in the mood to eat, so count me in. See you soon."

He disconnected and nearly had to slap his hand against his mouth to keep from letting out a cheer. So much for his quiet Saturday evening at home.

He broke into song before he ever hit the shower.

 Chapter 24

RACHEL TRIED TO COAX BEASLEY BACK INSIDE THE HOUSE AND glanced up just in time to see John's Taurus approaching. Her stomach flip-flopped, and she told herself it was excitement about telling him her mother's plan. Realistically, though, she knew it was more than that.

Beasley spotted John the minute he stepped out of the car and raced to greet him. Rachel smiled as she watched the two relate as if they spoke one another's language. John got along well with animals as well as people, a huge plus in Rachel's book. Come to think of it, Beasley had become much more attached to John than to Hayden. She pushed the thought away as irrelevant, but she continued to watch the man and the dog in the midst of their bonding.

"Hey," John said, finally breaking loose from the cocker spaniel and walking toward her. "How are you?" He grinned. "You made my day with your phone call, you know."

Rachel swallowed her smile and raised her eyebrows instead. "Really? Why is that?"

"Are you kidding me? It's Saturday night, and I expected to spend it at home alone, eating a TV dinner or something. And now here I am, welcomed by your dog, and looking forward to eating your mom's cooking. Plus your charming company, of course. It doesn't get much better than that."

Though Rachel managed to keep the smile from popping up, she couldn't stop the heat that rushed to her face. Her cover of being cool and disinterested had been blown. Might as well go with reality and let John know how excited she really felt.

"Thanks," she said, allowing her smile to surface. "I'm looking forward to it too. When Mom threw her idea at me earlier this afternoon, I knew I had to tell you about it right away."

"So tell me."

She shook her head. "Nope. The more I thought about it, the more I knew I had to let Mom do that. You'll understand then just how much she's supporting us in this."

"In our harebrained, farfetched idea, you mean?"

Rachel laughed. "Exactly." She turned toward the house. "Come on in. Mom's in the kitchen, cooking up a storm. She wouldn't even let me make the salad. She said she's missed cooking since Dad died and felt in the mood to make a nice dinner tonight."

"Sure am glad I get to reap the benefits of her cooking spree," John said, following her inside with Beasley at his heels.

A delicious blend of aromas, including garlic and cheese and chicken, greeted them as they stepped inside. Rachel's mouth watered, her lunch of tuna on rye long forgotten. No one made chicken casserole like her mom, though Rachel didn't think she'd tasted it since before she went off to college.

"John's here," she called out, leading her guest into the kitchen.

"So I see," Lynn answered, tossing them a quick glance before returning to chopping vegetables. "Welcome, John. Have a seat. Dinner will be ready soon. I just have to finish the salad and set the table."

"Are you sure I can't finish that salad for you?" Rachel asked.

Lynn shook her head. "Nope. I've got it covered. This dinner's on me."

Rachel and John exchanged smiles behind Lynn's back.

"Well, at least let us set the table," Rachel insisted. "That doesn't count as cooking."

Lynn laughed. "Okay, fine. You can set the table. We'll eat faster that way. And I have a fresh pitcher of sun tea in the fridge, unless you two would like something else."

"Sun tea is perfect," John said, taking the stack of dinner plates from Rachel and carrying them to the table.

In moments, they sat together at the table, offering a quick prayer of thanks and digging in. Rachel's taste buds operated at high alert from her first bite.

"Mom, this is fantastic. I'd forgotten how wonderful your chicken casserole was, but I think this is even better than ever."

"That's probably because you haven't had it in so long. But thank you. I'm glad you like it."

"Like it?" John beamed between bites. "I love it! This is amazing. You should open your own restaurant."

Lynn laughed and set her fork down. "Oh, now we're getting a little carried away here. Good, yes. Delicious, maybe. But my own restaurant? Not a chance."

"I don't know, Mom," Rachel said. "You told me Kathy Wilson said your flat apple pie was even better than Grandma's."

"I'm sure she said that for the same reason you said what you did about the casserole. It's been so long since Kathy's had that pie she's forgotten how really good it was."

"If you say so," Rachel said, pleased at the warm banter that permeated their meal. "But I'm with John. If you ever decide to open a restaurant, you've got my support."

"So, Mrs. Myers," John said, jumping in during the brief pause that followed Rachel's remark, "Rachel tells me you have an idea about the situation with the fence behind the church. I know I should have waited until you brought it up, but I have to tell you, I'm really anxious to hear what it is." He raised his eyebrows. "Is this a good time?"

Lynn smiled. "As good a time as any, I suppose. And it's really not that big a deal, just something that popped into my head as I thought about your dilemma in trying to convince Pastor Brunswick and the church board to tear down a perfectly good fence on the very slim chance that there might be seven dollars buried inside it."

"If you've got an idea that might help convince them," John said, "then it's a bigger deal than you think. Because right now I don't see it happening. You should have seen the pastor's face when Rachel and I told him about our hunch. Even though he eventually admitted that he too would love to see Last Chance's name cleared after all these years, he didn't respond too well to our suggestion of how that might happen."

"I can imagine," Lynn said. "Even if he were in favor of it, it would be a tough sell to the church board, whose responsibility is to use the congregation's money wisely. And that's what got me to thinking. The primary obstacle to getting an okay for this so-called harebrained scheme of yours is the cost. Now I don't have any extra money of my own; at least, I didn't until my brother died. But one of the things I discovered, in addition to inheriting this house and everything in it, is that Myron had a decent sum of cash set aside. The lawyer assures me that every penny of it is mine, to use as I see fit. And to be honest, it's more discretionary money than I've ever had in my entire life. So since I'm inheriting it from my brother, why not honor him by using a portion of it to try to solve the mystery surrounding Last Chance? It obviously meant a lot to Myron, and I think we should pursue it, if at all possible." She paused and shrugged. "Let's face it, we certainly haven't come up with any other ideas or leads. The fence possibility, as wild as it sounds, is all we've got."

Rachel watched John's eyes widen. "So you're saying you'd be willing to spend some of your inheritance to cover the cost of having the fence torn down?"

"Torn down and rebuilt," Lynn said.

John flicked a glance at Rachel, and the connection sent a lightning bolt of emotion from her toes up to her scalp. She knew she grinned like an idiot, but she couldn't stop herself.

"This is fantastic," John exclaimed, jumping up from his seat and leaning over to throw his arms around Lynn. "You are amazing. The absolute best!"

Lynn and Rachel laughed as John pulled away, his cheeks tinged pink as he realized what he'd done.

"Sorry. I didn't mean to overreact, but . . ." He shook his head. "But you really are the best, Mrs. Myers."

Lynn laughed again and shot a smile at her daughter. "You see? I've been trying to tell you that for years, and now you know it's true."

John resumed his seat, and the excited chatter continued while the still-warm casserole diminished.

Rachel thought she hadn't enjoyed an evening so much in a very long time.

"So you see," John said, his eyes fixed on the senior pastor leaning back in his chair behind the desk, "now you can take this to the board and let them know the cost won't come out of church funds."

Rachel sat beside John, across from Pastor Brunswick, holding her breath. The frown on the older man's forehead eased slightly, and she let her shoulders relax a bit. Was he convinced? Would he at least give it a try?

At last, he shifted his weight and tented his fingers in front of him, as if considering his options and preparing his response. When he finally spoke, he directed his words at Rachel. "What you and John are saying, then, is that your mother is willing to cover any cost involved in this venture out of her inheritance from your uncle, is that right?"

Rachel nodded. "Exactly."

He raised his eyebrows. "Aha. Well, that puts a slightly different twist on things, doesn't it?"

Rachel's heart rate elevated. This sounded promising.

"Tell you what," the pastor said, leaning forward before standing to his feet. "I'm due in the pulpit in fifteen minutes. The congregation is already gathered for the service and no doubt wondering why I'm not in my usual spot during worship. So I'm going to head out there right now and deliver my sermon as planned. I'll meet you back in here afterward and let you know what I think. We can talk more then. Agreed?"

Rachel felt her eyes widen and she turned to look at John.

He telegraphed his agreement with an almost indiscernible nod before answering. "Sure. We appreciate that, Pastor. We'll come back here after the service is over."

"Good," Pastor Brunswick said, picking up his Bible from the desk and heading for the door. As he reached for the handle, he turned back. "One more thing. Bring your mother with you. I think this is something we should all discuss together."

Rachel and John nodded in unison and watched the pastor exit his office.

"How do you think it went?" Rachel asked, turning toward John.

He shrugged. "I think it went well. At least I hope it did. Better than when we talked to him about it the first time."

"That's for sure," Rachel agreed, sighing as she stood up. "All right, then. Let's go find a seat. We sure don't want Pastor Brunswick looking out over the congregation and not seeing us sitting there."

John chuckled. "You can say that again."

He stood up and touched her elbow, steering her toward the door and out into the hall as the sounds of singing filled their ears.

✳

"I can't believe he agreed to it," Rachel said, glancing over at John in the driver's seat. She'd felt bad about letting her mom head home from church on her own, but then again, it was Lynn who encouraged her to accept John's invitation to lunch.

"Oh, go on," she'd said after they left the pastor's office and headed out into the noonday sun toward the parking lot. "I've got plenty of leftovers at home, and then I think I'll join Beasley for a quiet afternoon on the porch. I've got some reading I want to catch up on anyway. You two go out and have a nice time. Celebrate a little."

Rachel thought the celebrating was a bit premature, since all Pastor Brunswick had agreed to do was present the idea to the board. Even with Rachel's mother funding the project, there were no guarantees.

John smiled as he continued to steer his car down Main Street toward the little Italian place he'd convinced Rachel to try. "I can feel you watching me," he said. "And I have to agree with you. I can't believe he agreed to it either."

She laughed. "I'm just wondering what we've gotten ourselves into. Even if the board agrees to it—which is highly unlikely—what are they going to say if we don't find that money after all?"

John shrugged. "They'll probably say it was the most harebrained, farfetched idea they'd ever heard, and they'll never try anything like it again."

"You're probably right." She sighed. "But enough of that. There's nothing we can do or say until we find out what the board says at their meeting on Tuesday night."

"We can pray."

Rachel nodded. "Yes. We sure can. And I think we'd better. Meanwhile, where is this Italian place you told me about? My stomach is growling."

John chuckled. "You're going to love your lunch. I can't believe you haven't eaten there before. Then again, it's just a little hole in the wall, and it really hasn't been there that long. But everyone who's discovered it loves it."

"I'm sure I will too." She smiled. "So long as they smother everything in cheese, I know I will."

"Guaranteed," John said, turning into a crowded parking lot and aiming for the only available space. "And here we are."

"Just in the nick of time. I'm starved."

They exited the car and headed toward the entrance. As they walked, Rachel noticed that once again John had taken her elbow as they walked, gently steering her in the right direction. Though she knew where they were going and really didn't need his help to get there, she didn't pull away.

Chapter 25

LYNN UNLOCKED THE FRONT DOOR AND SMILED AT THE WARM greeting she received from her faithful dog. "You have no idea how glad I am to see you right now, Beasley," she said, bending down to ruffle the soft fur between his ears. "It's just you and me, old boy. Just you and me."

That seemed fine with Beasley, but Lynn wasn't so sure. Though she'd encouraged Rachel to go to lunch with John after church, she'd dreaded coming home to this big empty house alone.

There's something about Sundays, she thought as she rummaged in the refrigerator for leftovers. *They were my favorite days when Daniel was alive. Church together in the morning, then out for lunch or home for a cookout or a roast in the Crock-Pot.* She blinked back tears as her late husband's face swam in her memory. *Will I ever stop missing you, my love?* She sighed. *I imagine not, though everyone says it will get easier.*

She set the plate in the microwave and punched in the time before hitting START. While she waited for the triple-ding to signal her lunch was ready, she kicked off her shoes and poured herself a diet soda. Maybe one of these days she'd consume enough diet and sugarless drinks to offset what she ate and finally lose those extra pounds she'd been carrying around for years, though she sincerely doubted it. *I could if I really wanted to badly enough. Obviously I don't.*

By the time she grabbed some silverware and a napkin, the microwave sounded its alert. She used a potholder to carry the plate to the table and sat down next to the spot where Beasley had already settled in on the floor.

Listening to her beloved pet snore, she gazed down at the warmed casserole. It had looked so appetizing last night. Today it had lost its luster, but she thanked God for it anyway and scooped up a forkful. She was just about to shovel it into her mouth when the front door chimes sounded.

She frowned, as Beasley raised his head and let out a yip. "Now who do you suppose that is?" Lynn set her fork down, told Beasley to come with her, and headed for the door.

"Sorry to bother you, Mrs. Myers," Jason said as he slouched in front of the door, his body odor slightly less offensive today, "but I was planning to head into town this afternoon and I wondered if you needed anything."

His offer, combined with his unexpected appearance, left Lynn momentarily speechless. Why would Jason offer to pick up something for her in town when he didn't even have a car? The thought popped into her mind then that he had done exactly this sort of thing before she and Rachel arrived, stocking the kitchen with basic staples so they could get by until they had a chance to go shopping. She felt her cheeks flush at the realization that she hadn't even thanked him for his kind gesture or offered to reimburse him. Lynn knew from the provisions of the will that, in addition to a place to live, Myron had left his longtime groundskeeper a small monthly stipend, but it certainly wasn't enough for him to buy groceries for other people.

"I . . . why, no, I don't think I need anything, Jason," she said. "But thank you so much for asking. In fact, I just realized I never paid you for the food you bought for us before we came. If you'll wait a minute, I'll get my purse."

"No, ma'am," Jason said, shaking his head. "You don't need to do that. It was my way of saying thank-you to your brother for all he's done for me over the years. I don't need no pay for it—don't want it, as a matter of fact. But thanks for the offer."

Lynn waited, wondering what to say at this point. She ignored the prompting of her heart to invite Jason inside, and while she wrestled, he turned to leave.

"Well, I'd best be going," he said. "Didn't mean to bother you on a Sunday, but I thought you might need something."

As he approached the top step of the porch, Lynn followed him out the door. "Wait a minute," she called.

He turned back, a puzzled expression on his face.

"Have you had lunch? I just warmed up some casserole from last night, and I have plenty. Would you care to . . . to join me?"

The old man's eyebrows drew together, as if he couldn't believe he heard her right. "You . . . you want me to come inside and . . . have lunch with you? At your table?"

Lynn nodded. "Yes, please. I would like that very much. I should have invited you before this."

Jason stood his ground for a moment, and then Lynn saw

his shoulders relax. "Well, I suppose that would be all right. I like casserole."

"Good." Lynn stepped back and held the door open. "You go on into the kitchen and make yourself comfortable. I'll fix a plateful of those leftovers and stick it in the microwave, and we'll have you eating in no time."

Jason walked past her with Beasley following happily behind. Lynn thought this was probably one of the strangest invitations she'd ever extended to anyone, but somehow it felt right.

"Okay, so what do you think? Was that the best pizza you ever ate?"

Rachel restrained her smile, teasing John a bit with her eyes. "It was . . . okay," she said as they buckled themselves into the front seat of his car.

"Are you kidding me?" John's eyes registered something near incredulous. "It was perfect. Better than perfect." He leaned toward her. "And I didn't see you leaving any of it behind."

She laughed. "Busted! You're right. It was delicious, and I'd eat it again in a heartbeat. There. Is that better?"

"Much. I mean, seriously, we ordered a large and ate the whole thing. Did you really think I'd believe you thought it was just okay?"

She shrugged, enjoying the light, playful mood between them. "Probably not," she admitted. "But it was fun getting a rise out of you."

"Having fun at my expense. I see how it is." He sighed, long and slow. "Well, at least I know where I stand."

"Do you, now?"

"I believe I do, yes. But what can I say? It is what it is, right?"

Rachel laughed. "Whatever that means."

John's smile was warm, and his eyes lost their teasing gleam. "It means I just had a really great time with you," he said, his voice taking on a husky tone, "and not because of the pizza."

Rachel sensed the electricity in the air and couldn't decide whether she liked it or not. If she had an ounce of sense, she'd jump out of the car and run for her life. But at that particular moment, all good sense seemed to have abandoned her and left her welded in place.

"I did too," she said. "Had a great time, I mean. A really great time . . . pizza and all."

John reached across the seat and took her left hand in his. "I like being with you. I don't want it to end. Can we go somewhere, do something else?"

"Like what?"

He shrugged. "I don't know. Go for a ride, take a walk, go to the park . . ."

She grinned. "If we go to the park, will you push me on the swing?"

The surprise in his eyes quickly turned to delight. "Absolutely. But you have to push me back."

"Deal," she said, waiting for him to put the key in the ignition and get going. Instead he leaned even closer across the front seat, until she could smell the faint fragrance of spicy aftershave. Before she realized what was happening, she felt his lips on hers, and she closed her eyes, responding even as she told herself to pull away. Her heart raced as various snippets of thoughts tumbled through her mind. Would anyone see them? What would happen next? How could she now deny that she and John were more than friends and that they really were dating? And what would happen when she left Bloomfield?

No answers came to her, and when she and John finally separated and he started the car, she leaned her head back against the seat and hoped he'd kiss her again before the day ended.

 Chapter 26

LYNN KNEW SOMETHING WAS UP THE MINUTE RACHEL WALKED in the door late in the afternoon. Lynn watched her closely as she greeted Beasley and then crossed the kitchen floor to the refrigerator.

"Been thinking about that sun tea all the way home," she said, her back to Lynn as she poured the liquid into an ice-filled glass. "Sure am glad you had some made." She turned around, glass in hand. "Have you eaten yet?"

"If you mean supper, no. I did have a late lunch, though—leftovers from last night."

Rachel nodded. "I figured you would. John and I shared a pizza at that Italian place downtown. It was fantastic."

Lynn wondered how much of "fantastic" had to do with the pizza and how much with the company, but she smiled and swallowed her comment.

"John wanted me to stay for the evening service tonight," Rachel went on after taking another swig of tea, "but I didn't feel right leaving you here alone all day. If you'd like to go, though, we can still make it."

The twinkle in Rachel's eyes told Lynn her daughter would very much like to go back to church, and Lynn saw no reason not to do so. "Why not? Sure, I can change clothes and be ready in plenty of time."

Rachel's smile nearly split her face. "Great! I'll run upstairs and take a quick shower and change. Thanks."

Lynn nodded. "Should I heat up some of that casserole for you before we go? There's still some left."

"Some?" Rachel smiled. "If I remember right, there should be a lot left, even with what we ate last night. And I know you. You might have had a plate of it for lunch, but not much."

Lynn hesitated. Should she tell Rachel about Jason's visit?

"Actually, I had help with those leftovers," she said, watching her daughter carefully as she spoke. "Jason stopped by just as I was about to eat, so I . . . I invited him to join me."

Rachel's green eyes widened, and she set her glass down on the counter. "Seriously? You invited Jason for lunch? And he accepted?"

"Yes," Lynn said, "and yes. I invited, and he accepted, and though it was a bit awkward at first, we actually had a nice visit while we ate."

"Mom, you never cease to amaze me." Rachel shook her head. "If I'd had to guess who joined you for lunch, Jason would probably have been at the bottom of my possibility list."

"Well, it's not like I planned it," Lynn admitted. "In fact, I never would have thought of it on my own. It's just that he showed up at the door right when I got my plate of food out of the microwave. He said he was going to the store and wondered if we needed anything. That's when it hit me that he probably used his own meager income to supply our cupboards before we arrived, and it never even occurred to me that I should have offered to reimburse him. To be honest, I felt so bad about it that the next thing I knew I had invited him in for lunch. I'm sure he was at least as surprised as I was, but it all worked out okay."

"Amazing," Rachel said, snagging her glass and polishing off its contents. "But I'm glad to hear it. I always thought Jason was harmless—a little strange, yes, but definitely harmless. Otherwise, Uncle Myron wouldn't have had him around all those years."

Lynn nodded. Her daughter's words made perfect sense.

"Well," Rachel said, placing her empty glass in the sink, "I'm going to run upstairs for that shower now. I'll be down in a few."

"So what about those leftovers? Should I heat a plate for you before we leave?"

Rachel glanced at her watch before answering. "I don't think so. I don't want to risk being late. I'll just wait and grab something when we get home. Besides, I'm still full of pizza."

As Lynn watched her grown child depart the kitchen, she marveled.

Something's going on. She's awfully anxious to get back to church on time, and I doubt that it's just because she wants to be sure and get a good seat for tonight's service.

She smiled. It wasn't that she doubted her daughter's spirituality, but it was obvious the attractive youth pastor who had been her companion throughout the day was also the main attraction for the evening. Something was developing there, and Lynn wasn't in the least displeased about it.

The sanctuary was only about half as full for the evening service as it had been that morning, but Lynn was glad she'd decided to come. And, of course, she didn't even have to ask how Rachel felt about it. She'd been entirely captivated throughout the worship and teaching, her eyes straying only occasionally from the stage to the left side of the front row where John sat. No doubt both Rachel and John would have preferred sitting together, but Lynn knew that for the most part, the church staff tended to sit up front where they were more visible and easily located. Lynn thought it would be interesting to see what developed after they were dismissed.

"Mom," Rachel whispered, laying her hand on Lynn's arm as they rose to their feet for the final song, "do you mind holding on a little while before we go home? I need to talk to John a minute."

A minute? No doubt more than that. She smiled. "Not a problem, honey. Take as long as you need."

Rachel's relieved expression was her only answer.

In moments, the congregation began to file out of their seats and make their way down the aisles toward the back door. Lynn watched Rachel as she did her best to go against the flow toward the front of the room. Halfway there, John met her with a smile, and Lynn watched them step aside from the crowd and gaze into one another's eyes as they talked. It had been years—decades, actually—since Lynn and Daniel had been that young, but she could still remember the early days of basking in the glow of their budding relationship. Of course, in her opinion, that relationship had grown stronger and more binding over the years, but she couldn't deny that special feeling that accompanied its exciting beginnings.

As the crowd narrowed down, John and Rachel made their way toward Lynn, side by side. "Mom," Rachel said, "John would like to take us both out for a quick bite to eat. What do you think?"

Lynn raised her eyebrows. Both of them? She knew John was being kind, but she imagined he would much rather take Rachel alone, without her mother as a chaperone.

"You two go on," she said, waving them off. "Really. I'm a bit tired and would rather go on home. Besides," she added, directing her final comments toward John, "Rachel hasn't eaten tonight, and I know she's hungry. You two go grab something, and I'll head back."

"Oh, no, Mrs. Myers," John insisted, "we want you to come with us. Really, we do."

"It's true, Mom," Rachel added. "The three of us can go together. We won't be long—just something quick—and then you and I can go home. Please, Mom, come with us."

Lynn hesitated. Both of them seemed sincere in their invitation, and she had to admit she was hungry. "All right. You talked me into it, but just something quick and easy."

"Quick and easy it is," John said, offering her his hand to help her up and then tucking it inside his arm as they started down the aisle with Rachel on Lynn's other side. "In Bloomfield, that could mean any one of a half-dozen places. Rachel and I did pizza for lunch, and we could do it again if you'd like. Or there's the deli or the barbecue place or Burger Heaven. Your choice, Mrs. Myers."

"Burger Heaven sounds good to me," Lynn said, "though probably not the healthiest choice. Still, I have to admit I've been dreaming about a cheeseburger lately."

John laughed. "Burger Heaven it is. I have cheeseburger dreams a lot, so it works for me."

As the three of them exited the building and headed for the parking lot, Lynn risked a glance at Rachel. The look of joy and anticipation on her daughter's face warmed Lynn's heart, and she smiled as she wondered just what God might be up to in this situation.

By the time Lynn and Rachel arrived at home, Lynn could hardly keep her eyes open. It didn't help that her stomach felt stretched to the limits, but the burger had been delicious and worth every calorie.

She patted Beasley absentmindedly and plunked down in a chair at the table, kicking off her shoes. "I'm beat," she said, watching Rachel fill the kettle and put it on the stove. "And absolutely stuffed besides. Don't tell me you're going to have tea now. I'm too full to even think about it."

Rachel laughed. "Mom, how much room does tea take?"

"More than I've got. I can't fit one more thing into my stomach tonight, not even tea." She shook her head. "I know I've said this before, but I don't know how you do it."

Rachel grabbed a mug and dropped her favorite White Chocolate Obsession tea bag inside. "Tea isn't filling," she said as she turned to the cupboard and pulled the last of the leftover flat apple pie from the refrigerator, "but pie is. I'll have a hard time getting this down, but I'll make it."

Lynn laughed. "You really are amazing. You've always had a healthy appetite, to say the least. Thankfully, you have an active metabolism to go with it."

"If I didn't, I'd be in major trouble, wouldn't I?"

"Count on it," Lynn said.

"So what did you think?" Rachel asked, pouring water into her mug before carrying her snack to the table. "About John, I mean. Do you like him?"

Lynn raised her eyebrows. "What's not to like? He's a great guy. Funny, caring, intelligent, honest, great personality—not to mention handsome." She smiled. "Or maybe you hadn't noticed that."

Rachel's cheeks flushed as she held a forkful of pie suspended midway between her plate and her mouth. "Oh, I noticed."

"I'm sure you did. And it's obvious he's noticed you."

Rachel set the fork down and her eyes grew serious. "He has, hasn't he? There's a connection between us, that's for sure. Do you think I'm making a big mistake by seeing him like I am? I mean, we're going to be leaving Bloomfield soon, and then what?"

"No doubt John has thought of that too. I don't have an easy answer for you, honey, but then again, it's not like we're leaving to fly halfway around the world. We won't be that far away, and if something is to come of this relationship between the two of you, I'm sure God will guide you in how to work it out."

Rachel grinned. "I was hoping you'd say that because . . . well, I really like being with him. We just seem to . . . click. You know what I mean, Mom? Like we have the same goals and values."

Lynn nodded. "I'm sure you do. And no doubt, whether it's John or someone else, that's the type of man God has in mind for you one day. If that man turns out to be John, you'll certainly get no arguments from me."

"Even if it means I might have to move here to Bloomfield permanently?"

The question brought a jolt to Lynn's thinking process, but she held her reaction in check. She knew she mustn't let her aversion to change affect her thoughts or feelings about her daughter's future. "Even if it means a move back here to Bloomfield," she said, reaching out to cover Rachel's hand with her own.

Rachel smiled and then leaned in to plant a kiss on Lynn's cheek. "You're the best, Mom. The absolute best."

"Glad you think so," Lynn said, returning the smile.

# Chapter 27

RACHEL WAS UP EARLY MONDAY MORNING, SLIPPING OUT OF BED ahead of her mother for a change. As soon as she'd made some coffee, she poured herself a cup and sat down on the front porch to enjoy the morning sunshine. Beasley lay happily at her feet, his golden fur warmed by the early rays.

"Didn't expect to see anyone out here already," came a gruff voice, startling both Rachel and her dog. Beasley raised his head and identified the intruder, then hurried to his side for a greeting. Rachel stayed where she was, coffee cup clutched between her hands as she watched Jason approach the porch.

"You're right," she said. "I don't usually get up nearly this early. Can't imagine what got into me today."

"Morning's the best time of day," Jason said, stopping at the bottom of the stairs. "Full of possibilities and promises . . . if you don't waste 'em, that is."

Rachel smiled. "True. Absolutely true. Why don't you come on up and join me? I'll get you a cup of coffee."

"Oh, I don't want to be a bother. You just sit there and don't mind me."

Rachel set her cup down and rose from the chair. "It's no bother at all," she insisted. "How do you take your coffee?"

Jason frowned as if her question made no sense. "Black. Don't understand anybody drinking it any other way. What's the point? It's coffee, after all."

Rachel nodded and turned toward the kitchen, glad she hadn't added anything to her own coffee that morning. No telling what Jason might think of her if she had. She nearly had to swallow a giggle at the thought. Why did she care what Jason thought of her or how she drank her coffee? She sure hoped her mother's peer pressure issues hadn't rubbed off on her.

By the time she'd returned to the porch with a mug of steaming coffee, Jason had settled into one of the rockers, and Beasley had moved from his former spot next to Rachel's feet to the one beside Jason.

Fickle dog, Rachel thought, once again wrestling with a smile.

The familiar sound of one of their resident crows pierced the quiet as Rachel sat back down and retrieved her drink. The peaceful setting was growing on her, and she found her resistance to leaving increasing by the day.

How much of that has to do with Bloomfield itself, she wondered, *and how much with John Currey?* She wasn't even sure she could answer the question honestly.

"So, Jason," she said, "I understand you and Mom had lunch together yesterday."

The old man scowled. "I was just heading for town and stopped by to see if your mother needed anything, that's all," he said, a defensive note in his voice. "Wasn't my idea to come inside and eat."

"Oh, I'm sorry," Rachel said, leaning toward him as she spoke. "I didn't mean to imply that it was. Mom explained that you dropped by and made such a nice offer and how she then invited you in for lunch. I'm really glad she did. We should have had you over sooner."

"Humph." The old man seemed somewhat placated as he returned to his coffee, and Rachel found herself admiring her mother even more for having made it through an entire meal with a man who was obviously not much of a conversationalist. She'd just about resigned herself to sit in silence when he growled out a question.

"Learn anything about Last Chance yet?"

Rachel turned toward him, but he continued to stare out into the yard. How much should she tell him? Not that there really was anything to tell, as it was still all speculation. And if the church board met the next night and didn't approve moving ahead on their idea, there was no reason to mention it to anyone.

"Nothing yet," she said. "But I did go with John the other day to meet Last Chance's sister, Miss Pearl. We had a very nice visit."

"That's because she's a nice lady. The whole Justice family—nice, honest people." He shook his head. "That's why it just don't make sense that Last Chance would've taken that money. Nope, I don't believe he did. But what happened to it is still a mystery after all these years. Meant a lot to your uncle to solve it, but he died before he could."

Rachel wanted to assure Jason that she and John and her mother were doing their best to finish what her uncle had started, but she knew that would only precipitate questions she couldn't answer, at least not yet. "It sure seems that way, doesn't it? I can't imagine he took that money either, and I know you're right that Uncle Myron wanted to clear Last Chance's name."

"It would mean a lot to Miss Pearl," he said, setting his now-empty mug on the table between them. "She's the only Justice left in Bloomfield, and she was the closest to her brother. No wonder she don't want to talk about it." He rose to his feet. "Yep, it would mean everything to that fine woman to see her brother's name cleared after all these years. Well, gotta go work in my garden."

He headed to the steps after giving a final pat to Beasley. "Have a nice day," he said, and he headed for the cemetery.

Monday passed quietly, with Rachel and John limiting their communication to a couple of quick phone calls as they encouraged one another about Tuesday's board meeting. Though Monday was normally John's day off, he'd committed to spending most of it with some of the guys from his youth group, so Rachel ended up hanging out at home with her mom.

During their brief phone conversations that day, John assured her they had a much better chance of getting the board's approval now that Rachel's mother had offered to cover the expenses with some of her inheritance. Still, the decision was no slam-dunk, as Rachel well knew. Beyond the cost of such a project was the stir it would create around town. What in the world would the people of Bloomfield think of tearing down a perfectly good fence on the slim chance that a missing seven dollars and fourteen cents might be found inside? Rachel prayed the board would agree that exonerating one of its own would make the venture worthwhile.

By Tuesday, her stomach was in knots, and she was amazed that the situation had become so important to her.

"I'm heading over to the church," she announced to Lynn as they sat together over lunch. "I just can't sit here and wait all day until the meeting tonight. Do you need the car for anything? I can always walk or ask John to pick me up."

Lynn shook her head. "I'm not going anywhere. In fact, Chuck's supposed to stop by later this afternoon with a couple of final papers for me to sign, so I need to stay here anyway. You go ahead and take the car."

"Thanks, Mom." Rachel frowned. "So . . . final papers? Does that mean everything with Uncle Myron's estate is about settled?"

Lynn nodded. "It looks that way. We can probably head home by the end of the week, Saturday at the latest."

Rachel felt her heart plummet. Leave Bloomfield? That soon? She'd known it was coming, of course, but she'd hoped they could put it off a little longer.

"Okay," she said, deciding not to comment on their leaving. "Guess I'll run upstairs and change before heading over to the church. I don't think John will mind if I hang out in his office for a while."

Her mother's eyes twinkled as she smiled. "I don't think he'll mind at all. Give him my best, will you?"

Rachel smiled. "I will." She stood up to leave but turned back at the door. "You like John, don't you?"

Lynn's smile remained. "Very much. In fact, I think we had this conversation a couple of evenings ago, didn't we?"

Rachel felt her cheeks flame, and she nodded. "You're right. Well, I'm going to go get ready."

Lynn nodded, and Rachel hurried from the room and took the stairs to the bedroom two at a time.

John looked up from the pile of work on his desk as Rachel stepped into the doorway. "Hey," she said, offering a smile. "Hope you don't mind that I dropped by."

"Are you kidding me?" John nearly jumped out of his seat. "I'm having a terrible time concentrating today. All I can think about is that board meeting tonight. Did you come to keep me company?"

Rachel nodded. "Sure did. I figured it would be easier to wait together." She glanced at his paper-strewn desk. "But I don't want to keep you from your work, and it looks like you have plenty of it."

John laughed and pulled up a chair beside his, motioning for her to join him. "I do," he said, helping her settle in before resuming his own seat. "But if you're in the mood to help, I have things you can do."

"Seriously? That would be great. I've been feeling at loose ends since I got out of school. I'm not used to doing nothing. Bring it on!"

Laughing again, John moved a pile of papers in her direction. "These are the applications for all the kids who want to attend the back-to-school weekend retreat at the end of August. I need to go through them and make sure everything is filled out right—you know, nothing missing or illegible or anything— so there aren't any snags when we get ready to board the bus.

Seems there's always some last-minute thing that causes us to have to track down someone's parents for a signature or something. Here, let me show you what needs to be there."

John leaned close, and the now familiar scent of his aftershave started a faint buzzing in Rachel's ears. She shook her head slightly, hoping to dislodge it, but the buzzing seemed to run hand-in-hand with her upgraded heartbeat. Squinting her eyes, she determined to pay attention to his instructions. She didn't want him thinking she was an airhead or anything.

"Hey, there," came a familiar voice from the doorway. "How are you two doing?"

Rachel and John lifted their heads simultaneously, and Rachel couldn't help but wonder if they looked like a couple of mischievous kids who'd been caught with their hands in the proverbial cookie jar, though she knew there was no reason to feel that way.

Pastor Brunswick smiled down at them, apparently waiting for a response.

"We, uh, we're fine," John said, his face flushed. "I was just . . . showing Rachel how to check these apps for the weekend retreat. You know, to make sure they're done right and all."

The pastor grinned. "Good. Glad to see you're sharing the workload. That means I'm getting two for the price of one here." He paused and then added, "I imagine you two are anxiously awaiting the outcome of tonight's board meeting."

"Absolutely," John said. "What do you think, Pastor? Will the board agree?"

The older man shrugged. "I have no idea. I've tried to call this sort of thing before and usually end up on the wrong side of the decision. We'll just have to pray and wait. We're all good at that, aren't we?"

"That's for sure," John said as Rachel nodded her agreement.

"I'll check in with you later," the pastor said, and he turned to head down the hall. "Have a nice afternoon."

Rachel and John exchanged glances. "That was interesting," Rachel said.

"Exactly. Well, let's get to work. Maybe it'll help us keep our mind off the meeting."

"Maybe," Rachel said, though she seriously doubted it. She picked up the stack of papers and willed herself to concentrate, all the while wondering why the outcome of tonight's board meeting mattered so much. But there was no denying that it did.

 Chapter 28

THE DOOR STOOD PARTIALLY OPEN, AND LYNN RECOGNIZED the voices coming from inside. She rapped on the frame and pushed on the door until she could see the room's occupants.

"Mom," Rachel said, rising from her chair. "I didn't expect to see you here tonight."

"I hadn't planned to be," Lynn admitted. "May I join you?"

"Absolutely," John declared, standing up and coming around to the front of his desk where he scrambled to open a folding chair that had been leaning against the wall. "I'll sit here. You take my chair behind the desk. It's a lot more comfortable—well, a little more, anyway."

Lynn smiled her thanks and moved to the spot behind the desk, next to Rachel. So this is where the two of them had spent the last few hours.

"Wait a minute," Rachel said. "I've got the car. How did you get here?"

"Chuck dropped me off after our meeting." She glanced at John. "Myron's lawyer."

John nodded. "Sure. Chuck Harrison. Good guy. Lives over at the retirement home and has a real thing for Libby Birdwell. I heard he even took up golf just so he could spend more time with her."

Lynn smiled. "Really? Interesting. There aren't many secrets here in Bloomfield, are there?"

"That's for sure," John answered. "The only secret right now is what the board is deciding about that fence out back, not to mention a man's reputation."

"So you haven't heard anything."

Rachel shook her head. "Nothing. We've been waiting all afternoon. Didn't even go out to eat. John just picked up a couple of sandwiches and we ate them here." She frowned. "Oh, we should have gotten one for you. Have you eaten?"

"Not since lunch, but I'm not hungry anyway. I couldn't get the board meeting off my mind after you left. After Chuck and I finished our business and got everything signed, sealed, and delivered, I decided to ask him to drop me off here on his way home. It never even occurred to me to get something to eat first."

"I'll be glad to run out and get you something," John offered.

Lynn shook her head. "I'm fine, really. I'm not even sure I could eat anyway, at least not until we hear what the board decides. Did Pastor Brunswick give you any indication of how he thought it would turn out?"

"None," John admitted. "He said he couldn't call it."

Lynn sighed. "Then I guess we just wait—assuming you don't mind if I wait with you."

"Of course not," Rachel said. "We're glad you're here. This way, we can all get the verdict at the same time. Meanwhile, how did your meeting with the lawyer go? Sounds like things are all settled."

"They are. In fact, he said we can head back home anytime we want to. If anything else comes up, we can easily settle it from there, though it looks like everything's pretty straightforward at this point."

Rachel's smile faded, and the light in her eyes dimmed. "That's . . . good," she said, her smile thin.

Lynn watched as her daughter darted a glance toward John, who gazed back at her. When their eyes met, Rachel dropped hers. It was obviously going to be a hard sell on Lynn's part to convince her daughter to leave Bloomfield anytime soon—or at least to do so cheerfully.

Voices in the hallway caught their attention, and all three turned toward the open door. When a couple of board members passed by, Lynn knew the meeting had adjourned. In moments, Pastor Brunswick's stocky build filled the door. He looked tired.

"Well," he said, his face lighting up as his eyes landed on Lynn, "it seems every time I come by this office there's one more person waiting inside."

Lynn smiled. "Hello, Pastor. I thought I'd come down so we could all wait together. Am I right to assume you have news for us?"

"I do," he said, stepping inside and closing the door behind him. "Whether or not it's good news will no doubt depend on the outcome of the project, but at least the board has approved us to move ahead. And Lynn, I don't mind telling you, it would never have happened if you hadn't offered to cover the cost. But since you did, we finally squeaked out an approval—by one vote, mind you—simply because the yea voters thought it important to exhaust every possibility to find that missing money and clear Last Chance Justice's name."

Lynn felt her heart swell with joy, and she had to restrain herself from jumping out of her seat and throwing her arms around the pastor. The very thought that she even considered doing so brought a stab of guilt to her heart. Had she even noticed Martin Brunswick's attractive looks before this moment? And why in the world would that thought enter her mind?

Embarrassed, she shook off her thoughts and turned her attention toward Rachel, whose beaming face said it all. Not only was her daughter excited about the possibility of solving this decades-old mystery, but there was no way Lynn could drag her out of Bloomfield until the drama of tearing down and searching through the fence had been accomplished.

It appeared that Lynn and Rachel would stay in town longer than planned. And for whatever reasons, Lynn found herself nearly as pleased about that fact as she knew her daughter would be.

John had scarcely constrained an ear-splitting whoop when Pastor Brunswick delivered the news. He'd settled instead for a quick hug from both Myers women and a hearty handclasp and pat on the back with his senior pastor. Once the initial excitement had abated and the three of them were alone in the office again, John had suggested they go out to celebrate, and now the three of them sat at the deli, sipping decaf and pigging out on lemon cream pie, the house specialty.

"Can you believe it?" Rachel asked between bites. "They actually said *yes*."

John tried not to stare at her while he ate, but he knew he was losing the battle. He loved her animation when she talked, and the excitement and energy in her words and expressions. If he didn't get ahold of his heart soon, he knew he was in big trouble. Maybe he already was.

"So when do you suppose the actual demolition work will start?" Lynn asked, consuming her dessert with only slightly less enthusiasm than her daughter. "Pastor didn't actually say, did he?"

John shook his head. "No, but I got the impression it would be as soon as possible, especially since the board doesn't have to worry where the funds are coming from." He frowned as a possible glitch occurred to him. "That won't be a problem, will it, Mrs. Myers? I mean, you said the estate was pretty much settled, but I know sometimes it can take time for the money to actually be available."

"No, it won't be a problem. In fact, I asked Chuck about that when I saw him this afternoon, just in case things turned out like this. He said it could be available almost immediately—within days, if necessary."

Rachel smiled. "That's a relief. You know, I still can't take all this in. I mean, think about it. A few weeks ago, I was still in school, thinking I'd be working part-time this summer while I figured out what to do after that. The next thing I know, my job falls through and I'm on my way home. Then we get the news that Uncle Myron died, and now we're in Bloomfield, getting ready to tear down a fence to try and exonerate a man we never met—a man with the weirdest name ever. Last Chance Justice." She shook her head. "The weirdest thing is that we care so much about the outcome. I mean, none of us even knew the guy, but this is really important . . . to all of us."

John caught her eyes as she took him in with her sweeping glance, and he realized how very glad he was that both Rachel and Lynn cared enough about Myron Cofield's last wishes to not only donate the money to see them fulfilled but to stick around while they attempted to make it happen. John couldn't help but hope it took a good long while, too, because the last thing he wanted was to watch Rachel and her mother climb into their Toyota Corolla and roll out of town. They hadn't been here long, but he knew Bloomfield would never be the same if they left.

And neither would he.

Construction—or rather, destruction—on the fence began bright and early Thursday morning, with the demolition company agreeing to wait until the following week for Lynn to make the initial payment. She would give half down on Monday, and complete payment when the job was done. Of course, the same team that tore the fence down would then proceed to build it up again, as the board had insisted that be part of the agreement. The fence had been a part of the church property for decades, and no one was willing to do without it.

Lynn had come to the church with Rachel that morning to watch the beginning of the project, but as soon as she spotted her daughter and John connect, she saw her ideal time to leave.

"I'm going to head on back," she told them, raising her voice to be heard over the noise. "You don't mind bringing Rachel home later, do you, John?"

The youth pastor's eyes lit up. "Not at all, Mrs. Myers. Glad to do it."

Glad, indeed, Lynn thought, bidding them goodbye and heading toward her car. *Something tells me they'll get along just fine without me.*

She smiled as she climbed into the car and started the engine. She felt so good about things that she thought she might stop by the grocery store and pick up something special for dinner—maybe even call the church and tell Rachel to bring John home for a good meal that evening.

Pulling up in front of the market, she grabbed her purse and headed inside. It was a bit warm for a roast, but Myron's house did have an old air-conditioning unit, so why not break down and use it? So long as it kept the kitchen bearable, that's all that mattered.

She stood at the meat counter, comparing prices and weights as she considered the type of roast to buy, when she heard a familiar voice beside her.

"Why, Lynn, I thought that was you. Shopping for something special?"

Lynn turned and found herself nearly nose to nose with Kathy Wilson, whom she hadn't seen since the garden club luncheon. Lynn smiled. "As a matter of fact, I am. I was just in the mood to cook something really nice this evening, and what can be nicer than a good roast? I just love the way it makes the house smell, don't you?"

Kathy grinned and nodded. "Do I ever! Now that you mention it, I think I might want to fix one too. Frank loves my roast, and if I call Stan, maybe he'll bring Amber and come over as well." She leaned closer and nearly whispered, "Amber is Stan's fiancée, you know. It took them forever to figure out they belonged together. I even had to enlist the help of the garden club to get things moving between them. Remind me to tell you that story one of these days. It all ties in with the story about Gnorman."

Lynn raised her eyebrows and nodded. The garden club helped bring Kathy's son, Stan, and his fiancée together? Just how small and intertwined was this town? Could anyone ever escape peer pressure in such a claustrophobic setting? Is this part of the reason she'd been willing to risk such a big change years earlier when she'd left Bloomfield behind to marry Daniel? The biggest reason, of course, was that she loved him, but . . .

Her train of thought led her straight to John and Rachel, and she wondered at the irony of her daughter's relationship possibly being the catalyst to bring them back to the town she'd left behind so many years before. But why would she think that way? Even if Rachel ended up in Bloomfield, that didn't mean Lynn had to come back too . . . did it?

"Lynn, did you hear what I said?"

Lynn blinked. She'd forgotten all about Kathy. "I'm sorry. I didn't get that last part."

Kathy smiled. "I said to remind me sometime to tell you the story of how the garden club helped me get Stan and Amber together at last. I was beginning to think I'd never have a daughter-in-law, let alone grandkids."

"Sounds . . . fascinating," Lynn said, amazed that Kathy considered the garden club's meddling a good thing. Lynn had never thought of it that way before, even when she was a child and heard her mother talk about the club members as if they were family.

"Mom loved the garden club," Lynn said, wanting to steer away from the topic of the club members' meddling. "She really did."

Kathy nodded. "Of course she did. Who wouldn't? And she was a beloved member. Well, let's grab those roasts and get them home so we can start cooking, shall we?" She giggled. "Maybe we can get together one day soon and compare notes."

Lynn wasn't so sure she liked the idea or that she'd be around Bloomfield long enough to see it happen, but she went ahead and snagged a large package of meat and stuck it in her basket. Then she said goodbye to Kathy Wilson, who had left her with some new thoughts to occupy her mind as she headed back home.

# Chapter 29

WHEN JOHN DROPPED RACHEL OFF AT HOME AFTER A QUICK lunch at the deli, the young woman's eyes nearly danced with excitement. Lynn couldn't help but smile at the joy she saw reflected in her daughter's face.

"I didn't expect you back until this evening," she said. "Don't tell me you got tired of hanging around the church and watching the fence being torn down."

Rachel laughed. "Not at all. But John had meetings scheduled all afternoon, so I figured I might as well come on home. He promised to call me if anything turned up."

"Anything like a handkerchief full of money?"

"Exactly. Wouldn't it be great if they found it right away and didn't have to demolish the entire fence?"

Lynn nodded. "Yes, it would." She hesitated. "Of course, you need to keep in mind that they may very well tear down the entire thing and find nothing."

Rachel sat down at the kitchen table and picked up the glass of tea Lynn had fixed for her. "I know. I keep praying that won't be the case, but I know it could happen."

Lynn joined her daughter, pulling a chair close enough that she could lay her hand on Rachel's arm. "I've been thinking about this a lot too. The situation with Last Chance Justice matters to us because it mattered to your uncle. But it's more than that. It's almost as if God Himself put a desire in our hearts to see it through."

"I think you're right. But if that's the case, wouldn't we be assured of the money turning up?"

"You'd think so, wouldn't you? But that's human logic. And if there's one thing I've learned in my fifty-plus years of life, it's that human logic must always take a backseat to God's wisdom and purposes. So long as we know we're doing what He wants us to do regarding this money and fence issue, then the results are up to Him, not us."

Rachel set her glass down and focused on her mother. "You are so right on, Mom. I really needed to hear that to keep it all in perspective. Thank you."

Lynn smiled, her heart warmed by such a sincere compliment from her only child. "Well, I imagine it's safe to assume you already had lunch."

"Absolutely. John and I stopped on the way here."

"Why am I not surprised? You two seem to be hitting it off exceptionally well."

A hint of pink crept into Rachel's cheeks. "We are," she admitted. "So much so that it almost scares me sometimes."

Lynn raised her eyebrows. "So does that mean you've completely eliminated Hayden from the running?"

"He was never really in it. I like him—a lot. He's a great guy, and easy on the eyes too." She smiled. "But I never sensed the attraction to him that I have with John."

"And that attraction is a lot more than just John's good looks, isn't it?"

"Definitely. We share the same goals and passions. He's in full-time ministry, and that's what I want to do, too. He enjoys working with the elderly and with young people, just like I do." She paused and shook her head. "It's almost like God designed us to be on the same page."

"Which doesn't surprise me in the least. It's true that sometimes opposites attract, and your dad and I were perfect examples of that. But other times you discover God has planned for you to spend your life with someone who thinks and acts so closely to you that you can hardly believe it." She patted her daughter's arm. "Now don't get me wrong. I'm not trying to run ahead of God here and suggest that John is the man God has chosen to be your husband; only He knows that. But I will say I have considered the possibility."

"And what if he is?" Rachel leaned closer. "Mom, what if John really is the one for me? What will happen when we leave Bloomfield?"

Lynn chuckled. "Oh, honey, I'm sorry. I don't mean to laugh at your question, but do you really think God isn't big enough to bridge that gap? For heaven's sake, I left Bloomfield to be with your father, and no one knows better than you how much I dread change. So agreeing to marry him and move away was no light decision on my part. But I never regretted it, not for a moment."

"So . . . if John and I ever decide that God means for us to be together, you'd be okay with my moving back here to be with him?"

"Okay with it? Rachel, I'd be all for it." She grinned. "It would be a bit ironic, though, don't you think? I left Bloomfield for love, and you might return for that same reason."

"Love." Rachel spoke the word with softness, as the corners of her lips turned upward. "I have to be honest, Mom. While I was in college, I sometimes thought I'd never know what that word meant, at least so far as a husband-wife relationship goes. I resisted dating because it reminded me of trying on shoes in hopes of finding the right pair. Deep down, I think I was afraid I'd never find the perfect fit."

They both laughed then. "Oh, Rachel," Lynn said, shaking her head, "your honesty is so refreshing. Since you were a little girl, you've spoken your mind, and I love that about you. I guess we'll just have to wait and see how this situation with John plays out, won't we? But whatever happens, we'll know God's plans for your life are good, just as He promises in the Bible."

Rachel nodded. "I believe that, Mom. I really do. One hundred percent."

The call came midmorning on Friday. Rachel flipped her phone open and clicked the RECEIVE button the moment she saw John's name.

"Rachel," he said, a bit breathlessly, "I'm in my car and heading to your place. Can you be ready in five minutes?"

"Five minutes? Are you kidding me?" Rachel looked down at her tank top and shorts, glad she'd at least had the good sense to take a shower and wash her hair already.

"I'm not kidding at all. They've found something in the

fence, and you need to be here when they announce what it is. Your mom too."

Rachel's eyes widened. "Mom too? I . . . guess so. I mean, she's up and dressed and all, but—"

"Then be ready, both of you. I'm just a couple minutes away from Cemetery Drive."

Rachel disconnected her phone and scurried up the stairs to the bedroom, knowing her mother had been in there folding clothes just moments earlier.

"Mom?" she called, pushing the door open. "Mom, guess what?"

Beasley lay on the bench at the end of the bed, snoozing. At the sound of Rachel's voice, he raised his head, spotted Rachel, and then lay back down. Lynn, on the other hand, held a towel in front of her, a surprised look on her face as she stood facing her daughter. "What is it? Is everything all right?"

"I don't know," Rachel answered. "John didn't give me any details, but he's on his way over here now to pick us up." She paused for effect. "Mom, they found something in the fence."

Lynn laid the towel back in the laundry basket on the bed in front of her. "What was it?"

"He didn't say, but . . . what else could it be but the money? Mom, grab your things. We have to go."

"Go? Where? To the church?"

"Of course. Where else? John will be here any minute."

"Any minute?"

"Mom, stop echoing me and get your purse. We have to go. Now."

Obediently, Lynn turned to the nightstand next to her side of the bed and picked up her purse. "I'm ready. Let's go."

By the time the old Ford Taurus pulled up at the church, there wasn't an empty space anywhere in the lot or even out in front on the street. John parked as close as he could, and the three of them piled out and hurried toward the back of the church, where it seemed half the town of Bloomfield had already gathered, with more arriving all the time.

With summer in full force, children ran and played, chasing one another with squeals of delight. Adults gathered in clusters and chattered excitedly while construction workers huddled together beside the fence, now quite a bit smaller than it had been the day before. Lynn thought she wouldn't have been surprised to see vendors selling hot dogs and balloons before the day was out. And there, across the yard, was Bailey McCullough, snapping pictures for all she was worth. Something exciting must indeed have taken place.

Lynn spotted Pastor Brunswick about the same time that his eyes caught hers, and he headed straight for them. "You're back already," he exclaimed, chuckling as he directed his comments toward John even as he edged toward Lynn and took a stand beside her. "What did you do? Fly?"

John smiled. "Just about—as fast as my old jalopy would let me, anyway. So what's the latest? Do they know what they found yet? Is it the money?"

The pastor shrugged. "I hope so, but they haven't said. If it is, the handkerchief is no doubt at least partially rotted away by now. Whatever's in there, they're trying to remove it without losing anything, so it's taking longer than expected." He glanced around the packed church yard. "Meanwhile, as you can see, word has spread, and people just keep showing up."

"Amazing," John said. "Too bad we can't get a turnout like this every Sunday."

Pastor Brunswick chuckled. "Isn't that the truth?" He smiled at Lynn then, and she felt her shoulders tense and her stomach churn. She told herself it had nothing to do with Martin Brunswick's proximity. It was all about the discovery in the fence . . . wasn't it?

Of course it was. Had she wasted part of her inheritance on foolishness? With Rachel's college debts looming and work needed on two houses, had she squandered the money the Lord had provided for necessities?

But this is a necessity too, she reminded herself. *Proving a man's innocence and restoring his honor has to be every bit as important as fixing some old plumbing or slapping some paint on the side of a house.*

"So what do you think, Lynn?" Pastor asked, his brown eyes warm and twinkling with anticipation. "Do you suppose they've found that lost money after all these years?"

Lynn took a deep breath. "I hope so. And I suppose we'll know any minute now."

The pastor nodded and turned back toward the fence. "We should."

Lynn watched as John slipped his hand around Rachel's and squeezed, then left it there as the four of them waited together.

 # Chapter 30

RACHEL'S HEART RACED—FOR TWO REASONS, SHE ADMITTED to herself. First, of course, was the question of what had been found in the fence. Second was the fact that she stood there in broad daylight, surrounded by what surely must have been half of Bloomfield, with her hand tucked securely in John's.

She caught her breath as a stir seemed to make its way through the crowd. The foreman of the crew climbed on top of the remaining fence and stuck his fingers in his mouth to whistle for attention. Were they finally about to hear the results of the morning's discovery? Everyone in the crowd, even the children, ceased their activities and turned their attention toward the impending announcement.

"I have good news," the man announced, gingerly holding up what appeared to be a soiled cloth, full of what everyone in the crowd no doubt hoped were coins. "We've found the handkerchief with the missing money, and we only had to tear down a small portion of the fence to do it. Congratulations, Bloomfield. Your long-standing mystery has been solved."

Cheers rose up from all around the yard as children once again began racing around, whooping and hollering over the good news, despite the fact that most of them hadn't a clue what they were celebrating. The older citizens of the town, however, were obviously overjoyed at the implications of the discovery.

Last Chance Justice had at last been vindicated. Though he may have been a forgetful child who stopped to play on a fence instead of taking the Sunday school offering directly to the church office, he certainly had not been a thief or a liar. And that was the best news many in Bloomfield could have hoped to hear.

Rachel blinked back tears of joy as John squeezed her hand and her mother slipped an arm around her shoulder.

"Two celebrations so close together," Lynn mused. "Who would have thought?"

She sat at Bert's Barbecue, across the table from John and Rachel, waiting for a very busy Jolene to bring their lunch orders. The place was packed, as they weren't the only ones who had opted for a celebratory lunch. Lynn imagined most of the other eateries in town were full as well.

Lynn smiled, cognizant of the fact that Rachel had taken the seat next to John rather than her mother, the exact opposite of what she had done the last time the three of them went out together. The lines were drawn, and Lynn was pleased.

It's as it should be. Your will, Lord, not mine—though I wouldn't mind if this became a permanent thing.

"You look happy, Mom," Rachel observed. "This celebrating thing is good for you. We'll have to do it more often."

Lynn laughed. "I'm all for that. Seriously, though, how could we not be happy? Not only did they find the lost money, but they did so with only minimal damage to the fence. If they'd started at the other end, they would have had to tear nearly the whole thing down before finding it. As it is, they'll probably be able to repair it by the end of the day tomorrow. And I can't deny I'm pleased about how that will affect our inheritance money."

"Our money?" Rachel smiled. "That's your money, Mom, not ours."

"Oh, Rachel, don't be silly. Whatever I have is yours too. You know that."

"I do know that," Rachel said. "And I appreciate it."

John jumped in then, darting his gaze from Lynn to Rachel and back again. "I love the way you two ladies get along. Seriously, you've got a great mother-daughter thing going on."

"Thank you," Lynn said, reaching across the table to squeeze Rachel's hand. "Believe me, I know how blessed I am."

Jolene swooped by and dropped off their salads before taking an order at a nearby table. Lynn watched her walk away and shook her head.

"That woman is ageless. I don't know how she does it."

"My mom said the same thing when she came to visit a few months ago," John agreed.

In moments, they had offered thanks and dug into their greenery, but Lynn noticed a slight dampening of enthusiasm coming from her daughter's direction.

"Everything okay, sweetheart?"

Rachel raised her eyes to meet her mother's. She smiled. "Of course. Why wouldn't it be?"

Lynn shrugged. "Oh, I don't know. You just seem . . . less excited than a few minutes ago. Don't you like your salad?"

"My salad is fine." She paused. "It's just . . . well, I guess it just now hit me that with the fence and money situation resolved so quickly, there's nothing to keep us in Bloomfield any longer." With her eyes firmly fixed on Lynn's face, she asked, "Does that mean we'll be leaving soon?"

Lynn realized then how much her daughter had been counting on spending several more days there as the fence was demolished and then repaired. Now it seemed that would all be done in the next day or so, leaving no reason to stay on past the weekend, if that long. And she did have things to do at home, part of which was no doubt a huge pile of mail and several phone messages to answer.

"I imagine we will," Lynn said, watching not only Rachel's response but John's as well. Both appeared disappointed. "But that doesn't mean we can't come back. We're only a few hours away, you know." She paused and leaned forward, lowering her voice. "And to be honest, I haven't decided yet whether to sell Myron's place or the other one." She shrugged. "After all, there's no law that says we can't come back to Bloomfield to live, is there?"

John and Rachel's faces lit up as if connected to the same circuit breaker. Lynn felt cemented to her seat. What had she just done? Was she truly considering moving back to this busy-bee little burg where everyone knew everyone else's business and didn't think twice about interfering—a place where she always believed people had judged her for leaving town and where the peer pressure of her past could easily become a permanent part of her life once again?

Not if you don't let it.

She smiled at the silent words. That was it, wasn't it? She was a grown-up now, not a child or even a teenager. She didn't have to let peer pressure influence her life if she didn't want it to. And change? She'd been through more of that in the past few months than in all her previous years combined—with the exception of marrying Daniel, of course. And she'd survived, hadn't she? She most certainly had. So maybe she just needed to be open to whatever plans God might have for her now . . . even if they involved more change.

"Did you just say what I think you said?" Rachel asked. "Are you really thinking about moving back to Bloomfield?"

Lynn shrugged. "I don't know. It's all such a new thought to me, but . . . well, one I'm at least willing to consider."

John and Rachel exchanged an excited glance, and something told Lynn that even if she didn't decide to move back to Bloomfield, her daughter very well might.

Later that day, as the crew worked at restoring the fence, John and Rachel wended their way outside of town toward Miss Pearl's place. Rachel was so pleased that John had invited her to come along so he could deliver the news about Last Chance. She could only imagine what it would mean to a woman so close to the end of her earthly life.

Bear was up and off the porch, barking and growling in front of their car before John shut off the engine. But the minute he saw them climb out, he raced excitedly from one to the other, reveling in their affectionate greetings.

"Well, come on in," Miss Pearl called from the open screen

door. "I wasn't expecting you, but it sure is nice to see you folks again so soon after your last visit."

John and Rachel made their way up the rickety old porch, past their host and into the house, leaving Bear behind. Rachel couldn't help but notice that everything was in place, exactly as it had been the last time they visited. Miss Pearl was an impeccable housekeeper, even when she wasn't expecting company.

"Have a seat," Miss Pearl said. "I don't have no molasses cookies made today, but I do have some pickled figs. Made 'em yesterday, and they're downright good, if I do say so myself. Would you care for some?"

Pickled figs? Rachel had never heard of such a thing, let alone eaten them, but she wasn't about to be rude. "I'd love one. Thank you."

Miss Pearl laughed. "One? Child, nobody eats just one of my pickled figs. Why, once you get started, you can't hardly quit. Let me fix you a bowl of 'em. You too, Pastor."

Rachel saw John's smile, and she knew how much he appreciated this elderly saint who offered him such respect, even at his young age. Though Pastor Brunswick was regularly addressed by his title, it was a rare treat for the inexperienced youth pastor.

John caught her eye and winked, then quickly blushed. Rachel wished she were close enough to lay her hand on his reassuringly. Thankfully, their wait was minimal, and Miss Pearl had their bowls of fruit in front of them within moments.

"What do you think?" she asked, watching Rachel closely. "Bet you never tasted one of them before, have you?"

"Never," she admitted, "and now I know what I've been missing. They're delicious—sweet and yet tart and . . . I'm not sure how to describe them."

Miss Pearl beamed. "Got the recipe from my mama," she said, "and her mama before her. Our families been canning pickled figs for years. I got two nieces that make 'em too now, so I know the recipe won't be gone once I move on to heaven." She laughed. "Sometimes I think that can't be soon enough."

"Oh, Miss Pearl," John said, "don't be in such a hurry to leave us. We'd miss you around here."

"You might, and maybe a few of my distant kinfolk would too. But nobody else, I'm thinkin'."

A sadness seemed to dim the light in her dark old eyes, and Rachel glanced at John, wondering if he'd picked up the woman's change of mood. He apparently had because he quickly cleared his throat and began to talk.

"Miss Pearl, Rachel and I came out here to give you some news—good news. Something we just found out about this morning."

The old woman's forehead crinkled. "Good news? Why, I imagine I could use some of that."

John smiled. "We all could. And the entire town of Bloomfield got some as a result of what happened at the church yesterday."

Taking a deep breath, he poured out the story of how he had come to suspect that there was a connection between Last Chance and the fence behind the church. He told of enlisting Rachel's help and how her mother had then offered to pay for the venture. By the time he came to the part of the discovery of the missing money, tears trickled down Miss Pearl's cheeks.

"You found the money," she whispered when John finished speaking. "After all these years . . ."

Rachel slid her chair close enough to Miss Pearl's so that she could take her hand. She and John remained quiet until the old woman spoke again. "That boy," she said. "He always did have to stop and play everywhere. Never could make a clean shot from one place to another. My daddy used to scold him 'bout that. We shoulda knowed that's what happened. No way did he take that money, we all knowed that. But what happened to it, we just couldn't explain." She nodded and squeezed Rachel's hand. "But thank the good Lord, He answered my prayer. I been asking Him for years to let me live long enough to see my baby brother's good name restored, and He answered. Last Chance Justice won't never be called a thief or a liar ever again. He can finally rest in peace."

Rachel felt the old woman's shudder of relief, and she gave up trying to hold back her own tears, as they slipped from her eyes and down her face.

 # Chapter 31

"JASON HAS ASSURED ME HE'LL TAKE CARE OF THE PLACE WHILE we're gone," Lynn said on Monday morning, sipping her coffee at the kitchen table, directly across from Rachel. They had enjoyed a pleasant and relaxing weekend since rejoicing over the discovery of the money on Friday, but now it was nearly time to head back home.

Rachel nodded, her dark hair slipping from its semi-fastened "do" on top of her head. The two women hadn't been up long, and Lynn knew her daughter struggled with the idea of leaving the next morning. They'd talked about it long into the night, and she felt confident that Rachel understood the need to head home and catch up on some things. She also knew it wouldn't be long until Rachel returned to Bloomfield, possibly for good. Surprisingly, Lynn found she leaned toward coming back with her.

"I'm sure Jason will do a good job," Rachel said. "After all, this is his home too. He's perfect for the job."

Lynn nodded, even as she remembered her misgivings about

the strange old man when they first arrived. Now she was glad her brother had provided for his long-time friend and caretaker; it was the perfect solution for all of them.

"I'm going to do a last load of laundry this morning," Lynn said, "and then I'll start packing. What about you? Do you have any special plans for the day?"

Rachel's smile was wistful. "I do. Monday is John's day off, so he's going to pick me up in a couple of hours so we can spend some time together before you and I leave tomorrow. I may be gone most of the day."

"Good for you. That's exactly what the two of you should do. I'm glad John has the day off."

Rachel's smile faded and she took a swig of her coffee, though Lynn noticed the piece of toast on her plate remained untouched.

"We've all grown attached to this place in a short time, haven't we?" Lynn commented. "Even Beasley."

At the mention of his name, the dog looked up from his spot under the table and wagged his stump of a tail before going back to sleep.

"That's for sure, though I imagine he'll be thrilled to get home again."

"You're probably right, but I have to admit to having mixed emotions about it," Lynn said. "We had so many wonderful years there, and the house is full of memories." She sighed. "Sometimes that just makes it harder, though. It's like a constant reminder that your dad is gone and I won't see him again until I'm in heaven."

Rachel reached across the table and patted her mother's hand. "And aren't you glad you have that assurance?"

Lynn felt the hot tears bite her eyes. "Yes. However would I bear it if I didn't know that beyond a shadow of a doubt?"

"It's what makes life on this earth not only pleasant, but meaningful. Maybe that's why it's so important to me to spend my life helping other people realize and accept that truth."

"I imagine you're right, sweetheart," Lynn said, a swell of pride dispelling the melancholy feelings that had taunted her throughout the morning. "And who knows? Maybe God is opening up doors right here in Bloomfield for you to do just that."

Rachel's smile was sunnier now. "I think you might be right, Mom. I really do."

*

The day was perfect, making it even harder for Rachel to accept that they would leave Bloomfield the next morning. She and John stood beside his car, parked under a tree at the side of the road a few miles out of town, and strapped on their backpacks in preparation for a short hike. As she watched him cinch his straps, she determined to enjoy their time together and not dwell on tomorrow.

"You ready?" John asked.

She looked up at him. The sun glinted off his blond hair, and her heart raced at the tenderness she saw in his eyes. No longer did she have even the slightest doubt that he cared for her, as certain of that as about her own feelings for him.

But it's so soon. So quick! How can we possibly know what we feel or want in such a short time?

And then she remembered. It wasn't about what she or John thought or felt or wanted; it was about finding out what God had purposed for them—as individuals and as a couple. That was a point they would have to discuss if their relationship was to continue.

She smiled. "I'm ready. You lead, I'll follow."

He grinned. "I like that. I just hope you still feel that way by the end of the day."

She laughed and set off to match his pace, which she suspected he restrained for her sake. He'd given her the lighter pack, with only a few sandwiches and some fruit inside, while he carried everything else in his. She eyed that pack now, resting firmly between his broad shoulders.

If You give us the green light, Lord, I really do think I could follow him anywhere.

Chirping birds and the occasional rustling of leaves were the only sounds as they trudged into the woods, leaving civilization and Bloomfield behind. They'd been walking nearly an hour when they came upon a clearing next to a creek. The cool, clear water rippled over rocks as John spread the blanket that had been in his backpack. In moments, they had their lunch unpacked, sitting side by side, drinking in the beauty as they munched on their sandwiches.

"It doesn't get much better than this, does it?" John commented, gazing out at the water.

"It sure doesn't. Unless you think of how Miss Pearl reacted when she heard the news about Last Chance."

John turned toward her and smiled. "You're right. That really was incredible."

Rachel nodded.

"By the way, I heard this morning that the town is planning a big wingding next month to honor Last Chance. It'll be at the main park in town, with food and vendors and a petting zoo for the kids. The garden club is going to sponsor it." He smiled again as he leaned toward her, close enough that Rachel could once again smell his aftershave. "And Miss Pearl will be the guest of honor."

"Oh, John, that's wonderful!" Without thought, Rachel bridged the few inches between them and planted a kiss on his cheek. "Do you know what day yet? Because I wouldn't miss that for anything."

John shook his head, never taking his eyes from hers. "Not sure of the date, but we should know soon. And trust me, you'll be the first one I call with the news. If you can't get here on your own, I'll drive that old clunker of mine straight up to your place and bring you back."

Rachel laughed. "I do believe you would."

His eyes grew serious. "Count on it."

A crow cawed, but Rachel scarcely noticed as their lips came together and their eyes closed. It would be bittersweet to leave tomorrow, but she knew she would be back—and not just for the celebration at the park. Bloomfield was quickly becoming the home of her heart, and something told her that John would one day be a permanent resident of that home.

Lynn wandered through the old house the next morning, trailing her fingers across favorite pieces of furniture and remembering her brother as he was the last time she visited him—as well as when she was a little girl and she thought he was so grown up and mature. He was her protector then, her hero, but now he was gone, waiting for her in heaven with Daniel. The tug at her heart nearly started her waterworks flowing again, but she pulled herself together, determined to hit the road without giving in to another crying jag.

For heaven's sake, it's not like I'm leaving forever. I'm just going home to put out some fires and straighten out a few things before . . .

Before what? Before putting the house up for sale and moving back here . . . permanently? Have I really come that far in my thinking? Has the decision already been made and I'm just too stubborn to admit it?

Rachel knows what she wants. I just wish I could be more like her sometimes. Of course, she's young and has her entire life ahead of her. She's at the place where she needs to make decisions, and if those decisions involve moving or . . . marriage, or both . . . then that's as it should be. But me? At my age?

She sighed, catching sight of Beasley as she walked by the open door to the bedroom she'd shared with the cocker spaniel and Rachel for the past few weeks. The dog scarcely moved or acknowledged her as she passed. His naps had become more frequent and prolonged lately, and Lynn found herself wishing she could be more like him at times.

That dog can sleep anywhere, anytime. He can get up after sleeping all night long at the foot of my bed and then go right back to sleep after walking downstairs. He hasn't a care in the world, beyond waiting for me—or someone—to feed him each morning.

She smiled. *Then again, I don't suppose I'd want to sleep my life away, would I, Lord? Surely You still have work for me to do—a purpose of some sort. Don't You?*

A silent affirmation warmed her heart as she started down the stairway, lovingly running her hand down the smooth wooden banister. If she were even twenty years younger, she might straddle it and slide down—though she doubted it. She could picture Rachel doing it, though, and she smiled at the image.

Rachel would be a perfect pastor's wife, she thought. And not just in a supporting role. She'd no doubt be as active as her husband, pitching in to do whatever was necessary. And yes, she could surely see her gracious daughter ministering to senior saints, as well as to toddlers and teens. Rachel had always been a natural at giving herself away, and Lynn knew she was blessed to have such a child.

"Daniel," she whispered, knowing she couldn't really speak to him, but needing to hear his name, and glad Rachel had gone for a walk and left her to say goodbye to the house on her own. "If you were still alive, I wouldn't be wrestling with this decision, would I? Our world would still be back in our house where we spent our married lives and raised our daughter. But you're not. You've gone on ahead of me, along with Myron, and now I've got to make a choice. I know it's God and not you who will guide me in this, but oh, how I miss your broad shoulders and wise counsel."

She crossed the kitchen floor and stood in front of the sink, wondering if there was time for one last cup of coffee before Rachel returned and they hit the road. Surely there was, because even if her daughter got back before she finished, the girl would certainly not be in any hurry to leave. She nodded and made the decision to brew a fresh pot.

Lynn had just poured herself a steaming cup when she heard tires crunching on the gravel driveway. She went to the front door and pulled it open, not at all surprised to see John's Taurus pull up and stop just yards from the front porch. She motioned him to come on up and returned to the kitchen for a second cup of coffee while John and Beasley greeted one another. When Lynn stepped back out onto the front porch, she was surprised to see that John hadn't come alone. Martin Brunswick stood beside him, smiling at her as she regrouped and invited them to join her in the rocking chairs before retrieving one more cup of coffee.

"I had a feeling you might show up this morning, John," she said as they sipped their hot drinks. "And what a nice surprise that you came along," she added, turning her attention toward the pastor. His probing gaze unnerved her, and she quickly returned to the subject at hand. "Rachel will be back any moment, I'm sure. She just went out for a last walk."

John nodded. "I tried to stay away. Rachel and I said our good-byes yesterday, but . . ." He shook his head. "Well, as you can see, I didn't convince myself because here I am."

"You care about my daughter, don't you?"

John's cheeks flushed, and Lynn knew she had put him on the spot in front of his boss and pastor. But she needed to hear his answer before she and Rachel left town.

John lifted his head and focused his blue eyes on hers. "Very much," he said, his voice husky. "I know it's happened awfully fast, and I keep telling myself to slow down, but I . . ." He sighed. "The thing is . . . it's not the time factor so much as it is the God factor. You know what I mean? I've prayed and thought about this nearly nonstop since meeting Rachel, and I am almost one hundred percent convinced that God has brought us together." He frowned. "Do you think that's wishful thinking on my part?"

"Possibly. But that doesn't negate the probability of the God factor you mentioned. I always believed God brought me and Daniel together, even though it meant I had to leave Bloomfield behind to be with him."

"I couldn't agree more," Pastor Brunswick said. "I always felt that way about my marriage to Georgia, and also about our eventual move here to Bloomfield."

Lynn swallowed, surprised to realize that the man's comments about his wife only endeared him to her more. Martin Brunswick was indeed a fine man and a committed Christian.

John nodded, bringing Lynn back to the present as he said, "And it was the right thing for you to do, Mrs. Myers. You've never regretted it, have you?"

"Not for a moment."

"And now?"

Lynn sighed and leaned her head back. "Now? Now I believe God is calling me back to Bloomfield after all these years."

"Really?" The excitement in John's voice was evident, though Lynn resisted the temptation to peek at his expression. She couldn't help but notice, however, that the pastor sat forward in his chair as she spoke.

"Really," she said. "And I know Rachel is strongly considering it—moving here, I mean. How would you feel about that, John?"

He grinned. "I think I could get used to that real easy."

Lynn laughed. "I'm sure you could. Oh, and by the way, I heard from Kathy Wilson yesterday. It seems the garden club has offered their expertise and elbow grease to restore any landscaping that might have been uprooted by the fence excavation. Isn't that wonderful?"

Martin chuckled. "Why am I not surprised? That sounds like a perfect project for them."

John raised his eyebrows and nodded in agreement as he directed his comments toward Lynn. "It sure is. In fact, it sounds like you've become an honorary member of the club already, and you haven't even moved back here yet."

Lynn smiled. An honorary member indeed. Perhaps, once she and Rachel had truly resettled back in Bloomfield—and there was no doubt left in her mind that such a move was in the offing—she'd just have to check into becoming a full-fledged member, the way her mother once was. The very thought warmed her heart in a way she had never imagined possible.

She turned her face from John's and sat forward, taking another sip of coffee and listening to the familiar caw of what she'd come to think of as one of their own crows. Who would ever have thought that a cawing crow could bring on another onslaught of tears?

She blinked them away just as she heard her daughter's voice calling to them from the driveway.

"Well, look who's here," Rachel said, grinning as she approached them. "What a nice surprise!"

John jumped to his feet and hurried to welcome her with a hug. "I'm glad you think it's a good thing. I was wondering if you'd mind that I dropped by one last time. I just couldn't let you leave without being here to see you off. And besides, Pastor wanted to come along and say goodbye too."

Rachel gazed up at him, and Lynn knew her daughter fought her own battle with tears. "It's what I was wishing for the entire time I was out walking."

John kissed her on the forehead. "You got your wish." He paused for a moment, their gazes intertwined, and then he backed away. "The three of us were having a cup of coffee together. I know it's almost time for you to hit the road, but . . ." He turned and raised a quizzical eyebrow at Lynn. "Is there more coffee inside? Have you got time for Rachel to join us before you leave?" He glanced back at Rachel. "Unless you'd like something cooler."

She shook her head. "Coffee's fine. And knowing Mom, there's more in the kitchen."

"Of course there is," Lynn said. "And yes, we certainly have time for that."

With coffee all the way around, Rachel, Lynn, and Martin sat down in the rockers, with John perching on the porch railing. Before they had time to get comfortable, another voice haled them from the side of the house. Lynn turned, along with the others, and spotted Jason approaching them. Beasley hurried from his perch near John's feet and wriggled out to meet their newest visitor, and Lynn marveled at how quickly the dog had bonded to the old caretaker.

"Come and join us," Lynn called. "We're just having a last cup of coffee before Rachel and I take off. Let me run inside and get you a cup."

Jason shook his head. "Don't need any coffee. Just wanted to stop over and say goodbye. I hope you have a safe trip, and we'll see you back here real soon."

Lynn smiled. "Oh, I think you can count on that. John told Rachel yesterday that the town is planning a ceremony of sorts to honor the restoration of Last Chance Justice's good name, and we wouldn't miss that celebration for anything."

Jason nodded. "It's only right after all these years." He offered a rare and somewhat toothless smile. "Myron would have been there with bells on."

Lynn laughed. "He sure would have. But since he can't be, we'll all go in his honor. If it hadn't been for him, Rachel and I would never have started this quest to solve the missing money mystery, so we all owe a big thanks to my brother, don't we?"

"We surely do," Jason agreed.

"That's for sure," John added.

"Thank you, Uncle Myron," Rachel murmured.

"Amen to that," Martin said.

Beasley barked and wriggled his tail, and the rest of them—even old Jason—broke into laughter. The sound of it was just the confirmation Lynn needed to reassure her that she and Rachel would soon be back in Bloomfield . . . for good.

Mama's Flat Apple Pie

Preheat oven to 350 degrees.

Ingredients
3 cups all-purpose flour
1-1/3 cups shortening
1/2 teaspoon salt
2 medium eggs, separated
2/3 cup milk
3 handfuls flake-type cereal (i.e., corn flakes)
8 to 10 Granny Smith apples
1 cup granulated sugar
1 Tablespoon cinnamon
1 teaspoon nutmeg
1 Tablespoon orange juice
1 teaspoon lemon juice
1 Tablespoon margarine or butter

Blend together flour, shortening, and salt.

Add egg yolks to milk and mix with fork.

Add yolk mixture to flour mixture.

Divide the dough and roll out half of it for the bottom crust to fit a cookie sheet.

Sprinkle the bottom crust with cereal.

Peel and thinly slice apples and spread evenly over the bottom crust.

Sprinkle mixture with sugar, cinnamon, and nutmeg.

Pour juices over apples and dot with margarine or butter.

Roll out the top crust and place over the apples, sealing the edges.

Cut small slits in the top crust.

Beat the egg whites until stiff and spread over top crust.

Bake for approximately 45 minutes until golden brown.

Dear Reader,

As the author of many books, both fiction and nonfiction, I take my writing assignments seriously. I believe God has gifted me to be a communicator, and I must never take that gift for granted. I also believe He holds me accountable to how I use that gift, so I pray daily that every word I write will somehow glorify Him.

Jesus, of course, is my example because He told "parables with purpose." He didn't just spin interesting tales to entertain His listeners; He told stories they could relate to in their time and culture, but with the purpose of confronting them right where they lived, challenging them to change their hearts, their minds, and yes, their lives. I believe God wants all of us to do no less.

The Bloomfield Series is a collection of stories about regular, everyday, small-town people who deal with many of the same issues you and I deal with in our own lives. They are basically decent people, with charming characteristics—and some not so charming. On occasion they get on each other's nerves and fall into the trap of gossiping and competing with one another, but their faith always pulls them back to those things that are most important—their love of God and family, of the triumph of right and the joy of unconditional love.

Those are the points I tried to convey in *Last Chance for Justice*, as my main character, a midfifties, recently widowed former Bloomfield resident returns to the town to settle her late brother's estate, inheriting his "creepy" mansion near the cemetery in the process. Her just-graduated-from-Bible-college daughter, Rachel, accompanies her, and quickly finds herself as the center of attraction for two of Bloomfield's handsome young bachelors. In the midst of all that, Lynn and Rachel get caught up in the town's decades-old mystery involving some missing money and a deceased Bloomfield resident with the odd name of Last Chance Justice. Learning the meaning behind his name and discovering that Lynn's brother had been bent on solving the mystery before he died drives the two women to take up the cause and pursue the truth. The entire town of Bloomfield and its history will be changed in the process.

My prayer is that this sometimes humorous, sometimes serious tale of life in the charming little burg of Bloomfield will touch your heart and draw you deeper into that never-ending journey of truth, as we all make our way home to the One who is Truth Himself.

Blessings!

Kathi Macias

Discussion Questions

1. Lynn is already dealing with the loss of her husband when she receives news that her only sibling, her brother Myron, has died. Not only does that add to her grief, but she feels guilt over the fact that she has been so caught up in her own life that she hadn't spent much time with Myron and had no idea he was even sick. Describe a time in your own life when you felt such negative feelings compounded over circumstances.

2. The unexpected arrival of Lynn's daughter, Rachel, and her offer to accompany her mother to Bloomfield to settle Myron's estate not only bolsters Lynn's strength and ability to cope, but also adds a bit of a lighthearted air to an otherwise heavy story. How did you feel when Rachel was introduced into the story? Can you remember a time in your own life when someone showed up just when you needed that boost?

3. Old Jason is quite a colorful character in *Last Chance for Justice*. What emotions did his initial appearance in the book stir up in you?

4. Rachel is described as not only a physically lovely young woman, but a morally beautiful one as well. As she first met Hayden and John, what were your thoughts on what might happen? Were you rooting for one or the other? If so, why?

5. What were your thoughts and feelings as the story of Last Chance Justice unfolded? Did you find yourself thinking he was guilty or innocent?

6. The old house that Lynn inherited next to the cemetery had both its "creepy" and charming elements. Have you ever visited or lived in such a place? If so, what are your thoughts and memories about it now?

7. Lynn struggled with peer pressure, even at her age, though she may not have realized it until she returned to her hometown and began to reconnect with people she grew up with but hadn't had much connection with over the years. How about you? Do you remember the pains and pangs of peer pressure when you were young? Is it still an issue for you? If so, in what way?

8. What did you think of Bloomfield's Garden Club? Have you ever been involved in a similar organization? What were your experiences?

9. Rachel admires and enjoys the company of both Hayden and John, but very early on finds herself leaning toward one over the other. Why do you think that was?

10. *Last Chance for Justice* is full of some colorful and unusual characters: Homer Tatum, Jolene Trump, and Miss

Pearl. What did you think about these characters, and what if anything did you learn from them?

11. Not every story contains an animal as a prominent character, but Beasley certainly plays a prominent role in *Last Chance for Justice*. Did you enjoy reading about this lovable cocker spaniel? In what ways do you feel he contributed (or possibly detracted) from the story?

12. Several issues got resolved by the end of the book— Rachel's decision not to pursue a relationship with Hayden, the solving of the mystery of the missing money, Lynn and Rachel becoming friends with old Jason, Lynn reconnecting with her Bloomfield friends and making progress at overcoming her peer pressure issues—while other issues were left a bit open-ended, such as when/if Lynn and Rachel would return to Bloomfield and whether or not the brief, almost unnoticeable connection between Pastor Brunswick and Lynn might blossom at some point. How did you feel about the points that were clearly resolved, and were you bothered by those that weren't? Does it help to know that the series will continue, and are you hoping to see these issues addressed in future books?

Bloomfield

DEBBY MAYNE
WAITING for a View
★ EBOOK EXCLUSIVE

GAIL SATTLER
TaKE the Trophy & Run

GAIL SATTLER
WHEN PIGS AND PARROTS FLY
★ EBOOK EXCLUSIVE

If you enjoyed *Last Chance for Justice*, you can read about more of the quirky characters who live in Bloomfield in *Waiting For a View*, *Take the Trophy and Run*, and *When Pigs and Parrots Fly*. Plus, there are more titles coming as the series continues. Let's continue to put Bloomfield on the map!

Put the town of Bloomfield on the map.

Search for BloomfieldClub

BHPublishingGroup.com

B&H FICTION